THE SQUARE OF REVENGE

THE SQUARE OF REVENGE

PIETER ASPE

Translated by Brian Doyle

PEGASUS CRIME

NEW YORK LONDON

THE SQUARE OF REVENGE

Pegasus Crime is an Imprint of
Pegasus Books LLC
80 Broad Street, 5th Floor
New York, NY 10004

Copyright © 2013 Pieter Aspe

Translation © 2013 Brian Doyle

First Pegasus Books edition 2013

Interior design by Maria Fernandez

Library of Congress Cataloging-in-Publication Data is available.

ISBN: 978-1-60598-446-9

10 9 8 7 6 5 4 3 2

Printed in the United States of America
Distributed by W. W. Norton & Company

For my wife

O Fortuna,

velut Luna

statu variabilis,

semper crescis

aut decrescis;

vita detestabilis

nunc obdurat

et tunc curat

ludo mentis aciem,

egestatem,

potestatem

dissolvit ut glaciem.

—Carmina Burana

1

"I've had enough, Sarge. There's just no pleasing them. They hate me, and that's it."

"What do you expect, André?" said Versavel indifferently. "Life is a like rosebush. The stem with thorns comes first, then the flower."

André Petitjean was too young and probably a bit too naïve to understand the full implications of Versavel's words, and Versavel didn't really care. He was tired and wanted to go to bed.

"But she loves me a lot. A whole lot," the young police officer persisted, not cluing into Versavel's diffidence.

Sergeant Versavel smoothed his moustache, a gesture he repeated several times a day.

"Her father, there's an asshole if ever there was one. He won't even look at me."

"So her mother isn't so bad then," said Versavel.

"If only," Petitjean sighed. "The bitch won't let us out of her sight."

Versavel only kept the conversation going because time passed quicker that way.

"If I were you, I wouldn't let it get to me. Most parents feel threatened when some oddball turns up with his sights on their daughter."

"Thanks a million," said Petitjean frostily.

Versavel had no children and thanked his lucky stars for it. Kids these days were so thin-skinned. Silence filled the van for a few moments. Petitjean steered the Ford Transit through the desolate streets of Bruges, a look of grim determination on his face.

"You have to admit we're not kids anymore."

Versavel conceded with a dry nod.

"What's their problem? I work for the police! They know I've got qualifications. With a bit of luck I'll make detective in five years, and if I play my political cards right I could be commissioner *before* I turn thirty-five. *He's* a civil servant, don't forget. Twenty-eight years of loyal service. Think about it."

And I'm just a measly sergeant, Versavel wanted to say. *I wouldn't have minded a shot at commissioner myself.*

"And to add insult to injury, he's insisting that if I really want to marry his daughter, I have to buy a house first."

"And she does everything daddy tells her, good as gold," said Versavel, irked at the whiney tone the conversation was taking. He sneaked a peek at his watch. Thank God, only three thousand, nine hundred seconds to go and their shift was up. Most weekend nightshifts were fairly busy, which pushed the clock forward. But tonight of all nights, with rampant Romeo on his case, everything outside was eerily quiet.

"I've got a name for them, you know."

Versavel shook his head and stroked his moustache.

"A bunch of backward Catholic bastards," Petitjean cursed short-temperedly. "The misery started with the *inshicklical*. They should never have pitch-forked that Pole into the Pope's job."

"The what?" Versavel sat up straight.

"You know, the *inshicklical*," Petitjean reiterated, surprised that Versavel didn't understand him. "Come on, the letter that says we all have to recognize authority like good little boys and girls. *He* believes in all that stuff, one hundred percent. He works for the health service, Church-run, goes with the territory."

"Ah, that's what you mean."

"What else did you think?" Petitjean snorted.

"I see what you're getting at," Versavel yawned. "The Catholic Church has been responsible for more than a few headaches over the years."

"But I've made up my mind. This afternoon I'm asking her to marry me. What do you think of that?"

Find another bimbo, is what he had wanted to say, but instead he answered: "You might just manage to impress them. The petit bourgeoisie isn't insensitive to the occasional bit of bluff. Focus on appearances, André, and the rest will take care of itself."

He should have held his tongue.

"What do you mean by that?" Petitjean lashed out nervously as the pent-up tension of the preceding hours erupted. "Don't make fun of me, Sarge." His bulging eyes were spitting fire. Petitjean was clearly rattled and in his confusion almost lost control of the vehicle. Luckily they were doing a lap of the main square at the time.

"Steady on, steady on," Versavel barked, shaken at having missed the edge of the sidewalk by a mere ten centimeters. "I never said I was an expert, did I? I know nothing about women and even less about future in-laws," he hissed.

3

"So what did you mean with that 'impress them' stuff? What was that all about? This is a serious downer, man. Don't you get it?" said Petitjean accusingly.

It was now four minutes past six. His shift wasn't exactly flying by. Versavel had to think of something to kill the remaining time.

"What if you bought her a really expensive engagement ring?" he blurted.

It was a stupid suggestion, but Petitjean perked up like a drowning man catching sight of a boat on the horizon.

"Do you think an expensive ring might make a difference?" he asked, desperately enthusiastic. Versavel had no other option than to play along now.

"Absolutely," he said in a paternal tone. "In-laws need to be warmed up. Buy the ring your mother-in-law always dreamed of and present it to her daughter on a tray."

Petitjean had fortunately paid no attention to Versavel's claims of ignorance about women and in-laws moments earlier.

"Do you mean it?"

"You know I'd never mess with you, André."

Petitjean was satisfied with Versavel's answer and thankfully refocused his attention on steering the van.

They drove down Geldmunt Street toward Zand Square. Night patrols always follow a fixed route and a strict schedule. They were running ten minutes early. A drunk puking under the Muntpoort was in luck: they left him alone.

Petitjean was now clearly in the best of moods and Versavel heaved a sigh of relief.

"You're amazing, Sarge. Honestly, you always know what to do."

Versavel stretched his legs and imagined himself crawling naked under his duvet. Heaven!

"Later I'm going to buy the most expensive ring there is," Petitjean purred good-humouredly.

"You mean tomorrow. Today's Sunday."

"Okay, tomorrow then." He had apparently forgotten that he planned to ask his girlfriend to marry him that afternoon.

Zand Square, where the old neo-Gothic train station had once towered, was vast and empty. An early taxi cautiously overtook them. A train rumbled in the distance. Petitjean's bulging eyes twinkled in the early misty sunlight. His red hair seemed ablaze, and his angular face gleamed like polished marble.

"The question is," he volunteered, deadly serious all of a sudden, "where tomorrow do I buy a magnificent, expensive engagement ring? What kind of ring is going to impress those bitches? It's too late for mistakes, Sarge."

A merciless ray of sun forced Versavel to narrow his eyes. What a naïve bunch, the youth of today, he thought to himself. Naïve *and* thin-skinned.

"Where do I buy the right ring?" Petitjean muttered in a sort of self-induced trance.

Versavel let him dream out loud. He was more interested in the restoration work being done on the tower of Saint Salvador's. It was close to completion. Versavel loved Bruges, its atmosphere, its perfectly maintained monuments. There was no end to the pleasure it gave him, especially at moments like this, at the crack of dawn, when he felt he had the city all to himself.

"You have to help me, Sarge," Petitjean insisted. "You know Bruges like the back of your hand. Where do I buy the most exclusive engagement ring available?"

He had to repeat himself, twice. Versavel realized it made no sense to try to explain to the young Petitjean that his advice had been nothing more than an improvised response to an irritating question. He planned to ask the commissioner, in the course of the week, not to send him out on patrol with Petitjean anymore.

"We'll be passing Degroof's shortly," he said nonchalantly. "That's where all the wealthy Bruges folks buy their stuff."

"Honestly?" Petitjean seemed possessed by the devil. Pearls of genuine perspiration glistened on his forehead. "How much longer, Sarge?" he whined like a toddler waiting for an ice cream.

They passed Simon Stevin Square. A young couple was saying their passionate farewells under the awning of a bank. Versavel figured the girl couldn't have been much more than seventeen. *The world we live in*, he sighed.

"Sarge?" Petitjean bleated impatiently.

"We're almost there. Take it easy."

Petitjean slowed down just to be on the safe side.

The busiest street in Bruges was as dead as a secluded suburb, and without the customary halogen spotlights the merchandise in the shop windows had lost its edge.

"Over there," said Versavel, "next to the shoe shop." He pointed at the gilded sign dangling above the door, with the company monogram in elegant gothic letters. Most jewelers stored their collection in a safe at night and some even took their more expensive items home. But this wasn't the appropriate moment to bother his young colleague with such details.

"No harm in sneaking a quick look, eh, Sarge?" asked Petitjean, raring to go.

"Far from it. Take your time."

Petitjean parked the Transit carelessly in front of the jeweler shop and instantly jumped out. Versavel took the opportunity to close his eyes. People used to doing nightshifts know the procedure: a quick refreshing snooze, no more than a couple of minutes. Versavel even had the odd dream, over in a flash, less than twenty seconds. He woke abruptly when Petitjean slammed the driver's door. The young policeman shook Versavel violently by the shoulder.

"Sarge, Sarge," he croaked.

Versavel growled. In his dream he was about to chat up a shapely Spaniard who had been giving him the eye.

"There's nothing in the window, Sarge. The shop's empty," Petitjean stammered.

Versavel kept his cool, only just but still. . . . Of course the shop was empty. He glanced at his watch, important for his report, yawned and smoothed his moustache. It was ten past six.

"And there's glass all over the place," Petitjean added nervously when he realized Versavel was in no hurry to make a move.

Versavel took a deep breath.

"Jesus Christ," he groaned. "Why didn't I keep my big mouth shut?"

Petitjean heard what Versavel said but didn't quite understand what he meant. "What are we going to do now, Sarge?"

Versavel fished a flashlight from under his seat and got out of the van. He shivered. Dawn was always chilly, even in the summer. Petitjean scuttled like a lame rabbit to the other side of the street, formed his hands into a cylinder against the safety glass window and peered excitedly inside. Versavel pointed the powerful beam of his flashlight into the shop's interior. It took him barely five seconds to reach the appropriate conclusion. The window display was indeed empty and there was a pile of broken glass carelessly swept into a corner. But what concerned him most were two pairs of white cotton gloves beneath one of the tables.

"I think our luck just ran out, friend," he said sarcastically.

Petitjean stared at him vacantly. A surge of adrenaline suddenly made him shudder. "You don't mean . . ."

"Afraid so. Why now, of all times?" Versavel snapped. "You and your lame-ass problem."

Petitjean couldn't believe his ears. His sympathy for Versavel melted like an ice cube in a glass of tepid Coke. His colleagues had warned him: never trust a sergeant; when the shit hits the fan he'll drop you like a ton of bricks. Versavel had been making fun of him all night long. He actually didn't give a shit about his situation, which of course Petitjean found shocking.

"Don't move," Versavel barked. The prospect of bed and sleep vanished as he spoke.

"Whatever you say, Sarge." Petitjean stationed himself in front of the shop window and stared angrily into space.

Versavel hurried resignedly back to the Transit and radioed the duty officer. It took almost thirty seconds before the man responded. Bart De Keyzer had spent the last four hours snoozing on a folding bed and sounded like a crow with a head cold.

"ONA 3421 here, talk to me."

"Versavel here." He nervously drummed the Radetzky March on the dashboard.

"Good morning, Sarge, what's new?" De Keyzer tried to sound as awake as possible.

"Probable theft . . . Degroof's," said Versavel unruffled. "Steen Street," he added, knowing that De Keyzer was bound to ask him anyway. If you had said "city hall," he would have asked for the address.

"Signs of breaking and entering?" said De Keyzer after a pause.

"Negative."

Versavel hated De Keyzer with a vengeance. He was the youngest officer in the division, and everyone knew that had made promotion via one or other political back door. His father was a vice admiral no less, in the Belgian navy, and still this was the best he could arrange for junior.

"Are you sure it's theft?"

"Negative, but the entire shop has been cleaned out. There's broken glass on the floor, and gloves," Versavel responded curtly. As far as he knew, no one got along with De Keyzer. The man was stupid and arrogant and his skin was thicker than the rubber of a pre-war condom.

"Do you need back-up, Sarge?"

"Jesus Christ," Versavel cursed under his breath. "If I was you, I would phone the Deputy public prosecutor on call and the owner of the shop. Degroof . . . got it?" he snarled.

De Keyzer didn't react to Versavel's outburst. He knew the man and was in no doubt that he wasn't afraid to make subtle reference to the incompetence of an inexperienced officer in his official report. He's been watching too many American cop shows. They're always calling in the Deputy DA to do their dirty work, he thought to himself, but wisely held his tongue.

"Of course, spot on," he retorted, slightly indignant. "And I'll make sure you get to finish your shift on the double."

"Do that," Versavel sneered.

It seemed an eternity before Hannelore Martens finally heard the phone ring. She had only been appointed Deputy public prosecutor a couple of weeks earlier and this was her first night on call.

If anything happens, it's always early on Sunday morning, an older colleague had warned her. Hannelore Martens threw on her dressing gown, switched on the light, and rushed down-stairs. Her phone was in the living room by the window. She hoped nothing had happened to her father.

"Hannelore Martens."

Neither she nor De Keyzer had the slightest inkling that a common, garden-variety robbery was no reason to get a Deputy out of bed. Everyone in the division also knew that Versavel wasn't averse to the odd practical joke now and then, and Hannelore was new. A prime target.

"Duty officer De Keyzer, ma'am," he said in his best Flemish. "Sorry to disturb you, but it's a serious matter."

Hannelore Martens listened to Bart De Keyzer's detailed report, her heart pounding. The man had a rather irritating talent: he needed ten times the number of words Versavel, or anyone else, would have used to explain what was going on. When he was finished, she wasn't really sure what she was supposed to do. The name Degroof rang a bell. Should she inform the public prosecutor?

"Casualties?" she asked just to be sure.

"Negative, ma'am. There's not even a trace of the culprits." Her male colleagues had assured her that the only way to learn the ropes was on the job. But what should she do? Nothing, perhaps? Just wait for the report. But if that was normal procedure why had the duty officer phoned her?

Never hesitate in front of a subordinate and act firmly in every circumstance, the same colleagues had instructed her. She could hear De Keyzer breathing on the other end of the line. She wasn't to know that the duty officer, like so many other stupid and arrogant people, fostered an almost blind respect for his superiors.

"Might as well take a look for myself," she said with confidence, "now that I'm awake."

"Righto, ma'am. Would you like me to inform the owner?"

"Please. Tell him I'll be there in fifteen minutes."

"Okay, ma'am. I'll inform my people that you'll be taking personal charge."

Before she could say "thank you," De Keyzer hung up. The excitement made her shiver. She took off her dressing gown and headed for the bathroom behind the kitchen: nothing more than a cramped shower and an old-fashioned washbasin.

Her neighbor opposite, a retired postmaster with all the time in the world, slurped at his first cup of coffee. He was an early riser. The opportunity to admire Miss Martens's elegant silhouette in all its glory for a couple of seconds was an added, if unforeseen, bonus that morning. He never looked across the street on other days.

It seemed to take even more than an eternity for Ghislain Degroof to answer the phone, but De Keyzer let it ring for close to five minutes. If Deputy Martens hadn't been on her way, he would probably have given up earlier.

"Degroof," the man grouched. His legs were like lead and his voice hoarse from too many cigarettes.

"Bruges Police, Mr. Degroof. Duty officer De Keyzer. I've bad news, I'm afraid."

De Keyzer paused for a second to add extra weight to his message.

"A report has just come in from our night patrol. There's reason to believe your shop on Steen Street has been burgled," he said in a bureaucratic tone.

Degroof started to choke on his own saliva and turned away from the phone for a good cough.

"Mr. Degroof, are you still there?" De Keyzer asked after a couple of seconds.

"Of course I'm still here," Degroof rasped. "What in Christ's name does 'reason to believe' mean?"

"The duty sergeant informs me that the window and the display cabinets inside the shop are empty. He's not sure if that's normal. There's also broken glass and a pair of gloves on the floor."

"Of course it's not normal," Degroof croaked at the top of his voice. De Keyzer held the receiver away from his ear.

"Nonetheless, there's no sign of breaking and entering," he continued with caution. De Keyzer knew the Degroofs; or rather his father knew them. They were rich and extremely powerful. That's why he didn't consider it strange that Versavel had asked him to bring the Deputy up to speed. You could never be careful enough with the Degroofs and their like.

"The Deputy public prosecutor is on her way," he added with a degree of pride.

Degroof's head started to spin like carousel. He sat down and tried to assess the damage. Fortunately he was insured for every penny. The only reason his head was spinning was because he hadn't completely sobered up from the night before.

"Fine," he said. "I'm on my way."

2

GHISLAIN DEGROOF AND HANNELORE MARTENS arrived at more or less the same time. She had just parked her navy-blue Renault Twingo behind the police van when Degroof drove up in his pitch-black Maserati.

Versavel took note of their arrival. It was five past seven.

Hannelore Martens was wearing a white T-shirt and a long dark-brown skirt with an ample side split revealing a pair of shapely calves as she stepped out of her car.

"Good morning, Sergeant," she said brightly.

"Deputy Martens?" he asked in disbelief. He had heard that they were appointing magistrates young these days, but this specimen didn't look much older than twenty-five.

"Hannelore Martens," she said with as much polite firmness as she could muster. "How do you do, Sergeant?"

Versavel tapped his cap with his fore and middle fingers. At least she knew her police ranks. Not a bad sign. They were shaking hands when the final rumble of Degroof's Maserati made them turn their heads. Degroof had parked like a drunken cowboy.

"Degroof, I presume?"

Versavel spotted her derisive tone. "The very one," he said with a wink.

"Let's introduce ourselves to the injured party first, shall we?" she said cheerfully.

Versavel followed her. He found it hard to understand how a woman like her could wind up in the judiciary. She could have made a lot more money as a model.

Degroof junior was a tall thin man. His expensive designer frames half concealed an uneven pair of bulging eyes. His pointed angular shoulders protruded through his jacket. He walked with a stoop and looked ten years older than he actually was.

"Deputy Martens," she introduced herself with confidence.

Degroof seemed just as surprised as Versavel.

"I got here as fast as I could," she said.

"That's very kind of you, Deputy Martens." Degroof was clearly the perfect gentleman.

"My name is Degroof, Ghislain Degroof, Jr., to be precise, proprietor of Degroof Diamonds and Jewelry."

Versavel almost burst out laughing. Who else had they been expecting: Snow White?

"What in God's name is going on?" asked Degroof with an expression of painful indignation on his face.

"We should ask Sergeant Versavel," said Hannelore Martens. "He has all the details. Right, Sergeant?"

Versavel reported what they had observed in short sentences, prudently avoiding any mention of their real reason for stopping at the jewelry shop.

"It's common for night patrols to carry out the occasional routine checkup on their rounds," he lied straight-faced. Fortunately, Petitjean was out of earshot.

"There are no signs of breaking and entering. Everything appears to be locked up as it should," Versavel concluded with caution. "Perhaps Mr. Degroof could open the door for us. I'm sure there's more to be learned inside."

"Good idea," said Deputy Martens. "No point in hanging around. Let's take a look inside." She wanted to stay in control and be the one giving the final orders.

Versavel watched the jeweler carefully as he rummaged for his keys. He was wearing a crumpled pinstriped suit, casual moccasins without socks, and a hideous tie. His facial features were limp, his beard negligible, and he had serious bags under his frog-like eyes. There was the smell of strong drink on his breath. That explained the parking job, Versavel chuckled to himself.

As Degroof was unlocking the metal roller shutters, Hannelore Martens gave Versavel a knowing glance. Her first impressions of the jeweler didn't differ much from those of the sergeant. She didn't like the look of him one bit. It wasn't the hangover. Something disingenuous.

"Stay here," said Versavel to Petitjean when he made a move to go inside. "And don't let anyone through without my permission."

Petitjean nodded and did what he was told.

The roller shutter rattled upward with ease. Degroof opened the door, switched on the lights and made a beeline for an inbuilt cupboard, which was almost invisible between a pair of display cabinets.

"First the burglar alarm," he mumbled.

Hannelore Martens's intuition told her to stay where she was, but Versavel signaled that she was free to go inside.

"The alarm has a delay mechanism," he explained. "Degroof has one hundred seconds to disarm the system."

Degroof punched a four-digit code into the miniature keypad: 1905.

"There we are," he said, as if he'd just done something extremely complicated. "The coast is now clear."

Idiot, Versavel thought to himself. *Who says "the coast is now clear" after a break-in?* But the coast was indeed very clear. There was nothing left.

"Mon Dieu," Degroof whimpered as he looked around the shop. "They've taken everything!"

"Does that mean there's nothing under lock and key? That you didn't take anything home for safekeeping?" Versavel asked, surprised.

"With such an alarm system, that's no longer necessary, Sergeant. It cost me one and a half million."

He lunged indignantly to the other side of the shop and disappeared into a narrow corridor via a dividing door. Martens and Versavel followed, but before they reached the door they heard him shout "mon Dieu" for a second time.

Versavel was first into the corridor. He saw two doors to his right, both of them closed. On the left there was only one door, and it was half open. He noticed a pungent penetrating smell but couldn't figure out what it was. Hannelore Martens started to cough.

They made their way into a small workshop. Degroof was standing with his hands in his hair staring at a wall safe. The door of the safe was hanging from one of its hinges like a piece of modern sculpture.

"Curious," Versavel whistled. He produced his notebook and scribbled a few notes. Just as he was about to ask the jeweler a question, the shop phone started to ring. Like Lot's wife, Degroof had been rendered immobile, his hand frozen in front of his eyes in a bizarrely watchful, dramatic pose. Versavel returned to the shop and picked up the receiver.

"Sergeant Versavel speaking. Who's this?"

For a few seconds, there was silence on the other end of the line. The man from Securitas knew he was out of luck.

Every time the alarm was switched off, a signal was transmitted via a special telephone line to an emergency center almost sixty miles away. But the security guard had taken a couple of hour's nap that night, something he had never done before. He had promised his son a day out at an amusement park and his ex-wife refused to allow for the fact that he worked shifts. As far as she was concerned, he had visiting rights on Sundays and she made no exceptions.

"Freddy Dugardin from the emergency center. Is this the police?" he asked in the vain hope that the answer would be negative.

"Yes," said Versavel without intonation. He figured the man was nervous and could understand why. If the alarm had gone off that night or been disarmed and he hadn't heard the signal for one or other reason, he could expect to be signing up for unemployment on Monday morning.

"Nothing serious going on, is there?" Dugardin asked, close to desperation.

"The entire shop's been cleared out, my friend." As Versavel spoke, he suddenly realized that the alarm had in fact been on when they entered the premises. Degroof had disarmed it. That was why the guard had called. It was Sunday, and the system should have functioned normally until Monday morning. There should have been no interruptions, either right this morning or any time the night before.

"Did anyone disarm the system during the night?" Versavel inquired. In the meantime, he had opened his notebook and his pen was at the ready.

"One moment," said Dugardin. He feverishly typed the code for Degroof Diamonds and Jewelry into the keyboard in front of him on his desk: wv-BR-1423. After a couple of seconds the computer provided the requested information. Dugardin rubbed his face with the palm of his hand and started to breathe again.

"Sergeant," he said, audibly relieved, "nothing registered between midnight and now."

"And before midnight?"

"Just a second."

It took two minutes before Dugardin volunteered an answer.

"Mr. Degroof disarmed the system himself on Friday evening. He informed my colleague by phone."

"Friday, you say," Versavel repeated. "Stay on the line for a moment. Mr. Degroof is here beside me."

Versavel turned to Degroof. "Did you disarm the system on Friday evening?" he inquired. Deputy Martens had joined them and was listening carefully.

"Of course not," said Degroof, evidently affronted.

"Mr. Degroof claims he didn't disarm the system on Friday evening," Versavel told Dugardin. He used the word "claims" on purpose. He had been in the force long enough to know that people should never be taken at their word.

"Not so," Dugardin answered, a deal more confident. "He called at 22:23. You can listen to the tape. Just a second."

Versavel drummed a waltz by Strauss on the tabletop while he waited for Dugardin to rewind the tape.

"Here it comes," said Dugardin triumphantly. After a couple of buzz and whistle tones, Versavel heard the voice of Degroof. Like the rest of Bruges's prominent citizens, Degroof used a sort of sanitized West Flemish dialect, with the odd word of French tossed in here and there for good measure.

"*Allo, emergency center. Ghislain Degroof speaking. Sorry for the change, but I'm expecting an important client this evening so I've switched off the burglar alarm.*"

"*Understood, Mr. Degroof. Do you have any idea how long the system will be down?*"

"*An hour, an hour and a half. Is that okay?*"

"*So before midnight everything will be as normal?*"

"*Bien sur, mon ami.*"

"*Okay, Mr. Degroof, have a nice evening.*"

Degroof was straining at the leash with impatience and signaled nervously to be allowed to listen to the recording.

"Can you run the tape one more time?" Versavel asked. "Mr. Degroof wants to hear it for himself."

"With pleasure," said Dugardin.

Degroof grabbed the receiver from Versavel's hand. The sergeant stepped aside and angrily rubbed his moustache.

Dugardin pressed the start button, leaned back, and lit a cigarette.

As Degroof listened to the recording, the blood drained from his face and he turned deathly pale.

"But that's not my voice," he said disconcerted.

A curious Hannelore Martens turned to Versavel. For her, this was pure excitement. No one had ever told her that fieldwork could be so much fun. Degroof was still holding the receiver to his ear and was speechless. Versavel carefully took it back. Degroof shook his head and collapsed into a chair.

"Are we done?" asked Dugardin, relieved.

"Forget it buddy," said Versavel in what came close to an authoritarian tone. "If I was you I'd start writing my report, all the details, on the double. We're not done with you by a long shot."

"Of course, Sergeant," said Dugardin, happy that he was more or less off the hook with regard to his nap.

"If you ask me, something strange is going on," said Deputy Martens as Versavel returned the receiver to its cradle. The sergeant shrugged his shoulders.

"This is our bread and butter, ma'am."

"Is that so?" she reacted with a hint of indignation.

"But the man's lying," Degroof interrupted. "I didn't call anyone! I spent Friday evening at a wedding in Anvers, a nephew of Anne-Marie. We stayed the night. That's why the shop was closed for the whole weekend. I have a hundred witnesses who can confirm my whereabouts."

"Calm down, Mr. Degroof," said Versavel. "No one's accusing you of anything. You're the injured party, don't forget. We now know that someone called the emergency center in your name. We also know that whoever was responsible for this knew what you were doing this weekend. He apparently knew that you were busy with a family engagement. But more importantly, he knew how to disengage the burglar alarm."

Deputy Martens nodded approvingly. Sergeant Versavel knew his onions. Her picture of the force had changed. Her colleagues tended to be condescending when they spoke about the Bruges police.

Degroof stared vacantly into space and dabbed his forehead with a handkerchief.

"Relax for a while, Mr. Degroof. We'll take a look in the workshop first and then come back for your statement," said Versavel.

"Do you mind if I join you?" asked Hannelore Martens, determined not to be left alone with Degroof.

"Under no circumstances. I can't afford to make mistakes in front of a Deputy," Versavel joked. He was taking a risk, but fortunately she had a healthy sense of humor.

"I don't think there's much danger of that, Sergeant," she said with a wry smile. Her reaction pleased him.

They had barely set foot in workshop when Degroof stuffed his handkerchief in his pocket, grabbed the telephone receiver, and nervously punched in his father's number. The phone rang three times. Ludovic Degroof wasn't a late sleeper. He got up at six-thirty sharp every day without fail.

"Allo papa, ici Ghislain."

Ludovic Degroof listened to his son's confused account. When he was finished, he gave him detailed instructions.

"I'm going to call the commissioner tout d'suite. Restez là. I'll take care of everything."

He always took care of everything.

"Something stinks in here," said Hannelore.

"I was thinking the same thing," Versavel growled.

Versavel examined the wall safe. Whoever blew it open knew what he was doing. Versavel spoke from experience. He had spent part of his military service in bomb disposal, sweeping for mines.

"Is it empty?" she asked.

"More than likely." But he took a look inside just to be sure. "Nothing. Professionals never leave anything behind."

Hannelore started to cough again. The acrid stench refused to clear, in spite of the open door.

"It's like acid," she hacked. "I remember my father dunking his soldering iron in hydrochloric acid when I was a kid. It's the same smell."

Versavel nodded. He wanted to tell her she was an okay girl and that friendly Deputy public prosecutors were about as rare as white long-distance runners.

The workshop wasn't very big, no more than a hundred and thirty square feet. A bench against the wall opposite the door had been fitted with an articulated arm with a powerful magnifying glass and built-in lighting. Next to a bench vise a number of precision instruments were scattered in disarray. There was also a compact buffing wheel. This was apparently where minor repairs were carried out.

Versavel suddenly noticed the aquarium on the floor between the bench and the side wall. The thing was completely out of place and he didn't understand why no one had noticed it before. The walls of the glass container were roughly twelve by twenty and appeared to be the same on all four sides. It was filled with a cloudy liquid. A silvery scum floated on the surface.

"That's where the smell's coming from," Versavel snorted when he crouched and held his nose over the container. Hannelore crouched at his side. Their knees touched.

"Yuck, that's disgusting!" she yelped, turning up her nose.

"I think we should get Degroof in here," said Versavel.

She held out her hand and he helped her to her feet. Hannelore found Versavel a handsome man, amiable, the easy-going type, her type. She had always fallen for older men in her student days.

"Mr. Degroof," Versavel roared, "can we see you in the workshop?"

"Mon Dieu," Degroof blared when Versavel pointed to the tank. "Aqua regis, mon Dieu."

Degroof's pretentious "mon Dieus" were beginning to get on Versavel's nerves, so he resisted his initial urge to ask what aqua regis was.

Degroof yanked open a drawer under the bench and produced a pair of rubber gloves. He pulled on the left glove and dipped his hand carefully into the goo. His face was twisted with anxiety, as if he was afraid of finding something terrible at the bottom of the tank. A meandering vein started to swell on his forehead, making him even uglier than he already was and drawing particular attention to his uneven bulging eyes. He dipped his hand so deep into the sludge that the stinking fluid almost seeped into his glove. After thirty seconds rummaging around the bottom of the tank, he irately pulled out his hand. He had a wafer-thin strip of yellow metal between his thumb and his forefinger.

"Nom de Dieu," he grumbled.

"So?" Versavel asked, playing ignorant. "Did you find something, sir?"

Degroof glared at him in a rage and started to stir the grimy liquid in something of a frenzy. He didn't seem to care that the liquid came close to splashing into his glove as he stirred. Versavel and Hannelore were mesmerized. In a matter of minutes he managed to fish a small pile of unrecognizable twisted gold from the bottom of the tank.

"Are you suggesting that the culprit took nothing with him?" Hannelore inquired. She was slowly beginning to realize what was going on.

"Surely no one would take the trouble to break into a jewelry store just to destroy the spoils," said Versavel level-headedly.

"No?" Degroof squawked. "And what do you think this is?"

He held out his hand to reveal a pair of soiled precious stones.

"Barbarians!" he ranted. Without paying the least attention to Versavel and Hannelore, he continued to root around the bottom of the tank like a man possessed.

Versavel looked at Hannelore and realized for the first time that she was having a ball. Then someone in front of the shop shouted "hello." While Hannelore continued to watch in amusement as Degroof fished for what was left of various formerly extravagant bracelets, rings, necklaces, and earrings, Versavel made his way out to the front of the shop to see what was going on.

"Ah, Versavel, how's it goin', kiddo?" Officer Decoster blared like a broken trumpet in the broadest of Bruges accents. "Sorry we're so late, friend. But you know De Keyzer. It always takes more than half an hour before he's awake and then another hour to explain everything."

His colleague Jozef Vermeersch burst out laughing.

"You made it clear enough that we should be careful. Turns out Degroof's a bit of a protégé, if you get my drift," Decoster continued to blare.

Versavel raised a warning finger to his lips and nodded to the rear of the store. But Decoster wasn't interested. He and Vermeersch were cops without manners. If Versavel hadn't known better, he would have sworn that De Keyzer had sent the pair on purpose just to annoy him.

"It's always the same with those protégés," Vermeersch grinned. "That's why we stopped off at Decoster's on the way to pick up a pair of velvet gloves. You can never be too careful with those chic types. But I don't need to tell you that, eh, Versavel? Eh?"

Decoster produced one of his typical nervous whinnies. Versavel took him by the shoulder and brought his lips to within a few inches of his left ear.

"Dep-u-ty," he whispered, syllable by syllable, pointing in desperation to the back of the shop. Okay, she was still wet behind the ears, but a Deputy is a Deputy. Decoster confirmed with an exaggerated wink that he had understood the message and he treated Vermeersch to a jarring nudge in the ribs.

"What the . . . Jesus!" Versavel signaled that he should shut up.

"Petitjean's falling asleep at the door," said Decoster evasively, but Vermeersch still didn't get it. The important thing was that he was silent.

"Lucky his future father-in-law isn't in the neighborhood. Otherwise . . ."

"Do me a favor, Decoster. Don't start on about Petitjean. He hasn't stopped blabbing the whole night."

"Everyone takes his turn. That's fair, eh, Sarge?" Decoster teased. "I was landed with him twice last month."

Versavel wisely concealed the fact that he would have been in his bed at this very moment if it hadn't been for the ups and downs of Petitjean's love life.

"I think we should send him home," Versavel suggested. "He'll just get in everyone's way. Give him a lift to Hauwer Street," he said to Vermeersch, "then Decoster can help me with the police report."

"Can't the Deputy help?" Decoster joked. "Those guys are always rarin' to go."

"The Deputy's a 'she,'" Versavel clarified. "And not just any old 'she,' if you ask me."

"Thanks, Sarge." Three pairs of eyes flashed in the direction of Deputy Martens, who had returned unheard to the front of the shop. A few seconds of painful silence followed.

"Mr. Degroof thinks that the culprit dissolved the entire collection in an aqua regis bath," she said earnestly. "I suggest one of you help him put together an inventory of the damaged goods. In the meantime, if you could can call one of the forensic guys at the National Institute for Criminalities, Sergeant, that would be much appreciated."

They stood there a like a bunch of schoolboys caught red-handed. Even Versavel, who was rarely short for words, was speechless. This was the moment Hannelore had long been preparing for. Finally she had the chance to exercise her authority and reap the benefits of the degree she had worked so hard to obtain.

"Of course, ma'am," said Versavel. He knew her affability with them wouldn't last. But how would *he* behave if they had made *him* Deputy? It was a stubborn thing, class difference.

Just then, Degroof appeared from the back.

"I need to make a phone call. Will you excuse me?"

Versavel retreated, and Degroof sat down at his desk. He looked exhausted and dismayed. He had taken off his jacket. His left cuff was soaked with aqua regis. His eyes were blood-shot, and what remained of his hair stuck to his balding scalp. He was sweating like a marathoner, but that had nothing to do with the millions he had lost in the robbery. Degroof was afraid of what daddy would say.

"Let's go outside for a moment, gentlemen," said Hannelore diplomatically. The exercise of authority pleased her more with every passing minute. Degroof thanked her with an inconspicuous nod.

Once outside, she lit a cigarette. She offered the others the chance to join her, but only Decoster accepted. Both Versavel and Vermeersch were zealous non-smokers.

"Strange business," said Hannelore after taking her first drag and inhaling deeply. "If you ask me, magistrates should do more 'on the scene' work."

The three men smiled politely.

"We're not dealing with an amateur, that's for sure," Versavel observed. Decoster and Vermeersch appeared to have been struck dumb. "It's the motive that intrigues me. The whole thing seems absurd. Don't you agree, ma'am?" he asked.

A group of laughing Japanese tourists gaped at them inquisitively from the other side of the street. Their guide had made up one or other story on the spot. Guides always make something up if they don't know what's going on.

The Japanese immediately recorded the façade of Degroof Diamonds and Jewelry for posterity. The cameras and camcorders clicked and whizzed to their heart's content.

3

PIETER VAN IN'S TELEPHONE STARTED to ring after he had been in the shower for five minutes. He cursed under his breath, but didn't hurry himself. He took the time to rinse the suds from under his arms. He then stamped his feet nominally dry on the rubber mat, stood in front of the mirror in a cloud of steam, and shook his head. The fuzzy image in the steamed-up mirror wasn't a pretty sight.

He wrapped himself in his old, checkered bathrobe with a sigh of resignation.

It was Sunday morning, nine-fifteen. The light of the sun charily penetrated the faded curtains. Eight years of chain-smoking had given them an extraordinary patina, or was that too fine a word for nicotine deposits? The ivory ceiling and the drab wallpaper were no better off. They had once been white.

Van In dragged himself downstairs. The telephone was still ringing. The white beech stairwell connected the bedroom to the living room on the ground floor where the only telephone in the house was located. Van In hated telephones in the bedroom. He lit a cigarette before lifting the receiver.

"Van In," he barked.

"Hello, Van In, De Kee here, good morning." Nothing sounded more sarcastic than your boss wishing you good morning on a Sunday. "Sorry for bothering you so early."

The chief commissioner's sarcasm apparently knew no bounds. Van In took a bad-tempered drag of his cigarette. There was trouble on the way.

"I've just had a call from Ludovic Degroof. You know who I'm talking about?"

"Of course," Van In replied resignedly. *Everyone knows Hitler too*, was what he wanted to say.

"Good. Listen carefully to what I'm about to say, Van In." De Kee couldn't resist informing him that Degroof had called him out of bed. He was anything but comfortable with the entire business of police work arising outside of normal working hours.

"One of our night patrols observed a break-in a couple of hours ago at the son's jewelry store on Steen Street," De Kee explained. "I imagine you're asking yourself why I'm bothering you with a common break-in, and on a Sunday morning no less."

No, he wasn't. Van In was, in fact, asking himself why someone would bother *De Kee* with a common break-in on a Sunday morning.

"But there's more to it," De Kee continued. "According to initial findings, nothing was stolen. The culprit dumped the entire collection into a tank full of aqua regis. Ghislain Degroof, the jeweler, claims the acid destroyed the lot."

De Kee paused for an instant.

The first cigarette of the day usually tasted so-so, but this one tickled Van In's throat and made him cough.

"Hello, Van In?"

"A moment, commissioner," Van In hawked. It really was high time he stopped smoking.

De Kee betrayed a hint of irritation

"If Deleu hadn't been on holiday, I wouldn't have troubled you, of course. But I'm sure you understand that we need to deploy a seasoned detective in such circumstances, especially when someone like Degroof is involved."

Deleu was De Kee's son-in-law. Van In had shown him the ropes when he joined the force.

"Of course, Commissioner," he said, almost submissively.

Deleu was usually given the more sensational cases. If he screwed up, and most of the time he did, Van In was always on hand to clear up the debris. This time De Kee had no alternative than to turn first to Van In.

"So you don't mind standing in?"

"If I have to."

De Kee heaved a sigh of relief.

"Excellent, Van In," he said in good spirits. "I would genuinely appreciate it if you could get to the station as quickly as possible. Then we can start work without delay."

Van In was speechless. He was certain De Kee was calling from his apartment. *Degroof must be a serious heavyweight*, he thought to himself. *Lesser mortals wouldn't dare bother De Kee on a Sunday morning.*

"I'll be there in thirty minutes, sir," he said.

"Excellent, Van In. I knew I could rely on you." The line broke with a dry click.

Van In took a second bad-tempered drag. On the other hand, the extra money would come in handy. Double time for Sundays, and he was two months behind on his mortgage payments.

Van In stared for a full minute at the large contemporary mirror above the mantelpiece. He had given up the fight against his dictatorial vanity long ago. The carelessly knotted cord around his bathrobe had worked itself loose. The reflection of his chubby gut and sunken navel didn't exactly cheer him. He pulled a face, as he had in the bathroom moments earlier. Was this his reward for eight months of grueling training? Those women's magazines were right. Men enter senility, among other unpleasantries, when they turn forty.

He stubbed out his cigarette in a plant pot. The scrawny ficus plant trying to survive in it was on its last legs. He then let his bathrobe slip from his shoulders and stood in profile in front of the enormous mirror. He inspected himself anew with a critical eye. If he took a deep breath and pinched his buttocks, his belly looked flat and hard. Van In held the pose for twenty seconds, enjoying every one of them. Ritual complete, he climbed the wooden stairs to his bedroom heavy-footed. He had to. His clothes were still in the bathroom.

"Fucking Duvels," he grumbled as he wriggled into his pants.

To give De Kee the impression that he had hurried, Van In deliberately didn't shave.

From the Vette Vispoort where he lived to the police station on Hauwer Street was a ten-minute walk. Van In had sold his dented BMW three years earlier. You needed an expensive private garage in Bruges since it was impossible to park on the street, and Van In had decided after one too many tickets that it simply wasn't worth it.

"Good morning, Commissioner Van In," said Benny Lagrou with a toothless smile from behind the reception desk.

"Morning, Benny. Has De Kee been here long?" asked Van In nonchalantly.

Lagrou was old school, a heavy drinker and a gossipmonger. De Kee had taken him off the beat five years earlier. His usual job was "Lost Property," known among his colleagues as "Siberia."

"Did he call you in for the Steen Street robbery?" he said evasively.

"How long has he been here?" Van In reformulated his question.

"He stormed in half an hour ago," Lagrou whispered in a conspiratorial tone. "And I don't think he's in a good mood."

"Is he ever?" said Van In.

Lagrou grinned. More gums.

Van In pushed open the dividing door and took the stairs to the third floor. He was alone. Most people took the lift.

Chief Commissioner De Kee, a former barber who had worked his way to a Master's in criminology, responded almost simultaneously to Van In's discreet knock on the door.

"Enter."

The chief commissioner was behind his desk. He was short, like most dictators. He had put on his uniform for the occasion. Exceptional, since most of the time he wore expensive tailored suits. Vera, his mistress, painstakingly monitored his look.

"Take a seat, Van In," said De Kee in a toneless voice. He peered at him through non-reflective lenses in an eighteen-karat gold frame. He wasn't comfortable with his son-in-law's absence. He preferred to keep Van In on the sidelines.

"Cigarette?"

"Please," said Van In.

De Kee slid a packet of Players in Van In's direction, tax-free, naturally. Van In took his time. De Kee ran his fingers nervously through his thinning hair. A child could tell he was under pressure. He saw that Van In had noticed and immediately pulled down his hand.

"I want you to take control of the case, Van In. The most important thing is discretion. By that, I mean you should be as little trouble to the Degroofs as humanly possible. If you want to question anyone, don't do it here at the station. Do I make myself clear?"

"Of course, sir."

Van In knew that De Kee was indebted big time to Ludovic Degroof, as were three-quarters of the local politicians in fact.

"It's also not essential *per se* that the culprit or culprits be arrested."

De Kee was clearly uncomfortable with these words. Van In was astounded.

"And why not, if you don't mind my asking?"

De Kee took off his expensive glasses and rubbed the corners of his eyes with his thumb and forefinger. Van In was asking the kind of questions Deleu would never think of asking. But he had little choice. Someone had to set up an investigation.

"Pieter, my friend," he said in an unctuous tone. "Mr. Ludovic Degroof hates this sort of publicity. If you catch the culprits, fine. If you don't, no problem. Degroof is asking for a thorough police report, officially recording his losses and nothing more. He doesn't want us to waste a lot of time and energy on the case."

De Kee's sudden informality made Van In particularly suspicious. The chief commissioner always used titles and surnames.

"In other words, he needs us to recuperate his losses from the insurance," said Van In pointedly.

De Kee brushed off his remark with a gesture of indifference.

"How long have you been in the force, Pieter?" he asked as Van In stared at him in amusement. "Eighteen, nineteen years?"

"Nineteen," said Van In.

"Almost twenty, Pieter," said De Kee, correcting him. The cunning fox had a tremendous memory for detail and liked to flaunt it. "I presume you've seen a few things in your time?"

Van In nodded. He had heard this line before. Politics were usually involved.

"So you know the ways of the world, and that it's sometimes better not to stir the shit."

De Kee started to run his fingers through his hair again. Vera had dyed it only the day before with one or other expensive coloring. He didn't mind paying for it, nor for the Renault Clio and the apartment in Zeebrugge.

"I think I understand what you're trying to say, Commissioner." Van In felt like a schoolboy, and his teacher was a short, arrogant asshole.

"I hope you do, Pieter." He put on his glasses and stared Van In in the eye. De Kee liked to stare people in the eye. He was convinced that it gave him an air of authority.

"Do we have a deal?"

Van In moistened his lips.

"Do I have a choice?" he asked.

De Kee shook his head. "No, I'm afraid you don't, Pieter."

Van In thought back for a moment to his youth, to the unforgettable sixties, when he had never been forced to compromise. Those were the days. Nowadays he was burdened with alimony payments and a mortgage that was beyond his means.

De Kee got to his feet and looked out over Beurs Square. He had done what had been asked of him. If Van In screwed up, he could use him as the perfect scapegoat. Deleu's absence wasn't that bad after all. De Kee had a sixth sense that helped him steer clear of tricky situations.

"Shall we take a look at the scene?" he suggested. He checked the enormous clock above the door. It was nine-fifty. "Your colleague will be happy to be relieved of duty."

Van In stubbed out his half-smoked cigarette and made his way to the door. De Kee picked up the internal phone and dialed the cafeteria.

"Hello, Gerard. We're leaving immediately." De Kee's voice became thin and nasal and sounded like a slowly turning blender.

Gerard Vandenbrande was De Kee's private chauffeur. The chief commissioner had created the function himself the day after the mayor and his elected officials appointed him chief commissioner for life.

Gerard greeted De Kee and Van In in the prescribed fashion and dutifully held open the passenger door of the black Ford Scorpio. The Scorpio was just short of two years old. Nothing unique: De Kee had a right to a new official car every four years. The Scorpio's number plate, on the other hand, *was* unique: DKB-101. "De Kee Bruges," followed by the national police emergency number. The man's vanity was boundless.

"How's the baby?" asked Van In as he got into the car.

Gerard's wife Kaat had given birth to a child with Down syndrome six months earlier. De Kee was aware of the fact but hadn't gone to the trouble to get his own car out of the garage. Had he done so, Gerard would not have had to call his in-laws at the last minute and have them babysit. Kaat was a nurse and worked two weekend shifts a month.

Gerard discreetly shrugged his shoulders and took his place behind the wheel, a look of sadness on his face. Van In watched De Kee nod and Gerard stepped gently on the gas pedal.

The bronze fountain on Zand Square spouted powerful jets of water against a turquoise sky. The water splattered with comforting regularity into the basin. The enormous square was more or less empty, ready to catch the unsuspecting agoraphobe unawares.

Gerard turned into Zuidzand Street at a snail's pace. Zuidzand Street ran into Steen Street, a Mecca for Bruges's spoiled consumers. Degroof had set up business in an unexceptional building, although his collection was exclusive and as a result exorbitantly priced. It was said that Degroof junior designed the collections himself, but Van In knew from a reliable source that the man had a couple of young designers in his employ who were willing to sell him their inspiration and craftsmanship for a pittance.

A Volkswagen police van with revolving beacons had stationed itself in front of the store. Decoster and Vermeersch weren't averse to a bit of show now and again.

"Who's in charge of the investigation?" Van In asked as he got out of the Scorpio.

"Guido Versavel," said De Kee. "He was finishing his night shift. But you know Versavel. There's no stopping the man," he added in what was close to a sneer.

"Versavel's an excellent officer," said Van In resolutely. De Kee looked at him in amazement but said nothing. He had spotted Degroof, who had left the store and was walking in his direction.

"Bonjour, mon cher Commissaire."

De Kee walked up to Ghislain Degroof with a distinguished smile on his thin lips. They greeted one another elaborately on the sidewalk in front of the store with pats on the back, incomprehensible French salutations, and what seemed to be an endless handshake. In contrast to an hour earlier, Degroof was conspicuously relaxed.

Van In was demoted on the spot to a useless establishment appendage.

Versavel appeared at the door and saved the day. The sergeant nodded approvingly and beckoned Van In with a languid gesture. He was happy to hand over the investigation to Van In. Working with Vermeersch and Decoster was getting him nowhere.

"Guido, you look tired, my friend."

"You'd be the same if you'd spent the entire night playing nanny!"

Van In raised his eyebrows.

"Petitjean," said Versavel.

"Is that poor bastard still not married?" Van In smiled. Everyone on the force had heard about the young officer's amorous crusade.

"Vermeersch and Decoster are taking photos in the workshop," said Versavel. "The Deputy's keeping an eye on them."

"The Deputy!" Van In groaned. "Why not bring in the attorney general? No publicity. Jesus H."

"What are you driveling on about?" asked Versavel.

"Never mind. So tell me, what's the situation?"

Versavel quickly filled him in. He also confessed that he had played a joke on De Keyzer, the duty officer. "I wasn't surprised when he walked right into it, but I hadn't reckoned on her doing the same."

"So she's as dumb as the rest of her magistrate colleagues," said Van In disdainfully.

"I don't know if she's dumb," muttered Versavel. "But she's certainly cute . . ."

"I'll be the judge of that, Sergeant," said Van In. "Since when did this sudden interest in the opposite sex emerge, by the way?"

Van In and Versavel had known each other for years, and Versavel had grown immune to his insinuations.

"I called Leo. He'll be here any minute," said Versavel, ignoring Van In's provocation. Leo Vanmaele was a forensics expert for the NIC. He was also one of Pieter Van In's closest friends.

"Excellent," said Van In.

"Come, let's go inside," Versavel suggested. His tiredness was slowly getting the better of him.

Van In's feet sank half an inch into the mouse-gray wall-to-wall carpet into which the Degroof Diamonds and Jewelry monogram had been woven.

"Call this art?" he muttered.

"Not impressed?" said Versavel, slightly surprised. Van In shook his head resolutely.

He took a careful look around. It was a small space, twelve by forty at the most, he figured. The walls, into which eight imitation gothic alcoves had been carved, were covered with old hand-cleaned bricks. The alcoves had glass doors and served as display cabinets for the jewelry. But on this particular Sunday morning there was nothing in the alcoves except the blue velvet display mats.

A pair of crystal chandeliers hung from the ceiling and a couple of tables at which Degroof received his clients were the only furnishings. Van In couldn't quite put his finger on their style. A mixture of all the French Louis put together, an excess of gold leaf, and yards of Cordovan leather. Each table had three chairs in the same indefinable style. The seats were covered in velvet.

Van In lit a cigarette.

"Maybe I should introduce you to our Deputy first," said Versavel by way of precaution.

"Do you have to?" Van In growled. "You know I don't like working with women. First they snare you, then they play the boss, and before you know it they're somewhere else spending your money."

Versavel knew what Van In had been through, but insisted nevertheless: "I think you should follow my advice this time. You only have to look at her and you know you can't win."

But there was no need to try to convince him any further. Hannelore Martens had heard voices in the front of the shop and had come to take a look. Versavel kept a careful eye on Van In. He was mesmerized, as Versavel had predicted.

"Deputy Martens, may I introduce you to Assistant Commissioner Van In? He'll be in charge of the case from now on."

The Deputy didn't seem to mind Van In's stare.

"Delighted to meet you, Commissioner Van In. I'm curious to hear your opinion on the case. If you ask me, there's something weird going on."

"I only just got here," Van In snapped. "Sergeant Versavel was just briefing me."

He could feel the sweat begin to appear on his forehead. It usually took a while before he was able to have a normal conversation with a strange female. He had to make a serious effort not to stutter. The sense of unease he had with women dated back to his adolescence. He was now too old to do anything about it. It'll subside soon enough, he thought to himself, in a feeble attempt at comfort.

"Can we confer?" She pointed at one of the tables. Without waiting for an answer, she pulled back a chair and sat down. She crossed her legs with elegance.

Versavel noticed that Van In was having problems and came to his colleague's aid.

"The chief commissioner is here, ma'am. He's outside, talking with the owner. Shall I call him?" His question knocked her off kilter for a few seconds. Representatives of the public prosecutor were expected to discuss matters with the most senior officer present. It was an unwritten rule.

"No, thank you, Sergeant. I'll find him myself. We'll talk later."

"Whew," Van In sighed as she walked out the door. "You could have warned me, man. Thanks a lot!"

"I tried." Versavel grinned. "But you wouldn't listen. By the way, have you forgotten what you did last year, cuffing me to that young German guy for half the night? Jesus, we were thigh to thigh. I had to control myself. You did that on purpose. It's not my fault she's cute."

Van In took a deep breath. The throbbing knot of nerves in his gut had started to melt.

"Okay, that's one all. Next time we arrest an Adonis, you get to frisk him naked, Versavel. Eh, kiddo?"

They both exploded with laughter.

4

LEO VANMAELE LUMBERED INTO THE shop at eleven-fifteen with the pretty Hannelore in his wake.

"The chief commissioner and Mr. Degroof are having a coffee together in Café Craenenburg, on the terrace," she said before Leo could get a word in. "Mr. Vanmaele here is from the judicial police, part of their technical team," she added in a school-teacherly tone.

"Good morning, Mr. Vanmaele," said Van In with a wink.

They had often guzzled Duvels together into the wee small hours, but she didn't need to know that.

Vanmaele had parked his screaming yellow Audi 100 in front of the shop window with two wheels on the sidewalk. He had had it sprayed yellow in a bet with Van In. If anyone managed to trace another yellow Audi 100 with Belgian plates, then Van In would have to pay for every Duvel they cracked together for a whole year. If Van In lost the bet, it was going to cost him a hell of a lot more than Vanmaele had coughed up for the spray job.

"Been a while since we worked together."

"Indeed, Commissioner," said Leo Vanmaele indifferently.

"So what's the story?"

"Person or persons unknown appear to have dissolved Degroof's entire collection in a tank of aqua regis." Van In took a step backward and pointed in the direction of Hannelore and Versavel. "That's all I know; I just arrived."

Hannelore thought Van In's approach was on the feeble side. Instead of doing something, all he could muster was "That's all I know; I just arrived." Would her colleagues at the courthouse turn out to be right in their claim that the Bruges police were only good for towing away illegally parked cars?

"Mr. Degroof is busy, or rather *was* busy, putting together an inventory of the jewelry he keeps in the shop," she said with a professional air. At the moment, the information she had to offer was completely irrelevant. She noticed how Van In shook his head in pity and held his tongue.

"I'll need to take a look at that tank of aqua regis." said Vanmaele. "And the safe, of course. Oxyacetylene or explosives?"

No one had told him about a safe, but there was no need. Vanmaele had plenty of experience.

"Explosives," Versavel chimed in. "I suspect he used Semtex with a water pillow to dampen the explosion. There's still some cellophane stuck to the wall."

Hannelore had no idea what Semtex was, but she flatly refused to ask for an explanation, not wanting to betray her ignorance.

"And no one heard the bang?" Leo looked at Van In.

"It would seem not. Nobody lives round here. The poor bastards with shops on Steen Street usually have a hovel somewhere
in the suburbs," he sneered. "But we'll check it out, of course."

"Passersby?"

"Maybe," Van In nodded. The entire operation had taken
place before midnight and there was always someone out for a
stroll. But Van In wisely held his tongue. De Kee had insisted
on discretion. Finding witnesses was the least of his worries.

"Why not send out a call on one of the independent radio
stations, or contact local television," Hannelore suggested. The
assistant commissioner's lack of initiative was beginning to annoy
her. Versavel and Vanmaele shared her thoughts to the letter.

"We could, yes, indeed," said Van In without evident
enthusiasm. "But let's take another look around here first. Mr.
Vanmaele can start the ball rolling by taking a sample of the
aqua regis and checking the tank for fingerprints."

The ever-cheerful Vanmaele pulled an ugly face. This wasn't
the Van In he knew and loved.

"Right away, Commissioner," he said, emphasizing the word
"commissioner." "I'll get my materials."

"And ask Vermeersch to take you back to the station,
Guido," said Van In to Versavel. "I imagine you're dog-tired,
but I'm afraid the paperwork can't wait. I need your report
before the day's out."

Versavel nodded. Van In wasn't himself. But he knew him
well enough. The man always had his reasons.

After Versavel had gone, and while Vanmaele was busy in
the workshop trying to find useable traces, Van In took a seat
at one of the tables. Hannelore observed him, barely able to
contain her increasing amazement.

After a couple of seconds, the silence felt like a lead blanket.
Keeping his mouth shut was more irritating than his shyness.

"Have you heard anything from your own people, ma'am?" he asked finally, in the hope that she would bugger off. A drop of cold sweat trickled from his neck down his spine.

"This is an exceptionally intriguing case," she said, her response unrelated to his question. "Do you mind if I join you? I've never been present at a police investigation before. If anyone in the office needs me, they'll know where to find me. I left Degroof's number on my answering machine," she added with a sense of pride.

Jesus H. Christ, thought Van In. *Jesus H. come to my aid.*

He said that a lot when he was in the shit.

She pulled over one of the chairs and sat down opposite him.

"Have you been involved in anything similar?

Van In shook his head. He looked at her full on for a second, but then immediately looked down.

"Dissolving jewelry in a bath of acid isn't exactly an everyday occurrence. Probably the work of an unbalanced mind. And there's nothing more difficult to get a handle on than a crazy person," he said, consciously despondent.

"You don't sound too optimistic."

"If we don't find any useable traces or reliable witness, I'm afraid there won't be any reason to be optimistic, ma'am."

"But it's early days, isn't it? We still have to launch the radio and TV appeal. I presume that's part of your planning?"

Van In was faced with a dilemma. He couldn't tell her what De Kee had confided in him. It was better not to wash the force's dirty linen in public. Passing on confidences to a magistrate was tantamount to committing treason. His relationship with De Kee may not have been warm and hearty, but he still wasn't planning to take this Deputy into his confidence.

But if she harped on any longer about an appeal on independent radio he would have to do something about it. Hannelore Martens may have been as green as pool-table baize, but she was also obstinate and persevering. He tried in desperation to think of an excuse to have her drop the idea.

"I think it would be better to wait first for the results of the inquiry."

He suddenly sensed the warmth of her knees beneath the table. He hadn't realized they were sitting so close.

"Nonsense," she laughed. "The media are gagging for juicy reports like this. And don't forget, their cooperation often uncovers useful information. The Dutch police have solved any number of cases with the help of the media. Bruges isn't the sticks anymore, is it?"

"I'd have to run it past my superiors first," said Van In tensely.

"Fine, Commissioner. But I want you to keep me up to speed. Do we have a deal?" She grabbed a brown envelope that was lying on the edge of the table and scribbled something in haste.

"Here, my address and telephone number."

Van In accepted the envelope. It was just an ordinary envelope, without a stamp or imprint. Hannelore had used the back. He glanced at the address and telephone number, which she had written in sturdy capitals. Just as he was about to slip the envelope into his inside pocket, he noticed three words scribbled on the front.

For you, bastard.

Van In ran his fingers over the envelope. Like everyone else, he had thought that Degroof or one of his associates had left it behind on Friday. He opened the flap and removed a small square of paper.

"What are you doing?" she asked in surprise. When she saw Van In staring at the piece of paper with raised eyebrows she got to her feet and stood beside him. She leaned forward and Van In peeked shyly at her out of the corner of his eye.

She was wearing a flimsy lace bra. He turned his head. *Jesus H.*, he thought.

"What's this all about? What made you open the envelope?"

"Because it says 'for you, bastard' on the front. It's hard to believe that Mr. Degroof gets this kind of mail on a regular basis," he said impatiently.

Van In looked at the square of paper from every angle. It made no sense.

"Do you think whoever was responsible for the break-in left this behind?" She had moved in even closer. Her unabashed cleavage was unavoidable. Van In thought it better to look the other way. He tried to concentrate on the twenty-five letters on the piece of paper he was holding between his thumb and his forefinger. The fact that there were twenty-five of them was all he could figure.

"Perhaps Degroof can help," said Van In cautiously. "Jewelers sometimes work with codes and the like. It's all Greek to me."

"But you said just then that you could tell from the text on the envelope that it had something to do with the case."

"No, I didn't," he snorted. "I said that it was hard to imagine Degroof getting mail with 'for you, bastard' written on it."

"But you still think the letter is from whoever broke into the place," she persevered obstinately.

"Could be."

"Could be," she repeated. "Who else could have left it, may I ask, Commissioner?"

She pulled the piece of paper from between his fingers and studied it for a few seconds.

"I presume Mr. Degroof doesn't correspond in Latin," she sneered.

Fucking intellectuals, said Van In under his breath. "I don't know too many criminals who draft their messages in Latin either, do you?" he replied with more than a hint of sarcasm. The discomfort refused to let go. The naïve self-assurance she radiated gave him goose bumps.

"Absolutely, Commissioner, spot on. Criminals don't tend to leave messages in Latin," she laughed, seeing the funny side.

Jesus, that too, Van In sighted. *She's a good loser and she's got a sense of humor!* His thoughts returned to the fleeting knee contact. Had she done it on purpose, or was she teasing him? Maybe she sensed that he wasn't really in his comfort zone. Van In was a realist, but a warm, tingling thrill ran through his body.

She walked around the desk, grabbed her chair, and sat down beside him. She placed the piece of paper on the table in front of them.

"'Rotas' means 'wheels,'" she said pensively. The word made up the top of the square.

ROTAS
OPERA
TENET
AREPO
SATOR

Intended or not, Hannelore was very close to him yet again. She smelled of Lux toilet soap and had a couple of freckles around her nose. Was she really a Deputy public prosecutor? Van In shook his head.

"So what do *you* think 'rotas' means?" she responded without taking a breath.

Van In jumped. He had strayed in his thoughts to the care-free moments he had spent with Sonja.

"Sorry, my thoughts were elsewhere." He wanted to light a cigarette, but changed his mind. For some non-smokers, one cigarette was enough to spoil a friendship and he wasn't pre-pared to take the risk.

"It looks like a puzzle . . . a sort of cryptogram. Don't you think, Commissioner?" Her voice changed tone like a screwed-up adolescent. In the space of a few minutes she had shifted from interfering bitch to impish schoolgirl.

"If you're right, then we must have a bit of a weirdo on our hands, or an idealist, or a combination of both." Van In sighed. He was suddenly grateful to De Kee. Time to put the case to bed as quickly as possible.

"Or someone who's been watching too much American pulp TV," she added cleverly.

"Jesus H. Christ," Van In groaned. "Spare me!"

"What did you say?" Hannelore glared at him. Her upper lip was trembling and it looked as if she was about to burst out laughing. Van In presumed he was now blushing.

"Typical police talk," he said, brushing it off.

"You don't say."

Van In understood that there was no point in trying to fool her. She would only insist.

"You're right, ma'am. It's high time I updated my vocabulary."

"Rags, Commissioner, rags. That's what I used to say when I was in the shit."

"You're kidding."

"No, honestly, it harks back to my student days," she recounted eagerly. "I turned up for my first oral exam in jeans, brand-new jeans no less. Can you guess what the professor said when he saw me?"

"No," said Van In innocently.

"'I don't examine rags. Come back in September for a re-sit. Run along.' I cried my head off!"

"You're kidding." He was barely aware of the fact that their conversation had become just as irrelevant as the anecdote she had just told him. They were in the middle of an investigation, after all. Another *Jesus H. Christ* was on the tip of his tongue. He was grateful no one else was in the shop.

"So where did you pick up the expression?" She poked him in the ribs with her elbow.

It was hard to tell whether Leo had been eavesdropping, but in any case his timing was perfect. He wheezed a little from sitting on his heels. His sleeves were rolled up and his piggy eyes flashed back and forth between Van In and Deputy Martens.

Hannelore put on a serious face. All this was new to her and she was having a whale of a time. She had long forgotten her colleagues' wise advice. Pulling her weight was fine for a while, but she couldn't keep it up. It wasn't her style. No wonder they all walked around at the courthouse with a miserable face.

"Find anything?" Van In inquired.

"No prints," Leo declared in a resigned tone. "And the gloves aren't much help either . . . recent design, available everywhere. Maybe a microscopic examination might come up with something."

"And the aqua regis?" Hannelore turned toward Vanmaele.

"What do you mean, ma'am?"

"Can't it be traced? If you ask me, there's a good ten gallons of the stuff in that tank. A sizeable amount for something that's not available in the supermarket."

"So you think there might be a record somewhere of such a purchase? If only. Aqua regis isn't as rare and exotic as the name suggests. It's just a mixture of one part nitric acid and three parts hydrochloric acid. Two innocent components you can buy in any drugstore without arousing anyone's suspicions. Jewelers use it to separate gold from other alloyed metals."

Leo grabbed a chair and sat down opposite Hannelore and Van In. He took off his glasses and launched into his explanation. Leo had started his career as a schoolteacher. He loved teaching, but the pupils at a variety of high schools hadn't shared his enthusiasm.

"Pure twenty-four-karat gold is soft and unworkable," he lectured. His round rosy cheeks were riddled with rosacea. "What we know as eighteen-karat or fourteen-karat is in fact an amalgam of gold and copper, silver, nickel, or palladium. The more the copper, for example, the yellower the gold. So-called "white gold" is a combination of gold and palladium or nickel. Eighteen-karat is an alloy containing 75 percent gold."

"Well, well," said Hannelore, "you learn something new every day!"

Leo thanked her with a broad smile. The lovely Hannelore was apparently everyone's favorite.

"Processing old gold, or 'scrap' as they call it, is a question of separating the components. And one of gold's more agreeable features is that it's impervious to acid. The procedure is child's play. You make a cocktail of two concentrated acids and dump in the 'scrap.' That's how jewelers recover the pure gold."

Leo Vanmaele returned his glasses to his nose as a sign that his lecture was over. He peered at the lovebirds in front of him through his thick lenses. For Leo, the situation was crystal-clear: something was blossoming between those two. His only problem was trying to understand how a woman like Hannelore could fall for the likes of Van In. His friend was forty-one, smoked like a nineteenth-century chimney, and drank like a Hummer in overdrive.

"So Degroof has nothing to complain about," Hannelore concluded.

"The gold can still be used."

"Absolutely, ma'am," said Leo with a little too much emphasis on the "ma'am." As if he wanted to underline the difference in rank.

"But ninety percent of the retail value of an exclusive piece of jewelry is in the design and the labor costs. Whoever did this caused a great deal of damage. If they had just taken it all, the insurance would have paid Degroof back to the last cent. Now it is more complicated."

"Revenge," said Van In cautiously.

"Exacted by a classically schooled psycho." Hannelore waved the square of paper in the air.

Leo didn't understand what she was talking about and paid no attention to her remark.

"If it was an act of revenge, then whoever did it was perfectly prepared," he said. "No amateurs involved here. Semtex was used to blow open the safe, and that's not the kind of thing you can pick up at the local bakery. The entire process of dissolving gold in aqua regis also takes more than twenty-four hours. Whoever was responsible must have known that the shop was closed on Saturday."

"And don't forget the alarm system. The culprit knew the code and the procedure followed by the security firm," said Van In.

Hannelore fished a pack of cigarettes from the ample hip pocket in her loose-fitting skirt.

"Are you a smoker, Commissioner?"

Van In could hardly believe his ears. "Yes, thanks," he said." Leo refused the offer with a resolute gesture of the hand.

While Van In was enjoying his first greedy puff, Hannelore said unexpectedly: "Strange that someone who knew the alarm code didn't know the combination of the safe."

Leo looked at Van In with the words *pretty-and-intelligent-who-would-have-thought* written all over his face.

"My compliments, ma'am. As my old school teacher used to say: a good score, my boy, is a step closer to the front of the class."

"Why didn't *we* think of that," said Van In.

"Because women just happen to be sharper than men, Commissioner," she bragged and beamed. "And not to forget the Latin puzzle, Commissioner, eh?" She slipped the paper across the table to Leo. "You studied Latin at school if I'm not mistaken, Mr. Vanmaele?" Van In didn't understand why they kept up the pretence and didn't just use first names. But Leo didn't seem to be bothered by it.

"That's correct," he smirked, pushing up his glasses and subjecting the piece of paper to a detailed examination.

"If we're talking about revenge," said Hannelore, "then it seems logical to me that we should be looking for the perpetrator or perpetrators in the immediate vicinity of the Degroof family. Revenge is an extremely personal matter. It's more commonly associated with crimes of passion than with burglaries, at least if you can call this a burglary."

She stared at Van In in expectation.

"I'll try to put together a profile of the culprit tomorrow," he said. It annoyed him that he couldn't speak freely. "The guys from missing persons might be good for ideas. But I'm personally not convinced we're dealing with a psycho."

"But just then you said . . ."

"That was just then, ma'am."

"Okay, everyone's entitled to a change of opinion. But what makes you think it's not a psycho? Intuition?"

"Indeed," Van In smiled, "male intuition in this case."

Bulls-eye, thought Leo. He had been listening in while trying to decipher the Latin text. The meaning of "rotas," "opera," and "tenet" was obvious, and he had also noticed that "arepo" and "sator" were "opera" and "rotas" in reverse. But he still couldn't figure what it was about.

"Not easy, Van In," he said, removing his glasses as a sign that he had given up. "It was all so long ago. I think we're going to need to consult a philologist. And if we translate it, does that mean we've figured it out? Did you notice that 'rotas' and 'opera' are also written backward, both vertically and horizontally?"

"So you also think it's a sort of puzzle?" said Van In, leaning forward and taking the paper from Leo.

"But there has to be some kind of meaning behind it. Criminals don't just leave messages behind for no reason, do they?" She brushed her hair behind her ears with both hands.

"Except in American pulp," said Van In, straight-faced. "Then anything's possible."

"Come on, gentlemen. Stop messing me around," she said indignantly.

"All we can do is wait for the results of the investigation. Face it, ma'am. We don't have any other option."

"And what about the radio appeal?" she asked angrily. Hannelore Martens clearly did have a volatile temperament.

There she goes again, Van In sighed. She was right, of course. Someone must have seen or heard something.

"Don't worry, ma'am. I'm sure the chief commissioner will agree to your proposal. But at this moment in time I think I'd be more useful back at the station. There's a load of paperwork involved in this, and I can't let sergeant Versavel deal with it alone."

"Fine, Commissioner, but I'll be following the case closely."

"Mr. Vanmaele probably wants to hang around here a little longer."

Leo nodded.

"Then I'll be going. By the way, according to Versavel, Degroof gave the keys to the shop to Officer Decoster. I'll tell him to wait until you're ready, then he can close up."

"Okey-dokey," said Vanmaele. "I can come back tomorrow with a van and a couple of helpers to bring the tank with the golden gunk to the lab. Then we can determine precisely how much gold was dissolved. I figure that's what Degroof wants to know more than anything else."

"So that's agreed." Van In got to his feet.

"I presume we'll meet again," he said to Hannelore.

"I very much hope so, Commissioner. It was a pleasure to make your acquaintance," she purred. Van In was never going to understand women. She shook his hand and held it firm for a moment. "And don't forget the radio," she winked. "I'm certain an appeal will lead to something, and apart from that I insist that it happens," she added sternly. "If they don't broadcast it tomorrow morning, I'll take care of it myself. On the record, of course."

Outside, Decoster and Vermeersch were having a hard time keeping the curious at a distance. The street was crawling with tourists and everyone wanted to know what was going on.

A thin young gentleman watched events unfold with evident amusement. His short, bald, and unstoppable sidekick took photos of the scene. He was a local reporter who never left the house without a camera. He had bought the story for a thousand francs from one of the officers keeping the crowds at bay.

Van In wriggled his way outside, doing his best not to draw attention. The heat of the summer sun coiled like a burning snake between the rows of houses. It was going to be a sweltering day. Festive flags hung unruffled from the city's façades, ready for the annual celebration of the Flemish Community the following day. Van In tried to pick up his pace but it was hopeless. There were tourists everywhere, slowing everything down, and they got out of the way for no one.

He kept close to the house fronts, using the walls as cover. His thoughts still fluttered around Hannelore Martens, like a butterfly over a bed of flowers. Van In was angry with himself. He had behaved like an idiot.

Okay, a bit of an idiot, he corrected himself. She hadn't exactly played the respectable Deputy public prosecutor either.

Versavel was in room 204, his back to the window, sweating over an old-fashioned mechanical typewriter.

"Aren't you tired yet?" asked Van In as he walked in the door. The sergeant barely looked up from his work. His coarse fingers continued to batter the broken-down Brother without pity.

"Another five minutes," he groaned.

Van In collapsed into the chair behind Versavel's desk and lit a cigarette. He ignored the "No Smoking" signs. They were for visitors only.

"And did you wangle a date out of her?" asked Versavel dryly.

"Jesus H. Not you too. Leo spent the whole time winking at me. Why should I? She was just out to impress. Beginners are always a bit weird."

"She couldn't keep her eyes off you," said Versavel, unperturbed. "I'd watch my ass if I were you, buddy."

There was a moment of silence, broken only by the clatter of the typewriter. Van In wasn't really sure why he was making a fuss. If it had been up to him, he would have taken her out that very night.

"So, done and dusted," said Versavel, relieved. He rolled a densely typed sheet of paper from the typewriter and placed it carefully on top of the pile he had completed earlier. "Well-earned overtime. It's all yours." He stood and stretched.

"You on duty tomorrow?" asked Van In. "De Kee insists that I take personal charge of the case, and it would be good if I could rely on your assistance."

"No problem," Versavel answered.

It was clear that he felt honored by the commissioner's request. He may only have been a sergeant, but he had proved himself more than enough in the past. Van In was one of the few officers who appreciated him.

"Thanks, Guido, but there are a couple of complications," said Van In in a confidential tone. "De Kee's under pressure from Degroof senior. He's insisting on absolute discretion and no publicity."

Versavel frowned, but said nothing.

"We can do discreet, can't we?" asked Van In.

"But then our pretty miss Deputy is determined to broadcast an appeal on local radio in the hope of picking up a witness."

"Is that so?"

Versavel nodded.

"That complicates matters even more." He didn't inquire any further, just accepted the absurdity of the situation as one would expect of an experienced policeman. "So, if you don't mind, I want you to pick up the phone tomorrow if anyone calls about the case. I'll ask them to broadcast the appeal between seven and nine. De Kee won't be in until later and we can only hope that Degroof doesn't listen to local radio. From the moment someone comes forward as a witness we're covered. We write up their statements, stuff them in the file and send it to Miss Martens. Then everybody's happy."

"I hope so, for your sake," said Versavel skeptically.

"Don't worry about me, Guido. I've survived bigger disasters."

"See you tomorrow, then. I'll make sure I'm here before seven."

"Thanks, Guido. Now go the fuck home, man."

"Have a good one, Commissioner."

Versavel slammed the door hard behind him and legged it down the corridor, whistling as he went.

55

Before rolling the first sheet of paper into the typewriter, Van In smoked a cigarette. He hated the mass of paperwork that was going to take up the rest of his day. He took a long draw on his cigarette, knowing it was nothing more than a pointless tactic to delay the inevitable.

5

GUIDO VERSAVEL CRUMPLED THE PLASTIC coffee cup he had been holding in his left hand and tossed it into the wastebasket. His aim was perfect. It was seven-fifteen A.M. He felt upbeat and rested. Nine hours of sleep and a hot bath had neutralized the fatigue of the previous day.

He had brought a small, portable radio to work and had tuned in to Radio Contact, a popular local broadcaster. The telephone operator had been instructed to transfer incoming calls related to the Degroof case directly to room 204.

In the meantime, Versavel took another look at the substantial report he had sweated over the day before. Few of his colleagues knew that he liked to turn his hand to a bit of writing in his spare time. Two of his stories had been published under a pseudonym, and he had somehow found time to finish his first novel. His love for writing explained why he always paid

particular attention to the style and form of his police reports—
something his colleagues never understood nor appreciated. He
didn't care that most of the cases they detailed were dropped.
For Versavel, having a fluent and correct command of his native
language was a point of honor.

The first tip arrived at eight-fifteen.

A man identifying himself as Armand Ghyoot claimed he
had seen a couple of Moroccans hanging around Steen Street
at ten-thirty the previous evening.

"And one of those habibis was carrying a sports bag," he
added with a chuckle.

Versavel thanked the man, assured him he had taken note of
everything, and hung up. Nothing helpful there, he thought.
The phone buzzed again ten seconds later, and so it continued
for quite some time.

In the space of one and a half hours, Versavel took thirteen
calls. Three were about the Moroccans, one about a black guy,
and two about Turks, all of which were more telling about
the people calling in than who might have melted down those
jewels. An elderly lady confused Degroof Diamonds with
Deloof Lawnmowers in Zedelgem. She had seen a truck pull
into the parking lot the night before and heard the sound of
breaking glass. Turned out later that Deloof Lawnmowers had
indeed been burgled that night, and Versavel made a note to
have someone look into it once this mess at DeGroof's had
been resolved.

Versavel also took a couple of calls from the requisite set of
jokers. One was traced immediately because he had been dumb
enough to use his own phone. There were still people out there
who didn't know that their telephone number appeared on a
display when they called the police.

Versavel shortlisted four interesting calls and drafted a brief
report for the attention of Assistant Commissioner Van In.

THE SQUARE OF REVENGE

On Friday at ten-thirty P.M., Mr. Dupon of 14 Dweer Street had taken his dog for a walk, as was his routine. He always followed the same trajectory, cutting through the Zilverpand shopping center to Geldmunt Street, and then the length of Saint Amand Street as far as Market Square. He then stops for a glass of his favorite draft beer—Geuze—at Café Craenenburg, sitting on the terrace if weather permits. At eleven, or there-abouts, he crosses Market Square and saunters in the direction of Burg Square, the heart of the city's historic district, where he lets his dog—a four-year-old Golden Retriever—run loose for fifteen minutes. In the meantime, Mr. Dupont rests his bones on one of the benches under the trees. Almost without fail, he admires the illumination of the city hall and the Basilica of the Holy Blood, a spectacle of which he never tires.

He then heads back home via Steen Street. With the exception of a couple of speeding cars, he passed no one on the way. That's why he so clearly remembers the two men standing by the door of Degroof's, he said to Versavel on his call. The younger of the two—Dupon figures around twenty-five—is holding open the door for the older man. They're both empty-handed. Mr. Dupon stops for a moment, pretending his dog needs to take a pee, so he can get a better look. Both men are in dark suits and each is wearing a gray tie. The older of the two, a man in his mid-sixties, has long gray hair. The younger man steps into a dark Mercedes station wagon, while the older man locks the door and rolls down the window shutters. Mr. Dupon continues on his way without suspecting anything further.

He had been listening to the news that morning on the radio and had immediately made the connection.

The second useable tip came from a Dutch couple who had decided to celebrate their twenty-fifth wedding anniversary in Bruges.

59

They had traveled by car from Almelo to Bruges on Friday, July 8. Their four children had paid for a romantic weekend. They are currently staying at Hotel Die Swaene, which some guides describe as the most attractive hotel in the Benelux.

After enjoying a five-course dinner at De Visscherie, an exclusive restaurant on the Fish Market, Judith and Stan Cornuit decide to go for a stroll, sauntering down to Market Square via Burg Square and Breidel Street. They fritter away some time admiring Quijo's window display, one of Degroof's major competitors. The young jeweler is upstairs in his work-shop putting the finishing touches to a last-minute order. Hence the light in the window display. Stan has saved four thousand guilders under strict secrecy and plans to spend it on a bracelet for his darling Judith.

After five minutes or so—Stan meanwhile had managed to spot a magnificent specimen—they saunter across Market Square like an amorous young couple, heading toward Steen Street. Stan remembers having seen another jeweler there that morning when they passed in the car. He's not surprised to see light burning. Two men are hard at work inside, removing jewelry from the window displays and carrying it to the back of the shop.

Both men are wearing cotton gloves and are taking the greatest of care. The younger of the two even waves at them when he sees their faces pressed against the window. The older gentleman trails in with a brush and dustpan and sweeps some fragments of broken glass into a pile. The young man helps him. Brushing broken glass together on a deep-pile rug isn't easy. The Dutch couple didn't suspect a thing. After all, why would they wave if they were up to anything illegal? The happy couple just assumed there had been an accident.

What a nerve, Versavel sniggered to himself, but you had to give it to them. When he thought about their barefaced modus operandi, he realized that it was probably the least likely to attract attention. He knew from experience that there wasn't much movement on Steen Street after ten-thirty. The intruders were probably well aware of the fact. Most shops switched off their window display lighting at ten, using an automatic timer. The days of wasting electricity without restraint were a thing of the past. Cutting back on energy consumption was now the height of fashion. It was also cheaper and environmentally friendly, and customers liked that sort of thing.

Even a police patrol would probably have noticed nothing amiss. If they had seen both men at work, they would have assumed the same as the Cornuits did: shop owners often have to work late into the night.

The Cornuits had observed the men for several minutes and were thus able to provide detailed personal descriptions. Versavel gave priority to their statements and made an appointment to see the couple in the course of the afternoon for a more comprehensive interview. He suggested two-thirty and hoped that Van In would be back by then.

The two other useful informants had heard a dull explosion somewhere between eleven and midnight. One said it sounded like a shotgun going off. The other, an elderly woman who lived in a shabby apartment around the corner in Kleine St. Amand Street, was shaken from her sleep by a hard, dry thud, which she put down to a faulty muffler on a passing car.

Versavel knew that Van In would be content with what his report contained. They had four useful witnesses at their disposal, and that was more than enough to keep Deputy Martens happy, especially since it was from the radio call-out she had so adamantly insisted upon.

De Kee hadn't shown up that morning. Van In had called him the evening before to say he had made an appointment at

nine with Ghislain Degroof for standard questioning. He would
stop by as early as possible to size up the situation. If everything
went according to plan, they could round up their inquiries by
Wednesday, type the whole thing up, and hand the file over to
the public prosecutor's office.

That, at least, was what Versavel thought.

Van In had had an exceptionally bad night's sleep. The
Degroof affair had dug in its heels, and he didn't like it. When it
came to crime, Bruges was a graveyard, a provincial backwater.
A comforting thought for the city's population, but exceptionally frustrating for a policeman. Spectacular crimes and real
tension were a rarity.

Van In had worked his way up to assistant commissioner
and head of the Special Investigations Unit, and in all that
time he had longed for an extraordinary case. When it didn't
materialize, his enthusiasm waned. He was sick of the routine
and small-minded intrigue that made up his day-to-day, and
had been so for years.

The more he thought about it, the more convinced he
became that the Degroof affair might just be the case he had
been waiting for.

The fact that De Kee was under pressure to sweep it under
the carpet left him uneasy. De Kee may have been a snob, but
he wasn't a pushover. Van In was certain that Degroof senior
had to have brought in heavy artillery to persuade the chief
commissioner to make such a decision.

And for what? Degroof's son was the injured party. The
events of the previous night were too lightweight to explain
Degroof senior's pressure. There had to be more to it.

And he was determined to get to the bottom of it,
whatever the cost, even if it was only to impress the pretty
Hannelore.

After his daily routine in front of the mirror, tensing his sagging abdominals and trying to picture how things had used to be, Van In rummaged around in search of his best suit.

He selected the floweriest tie of the three he owned and knotted it around his neck. Valentine's Day 1984, a somber memory. His last candlelight dinner with Sonja. She had reserved a table at De Zevende Hemel, an intimate little place on Wal Square with a very appropriate name. That night, he really was in seventh heaven.

The restaurant went bankrupt a couple of months later, as did his marriage. Sonja got the furniture and what was left of their savings. Van In borrowed a couple of million francs to compensate her for the house. The loan cost him twenty-four thousand francs a month on top of his mortgage payments. In total, he had to pay almost thirty-five thousand francs a month to be able to keep the house. But it was worth it.

It was his dream house. He had played in it countless times as a child, as he lived in the neighborhood nearby. Back then, an elderly spinster had lived in it, and she made him pancakes nearly every Wednesday. He had fallen in love with the Vette Vispoort, and the house at the end of Moer Street, with the upstairs room where he whiled away the hours reading. He loved the solid oak table by the window, the spiral staircase leading to the garden on the banks of the canal, the dark vaulted cellar full of cobwebs, the creaking wooden floor on the upper level. The house's tangible tranquility, combined with the light filtered through green windowpanes, never left him.

He made up his mind to live in the place when he was older.

The house went up for sale in 1978, when he and Sonja had been married for four years. Van In accepted the exorbitant asking price. Like him, Sonja was wildly enthusiastic. In their youthful naïveté, they took out a very expensive loan. She worked day and night to pay for their dream house. She was chef in an exclusive Bruges restaurant and earned a good deal more than he did as a rookie policeman. She worked herself to the bone.

But in 1984, when the worst seemed to be behind them, their marriage disintegrated.

Long evenings alone left Van In lonely and despondent. He had fallen for the charms of a young colleague and had enjoyed a short if passionate relationship with her. She was nineteen and seemed insatiable, until she realized that Van In couldn't do much for her career. He had just been promoted to the rank of inspector. She dumped him like a piece of dirt, and Sonja got wind of it precisely one day later. Any hopes of reconciliation were dashed.

Van In never figured out who had turned him in. Their marriage could have been saved, been beautiful, but now it was too late. And self-pity was nobody's friend.

His dark suit made him appear thinner, and that cheered him more than a little. He walked to the corner of Moer Street and made his way to the police station on Beurs Square.

Today you could tell where the real Flemish nationalists lived. The lion flag fluttered here and there throughout the city. Flanders was celebrating its annual feast, but it wasn't a Belgian public holiday. It was business as usual.

Van In marched into the station and asked at reception if a car was free. Officer Cardon, a pock-faced beanpole, handed him the keys to the Volkswagen Golf Van In usually drove.

"Thanks, Robert," said Van In.

"At your command, Commissioner," Cardon replied.

He briefly considered bolting upstairs to his office, but changed his mind when he caught sight of the clock in the corridor. It was almost eight forty-five. Radio Contact was scheduled to broadcast the appeal every half hour. He had tuned in quickly before leaving the house, and he was sure Versavel would be at his desk fielding any calls that came in. If there was news, it could wait until the afternoon.

He drove down Smede Street and took the main road out of the city in the direction of Gistel. Degroof lived in Varsenare, a small town between Bruges and Jabbeke.

Van In was familiar with the Grote Thems, the exclusive neighborhood where Degroof kept his official residence. The people who lived in the place had the right to call themselves respectable citizens. It was overflowing with doctors, real-tors, cash-rich businessmen, bank directors, and the privately wealthy. An aristocratic title was particularly appreciated in the Grote Thems, although Rotary and Kiwanis adepts, knights of the Order of Malta, and Opus Dei supernumeraries could also count on considerable respect.

It took Van In the better part of ten minutes to find Degroof's house. The street layout in the Grote Thems defied logic. It was as if its stuck-up residents wanted to give the impression that they each lived on a street of their own. He finally found what he was looking for after circling the neigh-borhood a couple of times.

Degroof lived in a mock-farmhouse, the typical habitat of moneyed folks who had built their homes in the nineteen seven-ties. Back to nature was the slogan in those days, and everyone who could afford it bought themselves an expensive plot of land and built their own rustic palace outside the city.

Degroof was no exception. He had spared neither money nor effort in the realization of his megalomaniac copy of a simple farmhouse. Two architects earned close to a half million francs each on the project. The result was in keeping with the finan-cial investment: a monstrosity made of expensive custom-made brick, with three garages, oak gates, and window shutters. In the middle of the impeccable lawn, there was a kidney-shaped pond in which a couple of swans swam in obligatory circles. Well-trained, thought Van In, sarcastically.

The VW Golf hobbled up the cobblestone drive, and Van In parked it in front of one of the garages. Before he had the chance to ring the bell, a young man, twenty or thereabouts, opened the front door. He was wearing an immaculate black suit and a bow tie, clothing that immediately betrayed his position in the household. His dark-brown skin, plump lips, and mysterious black eyes left no doubts as to his ethnic origins. It was well known that people weren't averse to a little cheap household labor around these parts.

"Assistant Commissioner Van In," he introduced himself with just a hint of authority. "I have an appointment with Mr. Degroof." The Indian conjured an indefinable smile. His pearly white teeth left Van In jealous.

"Moment please, sir," said the butler, almost accent-less, leaving him waiting at the door.

Van In felt uncomfortable in his suit. The collar of his shirt pinched and his tie was too tight. In spite of the early hour, it was already quite warm. They had forecast rain on national TV the day before.

The Indian reappeared in less than a minute.

"Mister Degroof can see you now," he said in what was close to a subservient tone. He bowed like a jackknife and gestured to Van In that he should go inside.

The hallway was substantially bigger than Van In's bedroom. Expensive Tibetan rugs graced the floor. Van In recognized them because he had been dreaming of buying one for years. He was crazy about their brown and ochre shades and simple geometric motifs. But that was where any agreement between his taste and Degroof's ended.

The walls were plastered with paintings in heavily gilded frames, mostly rural conversation pieces by unknown nineteenth-century "masters." The crystal chandeliers hanging from the ceiling with its artificial buttressing of recuperated oak beams were completely out of place.

The butler led him through a double door into the lounge. The room was at least six hundred square feet, and here, too, kitsch ruled the roost: a leather country-style lounge suite, Chinese porcelain in faux-antique displays, a leopard-skin rug in front of an open hearth lined with Delft tiles, more crystal chandeliers, medallion wallpaper, Val Saint-Lambert, bronze and copper metalwork. It almost turned Van In's stomach.

An enormous glass sliding door filled the left wall and gave out onto a terrace-cum-garden. Ghislain Degroof came toward him with a broad smile on his face.

"Commissaire Van In!" He welcomed him with open arms. "Such a pleasure to see you again," he said in the mangled accent he reserved for common folk like Van In. Van In shook his dry but limply slippery hand.

"I didn't want to bother you any more than necessary yesterday, Mr. Degroof. But I'm sure you understand that I'm duty bound to ask a couple questions. For the records," he added with a hint of sarcasm.

"Mais bien sur, I'm completely at your service." His French accent was equally painful.

Degroof was wearing high-quality, loose-fitting beige slacks, a white open-neck shirt, a pair of walnut docksides, and no socks. He seemed relaxed and ten years younger than the day before.

"Shall we take a seat on the terrace, Commissaire?"

"Of course," said Van In.

The Indian was standing immediately behind him and helped him take off his jacket. He was grateful that the room had no mirrors. His jacket was his camouflage.

The terrace was the same size as the lounge. A pergola with a splashing fountain cooled and refreshed the air. *It'll be hot outside the shade*, he thought. The oval impregnated mahogany table was still set for breakfast. Condensation dripped from a bottle of champagne resting in a silver ice bucket. He spotted of a couple of sun beds almost completely concealed by the commanding table.

Van In was taken aback, to say the least, when he suddenly caught sight of a woman's head sticking out above the table.

"Do we have visitors, Guy?" From the tone of her voice, she clearly hadn't been expecting anyone. She got to her feet and looked Van In up and down, evidently put out.

"May I introduce my wife Anne-Marie, Commissaire?"

Van In was frozen to the spot and Degroof's drivel was instantly transformed into background noise. Anne-Marie was wearing nothing more than a tiny bikini bottom. She walked toward him unashamed. Van In's eyes were glued to her form for a couple of seconds. He had little alternative. She was now just a few feet away. She had the body of a twenty-year-old girl, shapely everything, tight, tanned skin, an angular jaw line, a straight nose, and big gray eyes.

"My wife is a former model," said Degroof with the emphasis on "former." Her eyes appeared to flicker for a second.

Van In flushed hot and cold when she shook his hand. She was so close, her breasts touched his shirt.

"I'm here about, er . . . yesterday," he jabbered.

Anne-Marie could see that Van In was flustered and it seemed to amuse her.

"You should have told me we were expecting someone, Guy," she said reprovingly.

"Mais cherie, I announced it to you."

The fact that his wife was almost naked in front of Van In didn't seem to bother him in the slightest. Worse than that: it looked as if he had orchestrated the entire tasteless scene.

"Perhaps we could use the table, Commissaire," he said finally after a couple of uncomfortable seconds.

"As you please." Van In tried to look the other way.

"Coffee?"

Anne-Marie turned and made her way back to the sun bed, deliberately swaying her hips.

"Or would the Commissaire prefer a glass of champagne?"

She moved out of eyesight and Van In breathed a sigh of relief.

"Why not," he said gratefully. The sweat was streaming down his back, and it wasn't only because of the sun.

"You too, ma chère?" Degroof sneered. His wife rolled over, lying on her side now facing the table.

The Indian draped a spotless napkin around the champagne bottle's neck and poured three glasses. He served Anne-Marie first, followed by Van In and Degroof. He then withdrew discreetly.

"Santé, Commissaire." Degroof raised the glass to his lips and sipped sparingly.

"Your health." Van In followed his host's miserly example. Champagne wasn't designed to quench the thirst.

"Surely you're not here to tell us that the case has been solved, commissioner," Anne-Marie whined. He wasn't sure how to respond. "Or is it one of those cases that solve themselves? Literally . . ."

Van In smiled out of politeness, but a sense of resentment was fermenting inside him. They were clearly mocking him, and that made him mad.

"Come, come, cherie, let the Commissaire do his job," said Degroof appeasingly. She snorted and turned onto her other side. Van In seized the opportunity to take a seat, opting for the safety of the opposite side of the table, with his back to Anne-Marie.

"My wife has a *sens de l'humour*, it's a little special," said Degroof in an old-buddies tone of voice.

He collapsed into a chair and stretched his legs lazily under the table. He didn't touch the champagne. Van In flouted etiquette and tossed back half his glass.

"But now to business, Commissaire," said Degroof as Van In returned his glass to the table with a gesture of regret. "Fire away with your questions. I'm all ears."

Van In cleared his throat and took out his notebook.

He hadn't yet decided how he was going to approach Degroof, not certain whether every word would be transmitted via Degroof senior right back to De Kee.

"I believe we're dealing with an extraordinary and bizarre crime," he said, starting in neutral. "Had the perpetrator, or perpetrators, taken everything with them, then their motive would have been obvious. They would also have had to get rid of their pickings, a delicate point, bearing in mind that the objects were exclusive and as a consequence hard to sell in their totality. Only a handful of key receivers would have been interested in such a transaction."

"You're telling me," Degroof nodded enthusiastically.

"I presume the value of the jewels runs into the millions."

Degroof's accountant was putting an inventory together at that very moment. Little attention had been paid to the matter the day before.

"Between twenty and twenty-five million, Commissaire. The safe contained the collection for an exhibition in Antwerp."

Van In took note of this new piece of information and continued.

"In my humble opinion, the motive behind such a meaningless act has to be revenge or jealousy, Mr. Degroof. Unless we're dealing with a crazy person."

Degroof leaned forward, planted his elbows firmly on the table, and rubbed his chin.

"Who knows, Commissaire," he said, with a hint of perverse pleasure.

"Do you have enemies, Mr. Degroof?"

"Enemies? Anne-Marie," he yelped. "Do we have enemies?" Van In took advantage of the question to look in her direction. He couldn't stop himself. But she didn't turn around.

"Everyone has enemies," she answered abruptly as she turned the page of a magazine, evidently bored.

"Bien sur, but enemies capable of such a crime? I don't think so, Commissaire."

"A jealous competitor perhaps?" Van In suggested. "Give it some thought, Mr. Degroof. Something from the past? Were you ever the victim of blackmail? Were you ever approached by the Mafia? Has anyone offered you paid protection recently?"

"Mais non, Van In," Degroof blustered. "Here in Bruges? I can't think of anyone who . . . besides, why didn't they take anything with them?"

Van In spotted a moment of nervous hesitation in his eyes. And why the sudden use of his name instead of his title?

Van In cursed himself for asking the questions one after the other. Now it was impossible to tell which of them had put Degroof on edge. It made no sense to repeat them. Spontaneous reactions were a one-off thing.

"The perpetrators knew the code to the burglar alarm. They had a key and were clearly aware that you still received clients after hours from time to time," said Van In, all in one breath. "The Securitas guard even claims he recognized your voice," Van In continued, chancing his luck.

"I told you already. I did not call Securitas that evening. I also made a statement to that effect to Commissioner De Kee," he said, evidently irritated.

Hold on, easy does it, Van In thought to himself. He's getting worked up.

"But you still received clients after hours on a regular basis. The people at Securitas were familiar with the entire procedure. If I'm not mistaken, they're obliged to call you every time the alarm is switched on or off at an unusual hour. That's precisely what happened yesterday."

"Of course, Commissaire. But I did not call Securitas on Friday evening," said Degroof in a sugary tone. He was back in the driver's seat. "And what in God's name does that have to do with anything?"

"It proves that the perpetrators must have been watching you and the store for quite some time and that they were more than likely working on a tip from someone you know, family, an acquaintance," said Van In, determined not to let Degroof see he was talking bullshit and knew it. "I presume you aren't the only one who has access to the code?"

"Mon Dieu, mon Dieu," Degroof grumbled. "Who are you accusing?"

"Jesus H. Christ," Van In muttered.

"What was that?"

"Nothing, Mr. Degroof, nothing at all. A lapsus linguæ."

While Degroof was doubtless trying to work out what "lapsus linguæ" meant, Van In continued. "I only need this information for the file. Without it, the Deputy public prosecutor will just send it back and we'll have to start over."

"Bon," said Degroof, who understood what he meant. He relaxed back into his chair, stretching his legs under the table. "My father knows the code, my business manager, and Idris," he declared with a certain nonchalance.

"Idris?" Van In frowned.

"The houseboy," Degroof reluctantly explained. *Why Idris?*, he wanted to ask, but instead he said: "Who is your business manager?"

Degroof took a sip of champagne.

"Georges is beyond suspicion. You can count him out. I've known Georges Hoornaert for years. Anyway, he's on vacation in the Fijis."

Van In noted the name and scribbled a question mark after "Idris."

"Satisfied, Commissaire?"

Degroof smiled to reveal a set of pearly white teeth not unlike the houseboy's. But Degroof's were made of porcelain and his dentist had spent the fee on a Peugeot 204 for his daughter, who was at university in Leuven.

"One last detail, Mr. Degroof. Did the same people also know the combination of the safe?"

Degroof kept his emotions under control this time.

"No, only Papa and myself know the combination."

"I see," said Van In. "And how long has the store had electronic protection?"

Degroof pursed his thin, bloodless lips.

"Seven years," he answered after a couple of seconds. "The insurance people insist on it these days."

"And the alarm code hasn't been changed in that time?"

"Every year, Commissaire. Comme precaution, n'est-ce pas?" he said, a little too quickly.

"I imagine the safe was installed earlier and that its combination has always stayed the same?"

"Précisément," said Degroof, audibly surprised.

Van In picked his nose, something he always did when he was satisfied. Degroof had apparently underestimated him, if only a little.

"Incidentally, Mr. Degroof. Do you know if your insurance covers this kind of risk? Loss, theft, that I can understand, but aqua regis? Most policies don't cover that sort of thing, do they?"

"Indeed," said Degroof. "I'm not covered for what happened with the aqua regis. But now you're probably asking yourself why I'm so relaxed, n'est-ce pas?"

Van In nodded. Degroof had neatly anticipated his next question.

"Well, let me explain," he said with a hint of pride. "When they informed me yesterday about the robbery, I called Papa. At least, that's what we were thinking, you understand, that it was a robbery. I was furious, but not without hope. Papa assured me that we had the best of insurance and everything was fine. But when I realized back at the shop that nothing had been stolen and that the entire collection was at the bottom of a tank of aqua regis, I started to get nervous, very nervous."

"And then you called your father again from the shop," said Van In.

"How did you guess, Commissaire? Yes, I called Papa and . . . You should know, Papa has a solution for everything."

"Then your father called the chief commissioner," Van In guessed again.

"Précisément. With Monsieur De Kee as witness and an official analysis by the laboratoire judiciaire, I was free to deduct the entire loss from my taxes, one hundred percent," Degroof junior beamed. "As you know, Monsieur Vanmael is the expert on the case. Everything is being transferred to the laboratoire in Ghent in the course of the morning."

"Excellent, Mr. Degroof, excellent news," said Van In dryly. If Degroof had incurred no losses, the case was likely to be shelved even earlier than he had hoped.

"Another glass of champagne, Commissaire?"

Van In checked his watch. It was ten-fifteen.

"Why not?" he said with eager gratitude. "Krug isn't exactly on the menu every day."

He stayed with Degroof until the bottle was empty, and when he got up to say good-bye, his frontal lobes positively effervesced with overconfidence. He marched up to Anne-Marie brimming with self-assurance.

"An exceptional pleasure to have made your acquaintance, ma'am," he said, barely able to disguise the effects of the Krug on his voice.

And this time, yes, she turned toward him and leaned up on one elbow. Van In resolved to etch the image forever in his memory. She held out her hand and he came close to kissing it gallantly. Their eyes met. For a fraction of a second her boredom made way for icy determination.

"Good luck, Commissioner, and who knows, perhaps we'll meet again," she said in a slightly conspiratorial tone.

Degroof also wished Van In success and accompanied him back to the lounge. Idris took it from there.

Had Van In been sober, he would certainly have sensed that they had wanted to get rid of him. But the Indian servant gave nothing away as he accompanied Van In impassively to the front door. "Have a nice day, sir," he said with a sad smile and gently closed the door.

Idris followed the departing Golf from behind the window until it disappeared from sight.

6

Once inside the car, Van In hastily lit a cigarette and tried to organize his thoughts during the short drive from Varsenare back to Bruges.

He started with a sort of psychological profile of Mr. and Mrs. Degroof, although his mind wasn't exactly clear after five glasses of champagne.

Ghislain Degroof was an empty-headed weakling. It was clear that the father called the shots and the son simply ran the day-to-day business affairs. It was also Degroof senior who had insisted in hush-hushing the affair. Negative publicity, my ass! A robbery usually meant a load of free advertising.

Ghislain Degroof had clearly been taken aback when asked about potential enemies from the past. Van In was referring to either him or his father, of course, and Van In was convinced that Degroof had reacted differently to that second part of the question. It was perfectly possible that the perpetrators wanted to get at the father and not the son. Degroof senior must have made enemies by the dozen in the course of his career.

The champagne, on reflection, seemed to be more of a help than a hindrance when it came to his powers of reasoning.

And what about Anne-Marie, the voluptuous wife? She had obviously married him for the money. Did she perhaps have a lover intent on getting one over on Degroof?

And why give the burglar alarm code to the houseboy?

If he stuck to the facts, there were four suspects: Ghislain Degroof, Ludovic Degroof, Georges Hoornaert, and Idris. They were the only ones who knew the alarm code. But none of them had an acceptable motive, and Hoornaert even had a watertight alibi.

There was nothing substantial to go on. Where do you begin when a case appears to have no suspects and no motive?

Two lines of reasoning remained. Either someone else had gotten hold of the code without Degroof's knowledge, or the perpetrators had cracked the system. The latter seemed the least plausible. And then there was the letter with the Latin text that made the entire affair feel like a student prank.

He nervously lit another cigarette. Versavel would probably have more news.

A long line of traffic had built up at the Smedenpoort, a surviving medieval gate that stood at the city's entrance. It was eleven forty-five A.M. and he knew that Versavel would go home at noon on the button. They had agreed to meet, but Van In urgently wanted to talk to him. But there was no point in getting overly anxious. The traffic wasn't going anywhere.

He understood why so many people hated driving in Bruges. Hardly a day went by in the summer months when the city center didn't grind to a standstill because of one or other event.

Only the day before, they had shut down the city for the best part of the afternoon for the annual marathon on June 11. The finish was on Burg Square, and driving in the city center at any point that day was more or less impossible.

What was the reason for today's holdup? The forty-sixth anniversary of brass band "The Sound of the Polders," or a historical reenactment of a visit by Jan van Eyck's great-nephew to his grand-uncle's atelier?

The constant flow of oncoming traffic made passing impossible. He decided to contact Versavel on the radio. It wasn't the best option. He hated the fact that everyone would be listening in.

"ONA 3446 calling ONA 3421, over." The connection crackled and peeped and it took all of thirty seconds before someone answered.

"ONA 3421 here, Sergeant Saelens, over."

"Afternoon, Robert. Van In here. Do me a favor, Robert: will you run up to 204 in a moment and see if Versavel's still at his desk?"

"No problem, Assistant Commissioner," Saelens replied obligingly.

Sergeant Saelens was one of the few who used the title assistant commissioner. The majority simply called him commissioner. It was shorter, and assistant commissioners tended to prefer it. As in every police division, rank was rank, even if it wasn't official.

"Ask him to wait for me. I'm stuck at the Smedenpoort in a fuck of a traffic jam."

"At your service, Assistant Commissioner. Is there anything else?"

"Maybe you can try to get your hands on the officer directing traffic out here? It already seems like an eternity."

"Consider it done."

"Thanks, Robert."

"My pleasure," the loudspeaker crackled.

Two minutes later, the line of traffic finally started to move. Saelens deserved a pat on the back. Van In nervously stepped on the gas and tore around the corner.

Versavel was waiting for him in the courtyard in front of the police station. From a distance, he didn't look a day over forty. In contrast to Van In, who had been living on junk food and Duvels since his divorce, Versavel took care of his body and went to the gym. There were even rumors that he had his uniforms and shirts taken in by a seamstress to give them a more fitted look.

"Where's the fire?" Versavel jibed as Van In got out of the car.

The sergeant grinned from ear to ear. That perfect set of teeth almost sickened Van In. He was determined to have his own ivories restored, but that was for next year. He looked forward to being able to smile in public for once.

"Question marks, man, massive question marks," Van In groused. "What about you? Any progress?"

"Three eyewitnesses and a couple of neighbors who heard an explosion," said Versavel, proud as a peacock. "And De Kee knows nothing about it. He didn't even show up this morning."

"Typical De Kee," Van In sneered. "He'll have been playing the Flemish Lion with his Vera. So much the better, then he won't have been listening to the radio."

"There was a call from Leo."

"And?"

"He wants to have a word this evening. Six-thirty in l'Estaminet. He was really insistent. Kept reminding me to tell you."

"Did he say what it was about?"

"Negative. Anyway, I was too busy taking calls from potential witnesses."

Van In looked at his watch. The station courtyard was full of cops, most of them heading home for lunch.

"Fancy a juicy steak, Guido? My treat. Then you can fill me in on the details."

"No problem," said Versavel. "Name the place."

"What about the gypsy's place in the Wool Market?" Van In suggested.

Versavel gave him a questioning look.

"The Old Swan or the Three Swans. Whatever they are calling it these days?"

"Ah, you mean Huguette's place," Versavel nodded.

"That's the one. No microwaves, and the fries are the real thing. I'm sick of pizzas and hamburgers."

Van In was about to get back into the Golf, but Versavel grabbed him by the arm.

"Not in this weather," he said disapprovingly. "We walk."

Van In ordered a Duvel as aperitif, Versavel a Perrier. In the meantime, a couple of twelve-ounce steaks were browning with real butter in the kitchen.

"The Dutch couple was a bull's-eye," said Versavel. "They watched the perpetrators at work for a couple of minutes. I've arranged to meet them later in their hotel. They're at Die Swaene."

"From one swan to the other," Van In joked. "When are they expecting us?"

"Two-thirty."

"Perfect. Then we can take our time," said Van In, contentment written all over his face.

Huguette's traditional approach to preparing food meant that the fries and the béarnaise sauce took a little longer than in most other restaurants. She kept the steaks warm in a hot oven in readiness. Van In sipped at his second Duvel as the steaming plates arrived at their table. Both men fell silent as they tucked in with relish. Van In hated people who could ruin a decent meal with too much yapping. Americans were unrivaled. They could spend hours over a chicken thigh.

Van In tore in to a serious helping of béarnaise, dipping his fries in it and enjoying every bite. The steak was perfect: a dark crust on the outside, red and juicy on the inside. The oven's intense heat had kept the meat warm to the last nibble.

Van In finished before Versavel and eagerly lit a cigarette. Versavel was a fervent non-smoker, but it didn't bother him. The world was awash with rabid nicotine haters, but Versavel was unique among them.

"Don't you think they took some enormous risks?" Van In asked out of the blue. "Especially when you know how much work they put in to preparing their stunt."

"Maybe they're less professional than we thought," Versavel replied as he popped the last chunk of meat into his mouth and ground it between his powerful jaws.

"Or they had no alternative. They had to do their thing relatively early."

Versavel neatly rested his knife and fork on his empty plate. "What do you mean?" he asked, all ears.

"Well, the perpetrators had the code and the keys at their disposal and they knew Degroof sometimes received customers after hours."

"But never after midnight," Versavel concurred.

"Precisely. They had to go to work early or the people at Securitas would have smelled a rat."

"And by working in the open as they did, they probably didn't run much of a risk. I thought the same thing," said Versavel. "Even with people watching them, there wasn't much danger. You know the people of Bruges and how much they love to cooperate with the police."

"It's not only in Bruges," Van In sighed.

"Tell me about it. If the security cameras don't pick it up, you can forget it. Nobody wants to stick their neck out. It's all over the TV in the States."

Van In nodded. He'd seen the shows.

"People don't care. And you can be sure our buddies in the store counted on that indifference." He gestured to the waiter with his glass. Another Duvel. "Something might surface if we take a browse in Degroof senior's past."

"What about De Kee? I thought we were just going through the motions."

"De Kee can kiss my ass. Anyway, what can he do? Stop me from doing my job? He retires in a couple of years and there are local authority elections in October. Do you think the mayor's likely to carpet me for doing what I'm paid for? Candy-ass wouldn't dare," Van In thundered. "Certainly not before the elections."

The combination of champagne and Duvel was having a remarkable effect on Van In's assertiveness. Even Versavel had rarely seen him in such good form.

"Maybe there's politics behind it," he ventured.

"Could be right, Sergeant. Why haven't we considered politics? Political feuds are always thrashed out in the strangest of ways."

Daniel Verhaeghe waited in line for a ticket at the Bruges train station. He was nervous.

A couple of French girls, complete with backpacks and camping gear, were having an animated discussion with the guy at the ticket-office window. He listened to them with stoic tranquility and then pointed listlessly in the direction of the information desk. Fortunately, Daniel's train didn't leave for another half hour. When the French girls finally cleared off without a ticket, the line started to move again.

"Liège, first class," said Daniel, doing his best to appear normal.

"Return?"

"No. One way."

He paid with a two-thousand-franc note and sauntered back to the main concourse. He checked the timetable for a second time just to be sure. He wasn't comfortable in the clerical outfit, and the Roman collar was getting on his nerves. Every couple of seconds he stuck his thumb between the collar and his neck to alleviate the painful pinching. He suddenly stopped in his tracks and fished a tiny bottle from his trouser pocket. He unscrewed the top with the pipette, took off his glasses, and routinely deposited three drops in each eye. He then stowed the bottle and sauntered further. He let himself be carried along by the flow of hasty travelers, laden with baggage and in a hurry to catch a waiting train.

In spite of the delay at the ticket office, which in reality had lasted less than ten minutes, he still had to wait a good fifteen minutes before the international train from Oostende to Cologne trundled into the station. Daniel didn't have too far to walk. Belgian Railways were very considerate: the first-class carriages always stopped in the middle of the platform.

Laurent had driven back to Namur that Friday night. But Daniel had insisted on staying in Bruges until today. He wanted to experience all of it, from start to finish. Laurent, after all, had organized the operation on *his* behalf.

When the train set off with a couple of jolts, he made sure he was alone in the carriage. He then waited five full minutes before producing his pocket flask and tossing back a couple of gulps of J&B. The whiskey was lukewarm and immediately resulted in a mild euphoria. Laurent had made him swear that he wouldn't smoke in public, but he couldn't resist. He enjoyed the prickle of the smoke in his lungs, and for once he was happy that Laurent wasn't around.

"Watch out, boy. You know what drink and cigarettes can do to you," he heard him say, concerned yet angry.

But Daniel Verhaeghe squarely ignored his mentor's advice. Drink and cigarettes weren't going kill *him*, he groused to himself. He was immune. Anyway, he needed the kick to control the adrenaline coursing through his veins.

Daniel tried not to look out of the window. The landscape whizzing past and the sun-drenched fields hurt his eyes. The collar pinched, but he didn't dare loosen it. He had to get used to the bloody thing. He had to play the part with as much conviction as he could muster. Daniel tried to sit still and concentrate on an advertising poster next to the carriage door.

They had started the ball rolling on Friday evening. The first phase of their plan had gone off without a hitch, he mused. It had almost gone wrong at one point, when an elderly couple seemed to spend forever watching them through the store window.

"Just keep going," Laurent had whispered. "Try to relax. If you hesitate, they'll think something's wrong. Think of the goal, boy. Ours is a sacred task, and no one can stop us."

And Laurent had been right. Laurent was almost always right. The best moment of all was when Laurent let him press the detonator button. The bang had been no louder than the pop of a champagne cork. The water bag in front of the safe had muffled the explosion, just as Laurent had said it would. Daniel's heart started to pound anew when he pictured himself depositing the jewelry in the tank of aqua regis.

And that was only the start, he smirked. They were going to ruin the bastard, and with him the scum he cherished so much.

Daniel was proud, proud and happy that his short life already had a purpose.

I want to experience all of it, he repeated to himself. *I want to see Ghislain's face on Monday when he discovers what has happened.* So he booked a room at the Holiday Inn on Burg Square. The hotel was Laurent's idea

"The police never check the luxury hotels," he had sneered. But he had insisted nonetheless that Daniel wear the priest's outfit. "Just to be sure."

Daniel had patrolled Steen Street that morning from eight-thirty A.M. Degroof hadn't shown up. At nine forty-five, Daniel started to get worried. Just as he was about to go back to the hotel and call Laurent, a light blue delivery van stopped in front of Degroof Diamonds and Jewelry. Two men in overalls and a short, chubby guy went into the shop. As he watched the men haul a couple of lidded tanks inside, he realized that their work had been discovered earlier than they had expected. He hurried back to the hotel, raced up to his room, and poured a double whiskey. Then he called Laurent.

"Take it easy, boy." Laurent's deep warm voice calmed him. "Everything went according to plan. The police discovered the break-in on Sunday morning by accident. *She* contacted me this morning. Our plan worked. We screwed them."

Daniel had broken into sobs. He had been crying tears of happiness for quite a while. Laurent had done nothing to interfere. The boy needed to get rid of his emotions. He had waited patiently at the other end of the line until the sobbing was over.

"We keep going. Freshen up, put on the outfit we brought with us, and catch the 14:07 train. I'll be waiting for you in the Liège station."

And Laurent was waiting as agreed. Daniel caught sight of his shiny bald head in the writhing crowd as it wormed its way through the swinging station doors. He held up a plastic bag and waved it in the air. Tears trickled over Laurent De Bock's tanned cheeks as he embraced the boy.

"You make a first-rate priest," he said with a smile as he quickly dried his eyes.

"Do you think so?" asked Daniel. He was overjoyed at being back in Laurent's company, and he swirled like a catwalk model.

Laurent looked around nervously. It was better not to attract attention.

"Come, boy. The car's parked in a taxi stand across the street. In the present circumstances, the last thing we want is a ticket."

They passed a trash container on the way to the Mercedes. Daniel pushed up the lid and dumped the plastic bag on top of a pile of crushed beer cans and stinking leftover food. The contents of the bag rendered the descriptions provided by Mr. and Mrs. Cornuit as good as worthless. In addition to the suit Daniel had been wearing until that morning, it also contained a white wig and a false Vandyke beard.

Laurent held open the door for his pupil. When he noticed Daniel blinking, he said: "Don't forget your eyedrops, boy." He sounded strict at times.

Daniel did what he was asked and then lit a cigarette. Laurent didn't stop him. He was going to have to bite the bullet extra hard in the coming days.

They didn't talk much as they drove through the center of Liège. Daniel half closed his eyes. The glare of the traffic and the blinding sun irritated him.

When they were outside the city, Laurent took a thick brown envelope and a pair of sunglasses from the glove compartment.

"The letters are in here," he said. "Enjoy."

"I will." A satisfied sneer appeared on Daniel's face. "I can't wait for tomorrow."

7

VAN IN PAID THE BILL at two-fifteen precisely. To his surprise, they were the last to leave the restaurant.

Huguette raised a freshly tapped glass of beer and almost emptied it in a single gulp. Van In always treated her to a glass before he left. It was his way of saying thanks for her excellent cooking skills.

"Cheers, gentleman," she shouted. "À la prochaine."

The two policemen sauntered toward Rozenhoed Wharf—where the tourists lined up for the canal boats, their jackets over their shoulders. It was swelteringly hot, and only tourists ventured out in this sort of weather. The natives were either on the beach at Blankenberge or Zeebrugge, or relaxing in the shade in their own back yard.

Bruges-born and -bred, Versavel admired the intimate architecture of the city while Van In grabbed a pack of cigarettes at

a nearby store. They were only a couple of minutes' walk from
their appointment, but Van In lit up nonetheless. Versavel had
long given up reacting to such things.

Hotel Die Swaene boasted a subtle combination of fine linen,
nostalgic floral wallpaper, subdued lighting, and dozens of little
courtesies. There was always fresh fruit in the rooms, a cheerful
bouquet of flowers in an art-deco vase, fragrant soap, quilted
toilet paper, and puffed-up duvets.

The manager's wife—blond, elegantly dressed, forty
something—manned reception. When she saw them come in,
she discreetly slipped her glass of sherry behind a Rolodex.

Van In introduced himself and his colleague. "Assistant
Commissioner Van In and Sergeant Versavel. We have an
appointment with Mr. and Mrs. Cornuit. I presume you were
informed," he continued stiffly.

"Yes, of course," she said. "I'll tell them you're on your way
up."

Fortunately there was no one else in the lobby. She lifted the
internal phone and punched in the room number.

"Mr. Cornuit," she said, feigning a Dutch accent. "The
gentlemen from the police are here. May I send them up?"

Van In could hear the Dutchman bellowing through the
receiver. He sounded enthusiastic, to say the least. The manageress looked around nervously and signaled that they should
follow her. She hoped their visit would be a once-only. There
are three things a hotel doesn't like: a corpse, food poisoning,
and a police visit.

The Cornuits had rented one of the more spacious rooms on
the first floor. Stan Cornuit opened the door in response to a
discreet knock from the manageress. He was wearing a moss-
green track suit and was a textbook example of your average
Dutchman. He was tall, well-built, and well-groomed. Stan
Cornuit was fifty-five but looked at least ten years younger.

Versavel was particularly impressed by the man's moustache, which was almost as luxuriant as his own.

"Pieter Van In and Guido Versavel. Bruges Police." He did his best to articulate.

Cornuit stepped back and invited them in with an exaggerated gesture.

"Come in, gentlemen." He had a warm, clear voice. "Odd, don't you think, that we happened to be in the neighborhood at that one moment. I said to Judith, didn't I, dear: sweetheart, what are those guys up to? Back home, we would have reported it right away, but in Belgium nothing's a surprise."

His thunderous laugh echoed down the corridor. The manageress smiled by force of habit and then disappeared on the double. She had done her duty.

Van In and Versavel took a seat by the window at Stan Cornuit's invitation. Each of the rooms had its own cozy sitting area.

"A drink, gentlemen?"

Without waiting for an answer, he lunged toward the fridge and produced a bottle of Bokma jenever.

"Cheaper here than back home," he proudly trumpeted.

It was the first time Van In had drunk jenever from a paper cup.

All three took a sip. Versavel observed against the light that Cornuit had poured himself a generous measure, at least double the amount he had served the others.

Just as Van In was about to speak, Judith stormed in from the en suite bathroom.

"Hello, hello." Her voice was loud and shrill.

She was wearing a silver streaked kimono. Judith was eight years younger than Stan and looked as if she had been plucked from a Weightwatchers commercial.

"The excitement," she said in a schoolgirl voice. "A couple of days in Belgium and this happens. The kids will go crazy when we tell them. I was just saying to Stan last night in bed . . ."

"Judith, honey. The gentleman aren't here to listen to our bedroom stories."

"Of course you're not. Don't let me get in the way," she said in an evident huff, taking a seat beside Versavel, her wings clipped, jealous. Her kimono blew open far above the knee as she sat, but she didn't seem the least perturbed.

Here we go again, Van In thought to himself, ill at ease. He focused on a couple of etchings on the wall behind her.

Stan finally settled and launched into his story. Versavel took notes.

By four forty-five, the Cornuits were done. Versavel had filled five pages.

The younger of the two burglars was more than six feet tall, a detail on which they were in complete agreement. They figured he was twenty-five, had blond shoulder-length hair and a Vandyke beard. He was wearing glasses with thick lenses.

"Coke bottle bottoms," said Judith, more than once.

Both men were wearing dark gray suits, white shirts, sky-blue ties, and black shoes.

"Mephistos," Judith insisted. "And one of them stopped to put drops in his eyes. Obviously some kind of medication." There was something sickly about him, now that she thought about it.

His older companion was the double of Einstein; another point on which they agreed completely. He must have been seventy at least, and he walked with a stoop. He couldn't have been more than five foot six, and he had heavy bags under his watery Bambi eyes.

"Spent a lot of time outdoors," she said. "My God, the perfect tan!"

The jenever bottle was close to empty when they parted company. The Cornuits were over the moon when Van In suggested that they extend their vacation for a couple of days. City hall would cover it. It would give him time to send a forensic artist to do a facial composite and it would give them an extra day to compensate for the inconvenience.

"City hall will cover it, eh?" Versavel sneered once they were outside. "I can see De Kee's face right now."

Van In shrugged his shoulders indifferently.

"The file has to be complete. Otherwise they'll think we didn't make the effort."

"Would Miss Martens dare give our Van In a rap on the knuckles?"

Versavel jumped aside just in time to avoid a sharp elbow to the ribs.

"Go see what Dupon has to say, and the two neighbors who heard the explosion. I want their statements on my desk by tomorrow morning, Versavel," Van In hissed. "Time for me to continue my investigations in l'Estaminet."

"At your command, Commissioner."

"Go soak your head, Versavel."

"You took the words right out of my mouth! See you tomorrow," Versavel waved.

"Eight A.M., on the button."

"We'll see," Versavel laughed. "Good luck with your *investigation*."

He took to his heels, turning right past the Fish Market, and disappeared into a horde of tourists worming their way along the narrow Blinde Ezel Street.

To compensate for the Duvels and the Bokma, Van In ordered a spaghetti Bolognese and settled down to eat it outside Brasserie l'Estaminet on the edge of Astrid Park. There wasn't a barfly in Bruges who hadn't savored the spaghetti at l'Estaminet.

Just as Van In was emptying his bowl, a canary-yellow Audi careered out of Minderbroeder Street onto Astrid Park. Leo Vanmaele was five minutes early for his appointment, and that wasn't typical of the man.

"Hoy."

Vanmaele looked for all the world like a blushing leprechaun: spherical upper body on a pair of short sturdy legs.

"Duvel?" asked Van In. He had two fingers at the ready in the form of a V. The bartender knew what it meant.

"Finally," Leo sighed. "I've lost the feeling in my legs."

"So your efforts weren't in vain?" Van In inquired, hoping for a positive response.

Vanmaele picked his nose unashamedly.

"The comedians hardly left a single trace," he said apologetically. "No prints, no hair, no splinter of fingernail. I had two of my team go through the place with a fine-tooth comb. The most relevant discovery was a jar of Vaseline in an adjoining room."

"Adjoining room?"

"Didn't you check it out?"

Van In shook his head.

"A fancy lounge opposite the workshop," Leo grinned.

"Ah, that explains it," Van In whispered. "Now I understand what the after-hours 'clients' are all about. We should look into it."

"A jealous former lover in his seventies with his grandson along for the ride?" Vanmaele laughed.

"You're right, Leo. Let me have the rest of your report."

"Experts from the NIC are looking at the detonator, or what's left of it. But I'm afraid the source of the Semtex can't be traced. They smuggle the stuff in containers from Northern

Ireland via Zeebrugge. Anyone with half a connection in the criminal world can get ahold of it. And without any idea of the number plates, a Mercedes station wagon is about as easy to trace as an in-focus photo of his majesty the king."

The foolish comparison brought a smile to Van In's face. "Don't tell me you brought me here for a Duvel session," he said reproachfully.

Vanmaele wiped the foam from his lips and vehemently shook his head. "I wanted to talk about that note with the Latin on it. A friend suspects it might have to do with one or other esoteric society: the Rosicrucians, for instance, or the Freemasons. Something of the sort."

"Did your friend have any idea what it meant?"

"Negative," said Vanmaele. "But he knows someone who should."

"Who?" asked Van In impatiently.

"The concierge at the Holy Blood Basilica."

Van In stared at Vanmaele in disbelief. "The concierge at the Holy Blood Basilica," he repeated vacantly.

"The very one," Leo nodded. "According to my friend, the man's knowledge of magic, alchemy, and all that secret stuff is close to encyclopedic."

"Speaking of alchemy," Van In muttered. "Wasn't that all about turning lead into gold?"

"Something like that," said Leo, sticking two fingers in the air. "I've arranged to meet him. He's expecting us at seven. His name's Billen. Sounded enthusiastic over the phone."

They settled the bill at ten to seven. The terrace was pretty full by that time. The bartender turned up the blues music a little louder.

Van In and Leo turned right and ambled toward Burg Square via Jozef Suvee Street and the Fish Market.

The southwest corner of Burg Square in Bruges houses an extraordinary shrine, a two-chapel basilica in which a relic of the blood of Christ has been preserved since the beginning of the thirteenth century. The Holy Blood Basilica welcomes no fewer than two million tourists a year. Few people are aware, however, that a nineteenth-century mansion is located at the back of the basilica, concealed behind its lofty walls. The door that gives access to the mansion is underneath the entrance to the basilica, a monumental staircase known as the "Steeghere" that leads to the upper chapel.

It took a while before anyone responded to the old-fashioned doorbell. Van In was about to tug the bell a second time when they heard sound of shuffling feet. The heavy door dragged against the floor and the young man had difficulty getting it open. He was wearing shorts and a bright multicolored T-shirt.

"Good evening, we're from the police. Is your father at home?" asked Van In. Leo noticed the young man's extremely curt smile.

"Frans Billen," he said, clearly amused. "Please, come in."

Concierges don't look the same as they used to, Leo thought to himself as they went inside. They followed Billen along a bare vaulted corridor, turned left and made their way up a flight of stairs to a second corridor.

"A bit of a maze," Van In observed lightheartedly.

"Yeh, that's what everyone says first time," said Billen, his tone suggesting that no one ever came back for a second time. He opened one of the many doors and switched on the light.

The room was spacious and tastefully furnished. The amply proportioned mouse-gray leather lounge suite must have cost an average sixth-month salary. The walls were covered with sandy-yellow textured wallpaper, in perfect harmony with an impressive antique cabinet. But the room was dominated by an enormous bookcase. An old framed poster of the Holy Blood Procession hung above the fireplace, and a flourishing variety of indoor plants graced an assortment of side tables.

"Make yourselves at home, gentlemen, while I open a bottle of wine," said Billen invitingly as he disappeared into the corridor. The same sound of shuffling feet as before.

"Oddball," said Van In when they were alone. "Isn't this kind of luxury a bit too fancy for a concierge?"

"Not a bit." Leo caressed the sleek leather sofa. "Concierges are in great demand in the States. Officially they're paid almost nothing, but if they're in the right place and they use their brains they can earn a fortune in tips. If you ask me, Billen knew what he was doing when he took on the job."

"Maybe you're right," Van In sighed. "Only fools work for the police . . . apparently."

Leo jealously inspected the contents of the bookcase.

"They say you can get to know people by the books they read, but here it's hard to know where to start. He seems to be interested in everything."

The sound of glasses clinking outside in the corridor betrayed their host's imminent return. Van In and Leo quickly settled on the sofa. Sparrows, blackbirds, and thrushes chirped in the garden outside. The sun's oblique rays gave the room a golden glow and a unique ambiance.

"So, here we are," said Billen.

He placed three slender wine glasses on the marble coffee table and nimbly uncorked a dusty bottle of burgundy. Leo was able to identify the wine from the shape of the bottle. Van In, who was a little closer, spotted the vintage: 1986.

Billen filled the glasses, sloshing the scarlet burgundy as he poured to give it the necessary oxygen.

"I presume I can tempt you to a glass of wine?" he asked, as if he had suddenly realized that there were people in this world who might not have been interested in the excellent Chambolle-Musigny he had fetched from the cellar.

"You shouldn't have gone to the trouble," said Leo. "All the same, both my colleague and myself know how to appreciate a good burgundy."

Billen nodded approvingly. Visitors who liked their wine were always welcome.

"Hendrik told me you wanted to ask about a Latin puzzle," he said calmly as he handed each man a glass. He spoke slowly and with an irritating nasal voice, and it was impossible to tell otherwise that he was from West Flanders.

Van In fished a copy of the puzzle from his inside pocket. Billen took the piece of paper, glanced at it quickly, and took a seat.

"Am I allowed to ask where this came from?"

Leo turned to Van In. They weren't in the habit of discussing the details of ongoing cases with outsiders, but Van In decided not to beat around the bush and told him what had happened in a couple of short sentences.

"Intriguing," said Billen. Two deep vertical furrows appeared on his forehead. "I think you've come to the right place." It sounded blasé, but it wasn't meant to. Frans Billen was a very modest man.

"Any idea what it might mean?" asked Van In optimistically.

"More or less. The translation is a question of interpretation, but I know what it is," he said with conviction. "This, good sirs, is the Templars' Square, their creed in a nutshell. The original text is carved in stone on a pillar in Ethiopia, in Axium to be precise. Christ is said to have leaned against it."

Leo's eyes almost popped out of his head and Van In rubbed his chin in disbelief.

The Templars, he thought. So they were dealing with a bunch of crazies after all.

Billen noticed their surprise.

"There's a lot of nonsense doing the rounds about the Templars. It would help if we tried to get handle on them first, then take a look at my interpretation."

Van In and Leo nodded in unison. They knew as much about the Templars as a retired padre knew about modern mathematics.

"Let me try to sketch the history of the order as a basis for explaining the text. But why don't we begin with the wine. It's not a short story."

Billen gave the example by raising the glass to his lips. Leo, who was more used to beer, fluttered his eyelids. This was the nectar of the gods . . . no denying it.

Billen waited until they had put down their glasses.

"We know from the history books that Philip IV, otherwise known as Philip the Fair, had the Templars arrested and that the pope of the day, Clement V, had reluctantly supported him. The judicial proceedings that followed the mass arrest served as a source of myth and gossip about the Templars that was to last for centuries. Philip was jealous of their power and wealth, and this led him to concoct a number of grotesque accusations. The Inquisition extracted the required confessions. It was claimed, for example, that the Knights Templar stamped on the cross and spat on it, kissed each other's anus, and indulged in sodomy and devil worship.

"It can be demonstrated on the basis of documentary evidence from the proceedings that only a handful of Templars actually confessed, but that would take us too far from our purpose. Suffice it to say that even the most gruesome torture failed to bring them to their knees. The majority of those who succumbed later withdrew their forced confessions. Sadly, Philip the Fair's version of events is what survived, not the truth."

Van In and Leo listened attentively. Billen was a passionate narrator.

"And the truth is a different story altogether. When Hugues de Payens and eight other noblemen founded the order at the beginning of the twelfth century, they had one goal in mind: keeping the roads that led to sacred places free of robbers and heathens and thus protecting pilgrims. They were monks in the first instance. Hugues was later supported by St. Bernard of Clairvaux, and the order acquired official status in 1128.

"Directly responsible to the pope alone, the Templars amassed a gigantic fortune in the shortest time. They enjoyed enormous respect and they became powerful, perhaps too powerful. Conditions of admission to the order were strict, its life was hard, and its discipline was unrelenting. For the nearly two centuries the Templars sojourned in the Holy Land, they performed their duties with excellence. Their permanent presence was remarkable in itself, especially when you realize that the order only reached a couple of thousand members at its peak.

"Moorish superiority was increasing, however, and after a while they were left with little choice: negotiate or face defeat.

"Peace negotiations naturally took place in the strictest of secrecy. The Church had forbidden compromise with unbelievers. Those on the home front were also unlikely to understand what they were doing and would probably condemn them in no uncertain terms. This is where we find the primary difference between the faith of the Templars and the faith of the official Church. The Templars were practical and broadminded for their day. They had long stripped the Church's teaching of its encrustations in search of the core of the faith, *le noyau* as they called it, its nucleus. They had shorn off the frills and absurd rules with which previous generations of popes and bishops had encumbered the message of Christ.

"The Christ they ardently believed in spoke words of love, fraternity, tolerance, and forgiveness, words that attracted the soldier monks more than the hodgepodge preached by the successors of Peter. They opted with determination for the most evangelical solution and tried to live in peace with the Muslims, for better or for worse—or at least those Muslims who had encountered the same message in the Quran. The Templars' greatest contribution has to be their conviction that we all worship the same God, that human beings are responsible for division, and that unity speaks for itself.

"The *Pax Dei* or Peace of God seemed to function well for a time. A fertile exchange of ideas and knowledge evolved between East and West. For example, the Templars imported windmills, algebra, exotic plants and fruits, and advanced medical techniques from the East.

"Everything went well until the order was torn apart from the inside by incompetent leadership, pride, and overindulgence. The Templars lost the Holy Land and returned to Europe without a purpose. They tried to return to their sources and renew themselves in the hope that they might one day retake Jerusalem. In those days they were even responsible for the French treasury. The Temple in Paris functioned as a sort of National Bank. Their exceptional status provoked the French king's jealousy. Philip the Fair, *le Roi Fraudeur*, was fed up having to go cap in hand to the Templars for money. He also found it difficult to swallow that the grand master of the order enjoyed more respect in certain circles than he did. So he decided to discredit the knights."

Billen interrupted his monologue for a sip of Musigny.

"Historians would burn me at the stake for less," he grinned. "And maybe they would be right. There are plenty of things I still can't prove."

He noticed that Leo's glass was empty, got to his feet and quickly topped everyone up.

"An exceptionally interesting story, Mr. Billen," said Van In, and before he could add "but" to the compliment, Billen interrupted.

"Thank you, but you still don't know much about the text, and I presume that's why you're here.

"You should know that the Templars left almost no documents behind. We have their Rule of Life, a copy of which happens to be preserved here in Bruges, by the way, details of the suppression proceedings, inventories, and this . . ."

Billen waved the piece of paper in the air.

"As I mentioned, we already know this inscription from Ethiopia. It was found in a mosque that had been converted into a church. What the Templars were up to in Ethiopia isn't clear. Links have been made in recent years with their search for the Ark of the Covenant, but that's another story altogether. It might be better if we concentrate on the text."

He got to his feet and fetched a notebook and felt-tip pen from a drawer in the bookcase. He tore a sheet of paper from the notebook and wrote down the puzzle in large uppercase letters.

ROTAS
OPERA
TENET
AREPO
SATOR

"There we are."

He handed the sheet of paper to Van In.

"Notice anything special?" Leo edged a little closer.

"A cross," said Van In hesitatingly, as if he was afraid of making a fool of himself in front of the concierge. Billen had written the letters forming the cross in bold.

"Spot on, a cross. And if you turn the Ts of TENET on their side you get a perfect Templar cross."

"Does that mean anything?" asked Leo.

"We're not done yet," Billen grinned. "There's more. If we puzzle around a bit, we get PATER NOSTER twice and we're left with the letters A and O."

"Fascinating," said Leo. Van In raised his eyebrows in amazement, not because he was impressed, but because he was clueless.

Billen noticed his reaction.

"Bear with me," he said. "It'll all become clear in a moment."

He scribbled a couple of words on the scrap of paper and handed it to Van In.

Van In read it aloud: "A PATER NOSTER O."

"God is the beginning and the end, the alpha and the omega. Pretty inventive, those Templars, don't you think?"

Neither Leo nor Van In reacted, so Billen continued, his enthusiasm unabated.

"As I said a moment ago, the Templars discovered the core of the faith in the prayer that Jesus taught his apostles. Our Father—Pater Noster. Get it?"

Leo nodded and Van In took a sip of the excellent wine.

"The 'Our Father' is the complete prayer. Its words are all-inclusive and the Templars didn't need anything else. But in spite of the prayer's simplicity, human beings are weak and find it hard to apply it in their lives. The core idea of the gospel, love your neighbor as yourself, seems to be even more of a problem.

"SATOR ROTAS OPERA TENET is the Templars' modest response to the PATER NOSTER. It means: the Sower (Creator) knows the burdens and vicissitudes (of life), because He is the beginning and the end. Everything comes from Him and flows back to Him. What he sows either bears fruit a hundredfold or lands among the weeds on the fire. The knights of the Temple thus gave expression to their humble respect and reverence for the love of God. Their reasoning was this: God sent his Son Jesus Christ into the world to preach a simple message of love. People heard the message and understood it, but found it difficult to put it into practice. And God is an understanding God, in spite of our human weakness. He takes into account the burdens and vicissitudes of life that so often lead us astray. Even with our many infidelities, He continues to love us."

Billen had been talking for close to half an hour.

Van In took advantage of the brief pause to light a cigarette without asking if it was okay. Billen had treated them to a handsome story, but he feared that his explanation of the letter square wasn't going to contribute much to solving the Degroof case.

The perpetrators were probably playing a game and nothing more.

"Do you mind if I ask you a question, Mr. Billen?" said Van In.

"Frans, call me Frans, Mr. . . . ."

"Van In."

He wasn't into the familiarity hype.

"Of course, Mr. Van In," said Billen. "Fire away."

"The story you just told us was fascinating, let me be clear about that. But would I be wrong to say that there aren't too many people as captivated by the topic as you would appear to be? I mean, is this sort of information accessible to the public at large?"

Billen leaned forward and slipped an ashtray to Van In's side of the coffee table.

"I think you'd be surprised at the number of people who are interested in the Templars and a whole lot more. Magic, freemasonry, Egyptian mysteries, Gnosticism . . . you name it. Esoteric societies are popping up everywhere, and their followers are completely convinced they have the answer to life's big questions. They say it's fairly normal for the turn of a millennium. And as usual, the gullible and the naïve are their first customers.

"But if we're talking about the Templars' Square, I don't think there are more than ten people in Belgium who would be familiar with what I just told you. If you ask me, whoever left the square at Degroof's wasn't a pseudo-new age freak."

Van In was about to ask how a simple concierge happened to be so well informed, but Leo sensed what he was about to do and shook his head. Van In held his tongue. Leo was much more diplomatic, and putting Billen under pressure wasn't going to benefit their inquiries. After all, the poor guy had nothing to do with the case.

"So, if only a handful of people know about the meaning of the square," Leo wavered, filling in the sudden and uncomfortable silence, "then the number of suspects has to be pretty small."

"If we presume they didn't leave the text behind as some kind of joke to throw us off the scent," said Van In, unable to contain his skepticism.

"That doesn't sound right, Mr. Van In," said Billen, sticking to his guns. "I'm close to convinced that the nature of the crime is proof that the perpetrators knew what the square meant."

"A payback with an esoteric tint? Your will be done, but if we don't like it, we'll take care of our own affairs. God understands what motivates us, and he'll take it into account on the Last Day?" Van In responded in an almost derisive tone.

"Who knows," said Billen unassumingly. "I've never looked at it that way. But believe me, Mr. Van In, I don't think we've seen the end of this. People who base their actions on a certain sort of symbolism—and what they did with the gold seems to point in that direction—usually think long and hard before they make a move and aren't likely to limit their plans to a once-only incident."

Leo nodded approvingly and Van In was obliged to agree. He had come to more or less the same conclusion himself, and he was also at a loss for a different explanation.

"I also have a sense that the symbolism was at least as important to them as the deed itself. Degroof probably knows exactly what it all means."

Van In took a mental note of Billen's words. The man was in a different league, far too astute to be a mere concierge.

"Another glass of wine, Mr. Van In?"

Van In fished his cigarettes from his pocket and placed them on the coffee table.

"Why not, Mr. Billen," he said good-humoredly. "Maybe you could fill us in on the Ark of the Covenant. Now that we have the time."

8

LAURENT DE BOCK AND DANIEL Verhaeghe spent the night in a Swiss Cottage-style chalet near Namur. In spite of the stress and tension that had marked the previous few days, Daniel slept like a log.

Laurent woke his pupil at seven-thirty with a shake.

"Time to get up, my boy," he said, in a gentle but imperative tone. "We've got a busy schedule ahead of us today."

He caressed Daniel's forehead with the back of his hand and shuffled back to the kitchen. The coffee was ready and Laurent popped two slices of bread in the toaster. Daniel appeared five minutes later. The kitchen ceiling was low and he had to stoop to avoid bumping his head on one of the beams. He looked gaunt and tired in his pajamas.

"Your eyedrops are next to your plate," said Laurent as he filled a huge mug with coffee and a lot of hot milk.

Daniel tucked in, stuffing his face like a ravenous wolf while Laurent nibbled guardedly on a piece of buttered toast. When the boy had had enough, Laurent cleared the table.

Daniel got dressed in the bedroom and Laurent transformed the rectangular table into an altar complete with crucifix and candles. Daniel wasn't exactly overjoyed when he saw what Laurent had been doing.

"Do we have to?" he sighed.

"One more time, my boy. We can't risk a single mistake. Do it once more for me. Then I'll be content."

Daniel closed his eyes for a second and took a deep breath. Laurent handed him the vestments one by one.

"First the alb, then you kiss the cross on the stole," Laurent instructed.

Daniel didn't argue. He popped his head through the hole in the chasuble and draped it over his arms and shoulders like an experienced priest. He then performed the ritual he had practiced every day for the last three months. Laurent watched carefully and congratulated him when it was over.

"Perfect, my boy. No one will notice a thing. I'm absolutely certain of it."

While Daniel smoked a cigarette, Laurent took a medium-sized Samsonite case from the wardrobe and filled it with clean clothes and underwear, shaving gear, a silver chalice, a breviary, a couple of novels, and towels. He also packed jeans, a sweater, and sport shoes should the boy have to get away in a hurry. Running in a clerical outfit would attract too much attention.

They climbed into the Mercedes at ten-thirty and drove off in the direction of Marche-les-Dames. The journey took no more than ten minutes. Laurent stopped the car a little short of half a mile from the monastery.

"If everything goes according to plan, I'll pick you up here on Friday evening," said Laurent. "And don't forget you're only allowed to leave the monastery if something goes wrong. But there's not much likelihood of that. I've prepared it all to the last detail. There are four other guests in the monastery at the moment. As a result, everyone is a potential suspect. But I'm not expecting Benedicta to sound the alarm."

"Rest assured, Laurent. *I* won't disappoint you."

The old man leaned to the right and kissed Daniel on the forehead.

"I know you won't, my boy."

Daniel got out of the car and took his luggage from the back seat. He held up his hand and made his way toward the monastery at a brisk pace.

"The best of luck, boy," Laurent whispered.

He followed Daniel until he disappeared behind the trees. He then turned the Mercedes and drove at a steady 30 mph back to Namur.

Daniel stood at the monastery gate, a little awkward, his spirits low.

"Monastère de Bethléem," read the sign. He repeated it four times. The eighteenth-century monastery was bathed in an unnatural tranquility. No twittering bird, no rustling leaf disturbed the silence. This was the least satisfying part of the plan, but Laurent refused to make exceptions. And Daniel had promised he wouldn't disappoint him.

He rang the bell and listened to its echo fade. He waited patiently for footsteps, for a sign of life. No one opened the door.

Daniel put down his suitcase and went in search of another entrance.

In the meantime he mentally rehearsed what Laurent had told him about "les petites soeurs de Bethléem." The order was relatively young. In 1950, during the solemn proclamation of the dogma of the assumption of Mary's body and soul into heaven, six pilgrims were overwhelmed by an extraordinary gift of grace and decided to establish a new monastic order.

The first community was founded in Chamvres, France. Their single goal was to join the Blessed Virgin Mary in venerating the Most Holy Trinity day and night, in complete silence and isolation. They sought inspiration from the first monks who gathered in the Egyptian desert in the fourth century, sharing a common life in individual hermitages.

The adopted the rule of Saint Bruno, who had founded the Carthusian order in Chartreuse near Grenoble in 1084. The rule was strict and the life of the monks was hard.

After waiting for ten minutes, and without finding another entrance, Daniel rang the bell a second time. He was dying for a cigarette.

A good fifteen minutes had passed, and after ringing the bell no fewer than four times, he pushed gingerly against the left panel of the door. To his surprise, it was unlocked. More disappointed than relieved, he made his way inside like a timid traveling salesman. The door closed behind him with a muffled click.

Daniel was standing in a spotlessly clean cloister corridor. The floor glistened treacherously like the surface of a Scottish loch. The walls were whitewashed and immaculate, and amber-colored shafts of light penetrated the enormous rectangular windows at regular intervals. For the second time that day, a flicker of doubt ran up his spine and wormed its way into his brain. Did they really have a right to revenge? Was Benedicta as innocent as the others?

He rested his suitcase carefully on the ground. In an instant the floor conjured a perfect mirror image. All this standing still was beginning to hurt. Daniel deliberately put an end to it and started to walk up and down. Each footstep offended the silence, like a dry twig cracking under a hunter's foot as he stalks his prey. But he didn't dare go far, so he went outside again and rang the bell for a fifth time, waiting on the threshold of the half-open door. The minutes crept past as he stood there, too timid to move.

Two wooden mailboxes graced the wall to his left, one reading "messages," the other "contributions," both in white letters. He started to lose track of time and decided to count to a hundred. If no one appeared, he would just have to head back to Namur on foot.

At ninety-eight he suddenly heard the squeak of hinges. A white figure hovered toward him from the half-light at the end of the corridor. The sister's face was partially concealed by a generous wimple. She stopped, leaving a distance of ten feet between them.

"Father Verhaeghe," said Daniel in a gentle voice, the loudness of which surprised him nonetheless.

"I'm here for a four-day retreat," he whispered. "I received notice two weeks ago that I could come today."

The diminutive sister nodded but said nothing in response to Daniel's words. Daniel felt as helpless as a wheelchair patient watching a child drown in a shallow ditch. Laurent had researched the monastery's customs in great detail, but he hadn't been able to find out how they welcomed strangers. "Be patient at all times," Laurent had insisted. So Daniel waited and tried to stare meekly into space.

"Welcome, Father," she said after a moment.

It was clear from her voice that she was French and that she rarely spoke Dutch. But she still did her best to pronounce each word correctly.

"Let me show you the way."

"Praised be the Lord Jesus Christ," Daniel responded, thinking she had quoted a verse from the Bible.

In less than five minutes she had shown him the cell in which he was to spend the coming days, the kitchen, the chapel, and the garden. She then accompanied him back to his cell and handed him two duplicated pages containing the house rules and the daily schedule.

"If you have any further questions, Father, you can leave them in the box by the entrance. You will receive an answer the following day under the door of your cell."

"Thank you, sister," said Daniel. "But there are a couple of things I would like to discuss with you, if I may."

"Sorry, Father, but I'm afraid our conversation has reached its end." She turned and ten seconds later disappeared around the corner.

Daniel was completely stumped.

The cell was sparsely furnished: a small alcove with a straw mattress, a table, and a chair. Fortunately, the window gave out onto the garden and the view was rewarding, to say the least. The nuns of Bethlehem had clearly managed to transform what had probably been a nondescript patch of ground into a breathtaking paradise.

Daniel deposited his suitcase on the chair, opened it, and arranged its contents on the table. He read the daily schedule standing by the window. Mass was at five-thirty, so there was still a little time to rest.

Laurent had packed a couple of novels. "To pass the time," he had said. "Unless you want to devote yourself to prayer?"

Daniel chose the thicker of the two, a nine-hundred-page doorstop.

The Quincunx, he read, half out loud. He kicked off his shoes and installed himself on the bed.

Van In appeared at the station that morning at nine-thirty. The Musigny from the previous day had had the same effect as a heavy dose of valium. He was still more or less anesthetized.

"Top of the mornin', Commissioner," said Officer Geerts at the reception counter in a thick Bruges accent, his malicious delight at Van In's hangover barely concealed.

"Morning, Patrick," said Van In confused.

Despite his condition, he sensed Geerts's mocking gaze burning a hole in his back. He turned instinctively and stared the surprised policeman in the eye.

"Something bugging you?"

Patrick Geerts, nicknamed "steamer" because he sweated like a pig, giggled sheepishly.

"Out with it," Van In barked. He didn't like Geerts.

The man was a sneaky bastard, prepared to sell his soul to De Kee to get into his good books.

"De Kee's been looking for you for more than an hour," he grinned unashamedly. "He called down just ten minutes ago. I don't think he's a happy camper, if you get my drift. You know what he's like if he's having an off day," the steamer snickered.

"Is he in his office?" Van In snapped.

Geerts nodded.

"Sure is. If you listen carefully, you can hear him pacing up and down."

Van In hurried up the stairs, leaving Geerts behind with a grin on his face. *The bastard must have found out about the radio appeal,* he thought. Van In's colleagues saw him as self-confident, not afraid to row against the tide. But his reputation was nothing more than a carefully constructed façade. Van In wasn't afraid to answer back either, but when it came to De Kee he was a little more submissive than he would have liked.

"Enter," was the hard response to his gentle knock.

De Kee stood with his back to the door, looking out over Exchange Square.

"I believe you've been looking for me, Commissioner," said Van In, trying to sound as neutral as possible.

"Take a seat, Van In," said De Kee abruptly without turning.

Van In took a seat and nervously winkled a cigarette from a half-smoked pack.

"I presume you haven't seen this morning's papers," said De Kee. He continued to stare out of the window. "They're on my desk."

Van In picked up one of the papers. The Degroof case had reached the front pages.

"Anonymous Alchemist Takes Revenge on Bruges Jeweler," he read.

"Keep reading," De Kee barked.

"Police reports are describing the incident as a well-orchestrated act of revenge against one of the most prominent families in Bruges. Ludovic Degroof, the father of the victim, is not unknown in political circles. For many he epitomizes the Christian People's Party and is the driving force behind numerous prestigious building projects in the center of the city."

Van In folded the paper and leaned back in his chair.

"I've no idea where they dug up such a story," he said with a truly clear conscience.

"You know good and bloody well that this isn't the only issue," De Kee rasped. "You have managed to make Mr. Degroof extremely angry." His voice sounded gloomier than usual.

Van In wasn't in the mood to beat around the bush any longer.

"Are we talking about the Radio Contact appeal we broadcast yesterday?"

"So you admit it," said De Kee dryly, his splayed left hand in his hair.

"I was under orders from the public prosecutor's office," Van In defended himself. It was his only argument.

De Kee turned and glared at Van In.

"Assistant Commissioner Van In,"—his first two words were unusually hesitant—"I presume you're adult enough to realize that you should have discussed a stunt like that with me first."

He sat at his desk opposite Van In and shook his head.

"I thought I made it clear enough, crystal-clear in fact, that this case was to be given no publicity. I even told you that Ludovic Degroof had made an explicit point of it, information I didn't have to share. You should also be well enough aware that we don't dance to the public prosecutor's pipes round here. *They* have to make do with whatever information *we* provide."

"But Commissioner," Van In protested, "the Deputy threatened to contact the media herself if I didn't do what she asked. God knows what might have happened. We managed to limit the radio appeal to between seven and nine in the morning. A friendly gesture. I had no other option. I was also convinced that a short radio report would make little difference."

"And you were wrong, my friend. The public prosecutor called me yesterday evening. If you had consulted me, there would have been no radio appeal. The case is set to be shelved. Get that into your head once and for all, Van In, and this is on Ludovic Degroof's explicit request. The public prosecutor has assured me that Ms. Martens will no longer be pressing the point. There even seems to be a problem with her definitive appointment as Deputy as a result of this whole mess."

"Jesus H. Christ," Van In muttered. This time he had screwed things up big-time.

"I thought you were smarter than this, Van In," said De Kee, his fingers in his hair yet again. Van In realized he wasn't the only one up to his neck in it.

"Even the mayor isn't happy with your exploits."

"The mayor!" Van In exclaimed.

De Kee leaned forward and folded his hands under his chin.

"The mayor is a socialist—opposed to Degroof politically
. . . is that what you're thinking? Forget it! Ludovic Degroof's
tentacles are everywhere, even in the mayor's office. And sometimes a mayor has no other choice than to knuckle under to the
Brussels club, even if he belongs to another party." De Kee could
see that Van In had realized the gravity of the situation. Perhaps
he had gone a little too far. The assistant commissioner wasn't
his best friend, but every now and then they had to toe the line,
chief commissioners, assistant commissioners and mayors alike.

"You mean the investigation's being cut short?" Van In
asked, still having difficulty believing what De Kee had just
told him.

"I have to admit, you're a master of the understatement,
Van In."

De Kee curled his bloodless lips into a thin smile.

"Personnel informs me that you have more than three hundred hours overtime to your credit," he said indifferently. "If I
was you, I'd start cashing them in, beginning today."

"All three hundred?"

"Let's say you're taking some time off."

"But that's more than two months," said Van In, quickly
doing the math.

"Two months is perhaps a little exaggerated," De Kee
conceded. "Let's agree to meet for a chat at the beginning of
August."

"You can't be serious, Commissioner. What will the others
think? I always take my vacation in September." Van In suddenly realized he was close to begging.

"Of course, I can't force you," said De Kee nonchalantly.

Van In sighed. It was all show. De Kee wanted to scare the
shit out of him, and the bastard had succeeded, in spades.

"But you'll have to explain yourself to the mayor's council.
The mayor himself is refusing to budge. And if I'm not mistaken,

suspension without salary is not what you want to hear right now," he added with another thin smile.

Van In refused to believe what he was hearing. *Almost anything goes with the Bruges police*, he thought to himself. *Weird stuff happens every day . . . but this?* His stomach shrunk as if he hadn't eaten in days.

"Chin up, Van In. It's not the end of the world," said De Kee as he watched the color drain from the assistant commissioner's face. "Look on the bright side. Two months vacation, man. I wish I was in your place."

"I still don't understand what's so bloody important about this case," said Van In, unable to control his temper. His reverence for the chief commissioner's authority made way for uninhibited anger-fueled defiance. De Kee took it to be nothing more than a final spasm, knowing that Van In had no alternative.

Van In clenched his fist and thumped De Kee's desk. He felt powerless. He was taken aback as a result when De Kee appeared at his side and gave him an almost paternal pat on the back.

"If I had been leading the investigation, my good friend, they would have sent me on vacation too."

Van In shook his head expressionlessly. He thought about the ideals of his youth and how he had renounced them. *Down with class difference, down with capitalism*, we chanted back then. And the powerful looked on in pity, let us spend our fury, and then they offered us a job. It was a simple tactic, but he had never thought about it before. *What would happen*, he thought, brimming over with bitterness, *if all the forty-somethings looking back on their lives decided to revolt a second time, even if they knew it was pointless and defeat was inevitable?*

"Come, on your way," he heard De Kee say. "Drink a couple of whiskeys and book a trip to Tenerife."

Van In got to his feet and left De Kee's office without a word.

As soon as he was alone, De Kee grabbed the telephone and punched in the number of Ludovic Degroof.

Daniel Verhaeghe spent his first miserable night in the hard and narrow monastery bed. He had no idea what the nuns might stuff into their mattresses to make their lives any more disagreeable. Needles and ground glass, he presumed.

There was nothing about the place that he liked.

Dinner the previous day had been a serious ordeal. He had made his way to the kitchen at six-thirty, following the schedule "sister doorkeeper" had given him. He saw no one on the way, and when he arrived the place was empty.

The layout in the small kitchen gave him some idea of what to expect. The air was filled with the smell of cheap soapsuds and stale bread, and there was a cupboard and a simple gas burner. A spotless sink glistened in the corner, the tap above it breaking the monotony of the white-tiled wall. A narrow kitchen counter took up most of the remaining space.

Thirty numbered containers were arranged side by side on the counter. Five wooden containers had been set apart to the far left. One of them had a piece of paper with his name on it, the other four the names of the other guests. The sisters apparently waited until the guests served themselves before coming to the kitchen for their own containers. On Sundays, everyone ate alone in their cell.

Each of the roughly four-inch-deep rectangular containers had the same disappointing contents: a couple of slices of coarse brown bread, a bowl of white spreading cheese, and a bottle of still mineral water.

Daniel had waited a couple of minutes, but when no one showed up he returned reluctantly to his cell with his frugal meal.

He had tossed the container onto his bed, but after an hour the hunger was too much and he devoured every last crumb. While he ate, he asked himself what kind of God took pleasure in this sort of thing. To get back at whatever divinity was causing his misery, he smoked five cigarettes in a row and finished what was left of the whiskey in his pocket flask. He had then scribbled a short note and deposited it in the box marked "messages."

He was curious to see if the sisters had already responded.

He walked to the front door in his bare feet. There was no response, as he had suspected.

He got dressed in a huff. The miserable rain outside lashed the tiny window. Sullen gray clouds had settled on the tops of the pine trees in the distance.

"Can it get any worse?" he grumbled.

The chill of the rain and the pangs of hunger made him shiver. He pulled the thin blanket from his bed and threw it over his shoulders like a cloak. He had overslept, that was clear. The nuns of Bethlehem had already started their day. He examined their schedule anew to see what they were up to.

Everyone rose at 4:45 for Matins, which he had evidently missed. They then collected breakfast from the kitchen and ate it alone in their cell. At 8:15 they chanted Terce alone in their cell. Sext was at 9:55 and the angelus was rung at 12 noon. The afternoon was set aside for meditation and Vespers were at 5 P.M. in the chapel, followed by mass. The day was brought to a close after dinner with Compline.

The sisters devoted the remaining hours to manual labor. They decorated porcelain cups and plates and used the proceeds to provide for themselves.

This was the life and work of the nuns of Bethlehem, day in, day out, in seclusion and prayer.

The only interruption to the routine was on Sundays when they ate together at noon and walked together in the garden for a couple of hours. This was the only moment in the week that they had contact with one another.

And anyone thinking such a place must be full of ancient oddball sanctimonious hypocrites would be completely off the mark. The majority of the sisters were thirty-five or younger, and most of them had one or more university degrees under their belt.

That's what Laurent told him.

Most of them were also from wealthy families.

Is the world really such a bad place? Daniel mused.

A bell clanging on the corridor made him jump. *Shit, ten past eight*, he cursed. Daniel hoped desperately they hadn't removed the breakfast containers. He would have killed for a cup of coffee and some decent toast.

The corridor was just as silent and deserted as it had been the day before. He crept toward the kitchen, like a shadow close to the walls. He felt a little guilty and didn't want to bump into anyone.

He cautiously opened the kitchen door and slipped inside. A single container remained on the kitchen counter, an accusing witness to his negligence. *Thank God the nuns like variety*, he sneered to himself. Breakfast consisted of rye bread, a bowl of milk, and a ceramic pot of pear jelly.

During his visit to the kitchen, someone had slipped a note under the door of his cell. *So they are keeping an eye on me*, he thought. Scribbled in miserly handwriting on an unsightly sheet of paper were the words: *Father, please be kind enough to preside at the Eucharist today at 17:25.* The time had been underlined.

Damn you, Laurent, he thought as he popped a chunk of rubbery rye bread into his mouth. Laurent had planned everything to the last detail as he had done before their nocturnal visit to Degroof's. Thus far, his planning had been immaculate.

To his surprise, Daniel found the rest of the breakfast more than edible. He cleaned out the pot of pear jelly with his finger.

At nine-thirty, when he was certain everyone would be in their cells, he stuffed his jeans and sweater into a plastic bag and quietly left the building.

Fortunately the rain had stopped. He changed into his street clothes behind some bushes a couple of hundred yards from the monastery and well out of sight. It was only a twenty-minute walk from the monastery to Marche-les-Dames. Laurent had forbidden him to leave the monastery, but Daniel was intent on making the most of every day he had left. The chances of his absence being noticed were close to nonexistent, and even if the sisters became aware of it they wouldn't ask questions. They clearly believed he was a priest, otherwise they would never have asked him to preside at mass that evening.

It started to drizzle around four in the afternoon as he slipped back inside. He thought it strange that sneaking in and out of one of the strictest and most isolated convents in the world had been so easy.

Instead of one plastic bag, he returned with three. The first contained his jeans and sweater. The second was bursting at the seams with drink and other provisions. He had guzzled half a bottle of whiskey in the course of the day, and at lunchtime he had tucked in to a healthy entrecote with fries. He didn't touch the food containers in the kitchen after that. *Let the sisters think I'm fasting*, he thought.

In the safety of his cell, he hoisted the bottle of J&B to his lips and gulped. He had to be careful, of course. Just enough to suppress the gnawing stage fright. He had to celebrate mass later and that meant a public, an expert public. He had rehearsed the ritual ad nauseam, but it still let him uneasy. Just the thought of it made his stomach turn with nervousness.

He took his last mouthful of whiskey at ten past five and
when the taste had subsided, he popped a couple of Fisherman's
Friends in his mouth and returned the box to his pocket. He
then hurried to the chapel, to his relief slipping unnoticed into
the sacristy via a side door. The sister sacristan had set out the
vestments with great care.

He pulled the spotlessly white alb over his head, his knees
knocking. There was no one with him in the sacristy to witness it, but he kissed the cross on the stole nonetheless. He
then popped his head through the opening in the chasuble and
draped it over his arms and shoulders just as he had learned.

When he was ready, he looked in the mirror. Real priests
always did the same. *Probably the only mirror in the convent*, Daniel
imagined. The idea that it was intended for the exclusive use of
the monastery's few male visitors made him smile.

As he examined himself, the singing in the adjacent chapel
fell silent. Daniel wasn't sure if this was the end of Vespers, so
he shilly-shallied by the door leading from the sacristy to the
chapel. Just as he was about to open it, a bell started to ring.
He decided to wait a little longer. He broke into a cold sweat
and yearned for a slug of whiskey and a cigarette.

After five minutes, the door was cautiously and noiselessly
pushed open. Sister doorkeeper shuffled into the sacristy.

"Good evening, Father."

Daniel nodded politely and even attempted a benign smile.
He took stock of the diminutive sister unobserved. The
wimple covered most of her face. He had studied the photograph of Benedicta Degroof for hours on end, but it wasn't
going to be easy to recognize her under a habit like this. Not
to mention the fact that the photo had been taken more than
sixteen years ago.

"Please follow me," said sister doorkeeper, her voice unexpectedly hushed.

Daniel raised his eyes to the heavens, took a deep breath, and followed her.

It was dark in the chapel. The sisters didn't have the money for electricity and only a small part of the monastery had been wired for it. What light there was came from five gothic windows, peering downward like eyes smoldering gently in the roughhewn stone.

The place was like a medieval fortress chapel and looked more fifteenth-century than eighteenth-century. The rib vaults, dark uneven floor tiles, and small cube-shaped altar reinforced the impression. The sisters had assembled in two rows along the side walls. Two nuns were holding on to a rope that was connected to a bell through an opening in the vaulted ceiling.

"In the name of the Father, and of the Son, and of the Holy Spirit." Daniel had learned the texts by heart just to be on the safe side, but he still had to give the impression he was reading it all from the missal. Laurent had surprised him when he said that few, if any, priests were capable of saying mass without textual support.

Every now and then Daniel looked up and scanned the chapel. But no matter how hard he tried, he was unable to identify Benedicta. All the sisters participated in the service with their head bowed, and a couple were even shrouded in complete darkness.

He was going to have to be patient until communion time.

Laurent had been right, as usual. It was the only way to get a good look at them.

Much to his surprise, the celebration went off without a hitch. But he was troubled by muted remorse at the consecration when he realized he was about to deceive these unsuspecting, trusting creatures. The bread they would be receiving today was just bread and not the body of the God for whom they had offered up their lives.

"And on the night He was betrayed, He took bread in his sacred hands, blessed the bread, broke it, and gave it to his apostles saying: take and eat, this is my body."

As Daniel spoke these words, he thought back to the night he and his mother had been betrayed. He was grateful to Laurent for warning him against such moments of weakness.

Distributing communion took the best part of five minutes, because the sisters prostrated themselves one by one on the floor before they received the host. Benedicta Degroof was last but one. He recognized her in an instant. She had been standing at the back of the chapel. Daniel etched her position in his memory.

Laurent had told him that the sisters liked to stay behind in the chapel after mass for meditation. He changed out of his vestments quickly nonetheless. All of the sisters were still present when he kneeled down at the back of the chapel.

It took a while for the first nun to leave. Benedicta was the third. She didn't notice the priest follow immediately behind her. Ironically enough, his cell wasn't far from hers.

Two hours later, Daniel slipped the first letter under her door.

9

On Wednesday morning, Laurent De Bock drove from Namur to Blankenberge on the Belgian coast.

Traffic on the freeway wasn't bad for that time of the year. The specter of the recession had its hands full, and thousands of potential holiday makers had been forced to stay at home for lack of vacation funds. The weather had also unexpectedly changed for the worse. A massive surge of coastal day-trippers was now extremely unlikely.

Laurent had no problem parking his car in one of the streets near the sea dike and found it just as easy to rent a hotel room. Hotel Riant Sejour turned out to be a modern three-star establishment with spacious and comfortable rooms. He reserved one for two nights and paid in cash. The gesture conjured up a smile on the hotel manager's face. She carried his suitcase to the elevator in person.

Five minutes later, Laurent stood by the window of his room and looked out over the rippling green-gray waters of the North Sea.

The tide was out. The beach looked like a vast barren plain longing in vain to be united with the infinite sea. A powerful storm had swept it clean in the space of a couple of minutes. Laurent grabbed a beer from the refrigerator and dragged a chair onto the balcony.

Down below, on the promenade, a sturdy few braved the weather, parading under brightly colored umbrellas. Dogs on their leads sniffed in the rain, pissing and shitting to their heart's content. Nobody paid any attention. The air on the balcony was muggy and perfumed. The smell of sun cream, pancakes, and wet raincoats was slowly but surely losing ground to the savage saltiness of the sea.

Laurent did his best to inhale the aroma of the sea alone.

"Sator rotas opera tenet," he mumbled.

Ludovic Degroof and the clan that supported him were finally going to pay for their deeds. This was Laurent's last chance to play the role of avenging angel. His life was coming to an end and the people he loved had been dealt the cruelest of blows.

With the rolling waves as his witness, he prayed the Our Father and asked forgiveness for the crimes he was now committing . . . God had abandoned him, but Laurent would remain faithful to the end.

Laurent De Bock sighed, sipped his beer, and gazed out over the waves. He was having trouble containing his emotions. De Bock, who thought he was familiar with the ups and downs of life, hankered like a little child for revenge and justice. He gripped his beer bottle tight and thought of Degroof. They were both more or less the same age.

Was it all really worth it, or was he doing this in the hope that it would ease his imminent death?

Van In spent the first evening of his compulsory vacation in his garden.

The rain had stopped and the sun had sucked up the humidity in the blink of an eye. Around six, the heat became so oppressive that he was forced inside in search of shorts and flip-flops. On the way, he grabbed an ice-cold Duvel and a pack of ripe cheese cubes from the refrigerator. He hadn't eaten since noon the day before, and now not even the Duvels were enough to suppress his raging hunger.

He installed himself once more in the garden in the shade of a parasol and devoured the cheese first before opening the Duvel and pouring it into its bulbous glass until the froth seeped over the rim.

When the doorbell rang, he jumped from his chair without taking a breath. Leo had managed some time off after all, he thought. Good thing he'd hauled a fresh crate of Duvel from the cellar that morning.

"I'm coming," he shouted.

Van In raced barefoot to the front door. The dejection that had plagued him the last twenty-four hours fell from his shoulders like a wet bath towel.

"Hello, Mr. Van In," said Hannelore a little timidly when he opened the door.

Van In was visibly shocked at the sight of her. *Of all people,* he thought. It was as if someone was squeezing his windpipe. His lips formed words, but they didn't come out.

"I hope I'm not intruding."

She looked radiant in her low-cut body-hugging outfit.

"Leo gave me your address. He assured me you wouldn't mind if I stopped by."

"Of course not."

It took all the effort he could muster to force these three little words from his lips. He stepped aside and gestured that she should come in.

"You have a beautiful place here," she said, meaning every word.

All Van In could think about was the mess in the kitchen. Apart from Leo, he rarely received visitors.

"I was out in the garden," he stammered. "But please, join me." Van In nervously led the way. Hannelore followed him through the open sliding door. She smelled of spring flowers and Pears soap.

"Take a seat . . . make yourself at home."

He sounded awkward and affected. A hundred thousand thoughts raced aimless and unanswered through his head. *What in God's name was she doing here?*

"A drink?" he asked in desperation. There wasn't much to choose from, and that irritated him. "An ice-cold Duvel, perhaps?"

She sat down at the oval garden table. Van In was too confused to notice the glint in her eyes.

"Only if it's *really* ice-cold," she said with an edge to her voice.

Van In scurried back to the kitchen like a rattled rookie, rinsed a moldy Duvel glass, and popped a couple of Duvels in the freezer compartment. Firecrackers popped in his head, and on his way back to the garden he almost tripped over his own feet.

"I envy you, Pieter Van In," she said admiringly as she savored the beer. "This is paradise at its immaculate best. What a house! And a walled garden . . . Unbelievable!"

It was *paradise*, Van In wanted to say, but that would have been inappropriate.

"So," he sighed. Van In deliberately took a seat on the opposite side of the table, and because he couldn't keep his eyes off her he focused instead on his glass.

"Leo told me all about you."

Hannelore didn't beat around the bush. Van In noticed for the first time that she kept referring to Leo.

"Leo?" he asked naïvely.

"Yes, Leo Vanmaele, the police expert from the other day. You hardly knew each other, or so it seemed. We had a long telephone conversation this afternoon. He tells me you've been the best of buddies for years. You studied criminology together in Brussels. And if the stories he dished up are anything to go by, college life was anything but boring," she said mischievously.

"Jesus H. Christ," Van In groaned.

She crossed her legs, and he broke into a sweat.

"Sorry, but the show with Leo was just a joke. I thought you . . ."

"You thought I was a know–it–all bitch."

Van In took a gulp of his Duvel and nervously wiped his upper lip. "The chief commissioner was already on our case, and when Versavel told me a Deputy had shown up . . . well, what can I say. You get my drift," he said apologetically.

"The Degroof case has been shelved," she said, suddenly serious. "The public prosecutor made that clear enough, and with convincing arguments. But I heard that you didn't get off lightly either, so I thought: poor commissioner . . . maybe he needs a little comforting."

"That's what I call generous . . ."

Her first name stuck in his throat.

"Has this kind of thing happened before?" she asked out of curiosity.

Van In took a deep breath. His heart was still pounding, but not so loudly. *I'll calm down in a minute*, he thought to himself. "Yes, but never with a trivial case like this."

"I thought the same thing, Pieter."

The way she pronounced his first name produced a warm, tingling sensation on his scalp. A moment or two, and he would be back to normal. At least that's what he hoped.

"I'm not planning to abandon the investigation," said Van In unprompted. The words had barely left his lips when he regretted having said them.

But she wasn't taken aback; on the contrary.

"Exactly what I was hoping for," she said. "The real reason I came was to ask you to continue your inquiries. And to offer my support, unofficially of course."

"What do you mean?" he asked, somewhat surprised.

"There's more to this than meets the eye, anyone can see that, and in certain circles Degroof has a lot less influence than some officials are inclined to think."

She gulped greedily at her Duvel. Van In automatically followed her example.

"Don't tell me it's political," he groaned.

"A possibility you should allow for," she observed.

"I've been trying to suppress that option for the best part of thirty-six hours. With this . . . ," and he pointed to the glass on the table.

She drew her chair closer and reduced her voice to a whisper.

"I want your solemn promise, Pieter Van In, that what I am about to say will never go beyond these walls."

Van In gazed into her eyes, bewildered. If she had asked him to streak naked across Market Square, he wouldn't have hesitated for a single moment.

"You have my solemn promise, Hannelore."

His secret was out . . . he had used her first name. "But before you make me privy to a bunch of state secrets, let me get us some more drinks."

"Good idea. You can't get enough to drink in this weather."

Van In ducked into the kitchen and returned a minute later with two more Duvels, a plate of cocktail sausages, some cheese cubes, and a pot of mustard, all neatly arranged on a tray. Hannelore didn't wait to be asked.

"Local elections are just around the corner, and everyone knows it's going to be a hard race," she said, popping a sausage into her mouth. "The Christian Democrats are ready to sell their soul for a shot at the mayor's office. The Socialists, on the other hand, will want to consolidate their position. But if you ask me, Dirk Van der Eyck, the new Liberal Party leader, is going to be a wrench in the system," she said, presuming he knew something about local politics. Van In understood what she meant, but he wasn't convinced that the people of Bruges shared her view of things.

"Do you think Van der Eyck stands a chance?"

"Don't underestimate him, Pieter. He has plenty of experience, and perhaps more importantly: he has the support of the Lodge, both here and in Brussels."

"But the Liberals didn't exactly shine in the European elections, did they?" Van In teased. Hannelore snorted disdainfully and stuffed two sausages into her mouth at the same time.

"Taste good, don't they?"

"Of course they taste good. I always get hungry when people get my hackles up. You don't believe me, do you?" she said threateningly.

Van In emphatically shrugged his shoulders. "I thought the voter decided who gets to run the show, at least in a democracy."

"Pieter, how could you be so naïve?" She apparently hadn't realized he was pulling her leg. "Everyone knows that the three major parties are going to share the lead, and two of them are going to have to form a coalition."

"And every party wants to appoint its own candidate as mayor."

"Exactly," she said. "It's all a question of playing the game without making mistakes and Van der Eyck is an expert. Don't underestimate the man, Pieter."

"That's the second time in five minutes."

"And with reason. Let me explain why I'm so convinced. Van der Eyck reached an agreement in principle with the Socialist Party yesterday. He's set to be appointed mayor, and his people are lined up to take charge of Tourism and Public Works. The Socialists get to share out the other responsibilities among themselves. On top of that, Van der Eyck has agreed to endorse every SP appointment for the next five years, and without conditions."

"You're kidding," Van In groaned.

Hannelore poured her second Duvel and dipped a couple of cheese cubes in the mustard pot.

"It's all true, Pieter."

"But where did you get this information, and what does it . . ."

"S-s-sh!"

She pressed her finger to her lips. Mischievous stars twinkled in her naughty-boy eyes.

"Come on, Hannelore. Don't chicken out."

It was Van In's turn to gulp greedily at his second Duvel. She fidgeted with the clasp of her necklace, stalling for time. Of course she had to tell him the whole story, but no one had told her she wasn't allowed to tease him a little.

"Even if the Degroof case does have something to do with politics, I still don't understand the connection you're trying to make with the coming local elections. Degroof senior isn't a candidate, nor is his son as far as I know."

Hannelore savored his ignorance.

"Good," she said suddenly. "Politics is a dirty business. The goal justifies the means, whatever it might be, and they'll try any trick in the book. Van der Eyck wants to cash in on the thousands of floating votes. He's determined to persuade the malcontented masses to vote for his party. Now that he's neutralized the Socialists, a bad turnout for the Christian

Democrats would be music to his ears. And even you should
know who calls the Christian Democrat shots here in Bruges.
Who's the party figurehead?"

"Degroof, of course," said Van In grumpily.

"Penny dropped yet?"

Van In didn't dare say no, so he nodded in the affirmative.

"Imagine something leaked about Degroof senior's past," she
continued with enthusiasm. "If there's a scandal attached, then
surely an experienced detective like you should be able to get
to the bottom of it. The mysterious act of revenge at Ghislain
Degroof's jewelry store is bound to attract press attention. And if
further actions follow, all we have to do is give the journalists a
couple of pointers and they'll be off like a pack of bloodhounds."

"But the case is closed," Van In objected. "And I'm on non-
active for the next two months."

Hannelore looked up in desperation.

"It was all crystal-clear in the report you sent to me yesterday.
Your analysis of the perpetrators was spot on, by the way."

"Jesus H.," Van In snorted. "I had a feeling they *might* strike
again, but it was just a hypothesis, nothing more, not a founda-
tion to build on."

"Oh, well, nothing ventured, nothing gained," she said, shrug-
ging her shoulders. "But if something happens to the Degroofs in
the coming weeks and we're ready for it, God knows what might
bubble to the surface. If we can scrape together enough muck by
then, it won't be hard to convince the press that the attacks on
the Degroof family are part of something bigger. Am I right?"

"So our Van der Eyck went to school with Machiavelli?"

"Didn't everyone?" she laughed.

"And she calls herself a magistrate," he said reproachfully.
"I was always led to believe that the judiciary were expected
to steer clear of politics, if you can call this sort of intrigue
politics."

She didn't appear to find his remark insulting in the slightest.

"Let me tell you something, Pieter Van In. I'm a woman. I worked hard for my degree. My parents worked themselves to the bone to pay for my education. They had no money and no connections. If I'd opted for court work I'd be grubbing for clients and I'd be up to my neck in debt. The public prosecutor's office needs new blood, urgently. It doesn't pay much, but it's steady work. If you want to build a career in this man's world, you need political support. It's the only way. Without it I'd still be making the coffee when I'm fifty for some lenient public prosecutor."

Rage and bitterness seethed in her voice. Van In was taken aback by her candor. The younger generation's relentless will to survive astonished him, as it had so many times before.

"I suppose you're right," said Van In. "Fly with the eagles or scratch with the chickens."

"Thanks for understanding," she said.

"And I genuinely appreciate your honesty, but aren't you forgetting one little detail?"

"Shoot," she said dryly.

"De Kee. If I understand it right, he's in Degroof's pocket. If anything should happen that might turn the spotlights on the Degroofs, I don't think he's likely to entrust the case to me."

"A minor detail, indeed," she concurred. "But De Kee retires in three years and it's a public secret that his son-in-law . . . What's his name again?"

"Deleu," said Van In spontaneously.

"Deleu, that's the one," she said. "Well, commissioner De Kee wants his son-in-law to succeed him. Not right away, of course. That would be too obvious. Van der Eyck put forward a scenario yesterday. De Kee retires in 1997 and is succeeded by Commissioner Carton."

"But Carton's fifty-nine," said Van In, surprised. If she was right, this was primed to be explosive news.

"Exactly. He keeps the chair warm until 2001, and then Deleu takes over. Get it? Carton is the Socialist candidate, and from 2000 Van der Eyck is no longer bound to his promise to approve every Socialist appointment."

"And De Kee knows about all this?" asked Van In vacantly.

"Of course he does. He was there yesterday when the deal was clinched chez Van der Eyck."

"God almighty." Van In gritted his teeth.

"What? No 'Jesus H. Christ'?" she jested.

"I said 'God almighty' because I'd rather sell my house than have to work a single day under Deleu."

"Not your favorite person, I gather. Done the dirty on you a couple of times?"

Van In didn't answer. Hannelore Martens had a little too much information.

"Don't worry Pieter. If you sort this out for us, the doors will be wide open for you at the judicial police, and that's a promise," she said softly. "Approved by Van der Eyck in person."

Benedicta Degroof was kneeling by her bed, trying to pray. Prayer was ordinarily never a problem, but tonight for one reason or another every sound made her jump. She heard Daniel's shoes creak as he bent down at her door. The rustle of paper made her cringe.

She knew who he was. The night before, she had had a dreadful dream in which her fate had been revealed. She concentrated on her prayers. God had never let her down. A door clicked shut not far from her cell.

Benedicta resisted the curiosity that tormented her for more than an hour. She then got to her feet, picked up the letter, and tore it open.

Sister,

Didn't Jesus say: First make peace with your brother or sister and then come to Me in prayer?

Didn't He say in the Sermon on the Mount: Visit the sick?

Didn't He accuse the Pharisees of being hypocrites and whitewashing tombs?

Didn't He say that sins against the Spirit can never be forgiven?

Well, dear sister, what kind of life do you live in this place?

Pride has made you blind. And pride is your inheritance, the inheritance of your accursed family.

Do you think of her from time to time? The one you helped to condemn?

Didn't she defend you when the beast wanted to take possession of you?

Didn't she freely offer to take your place?

These are the questions, sister, questions that are going to haunt you from today onward, questions to which you know the answer.

Sleep tight, sister.

Daniel

Benedicta's hands trembled as she read each word. If they had been slanderous words, she would have set the letter aside and prayed for the man who was responsible.

But what he had written was true.

Sixteen years inside the walls of Bethlehem had salved the wounds, but now a tidal wave of pain engulfed her heart.

She sobbed as she fell to her knees by her bed and spent the best part of the night in prayer.

10

ON THURSDAY MORNING, LAURENT DE Bock bought a powerful pair of binoculars at Priem's, a store devoted to hunting gear on Simon Stevin Square.

Van In sauntered across Market Square and they missed bumping into one another by a hair's breadth. But even if Van In had had a photo of De Bock at his disposal, he would probably never have noticed the amiable gentleman in the chaotic masses. In spite of the recession, city center Bruges was crawling with tourists.

With the patience of a saint, Van In wriggled through the dense crowd as it expanded at the speed of a glacier.

The conversation with Hannelore from the day before still preoccupied him. He was in the mood for a little undercover work, and he had a strange hunch about the Degroof case that refused to let go. He had also made up his mind to check Degroof's closet for skeletons.

He was determined to get to the bottom of the case. He had confided in Leo early that morning, and Leo had promised to initiate a discreet investigation within the judicial police. The archivist at the public prosecutor's office was an old friend and Leo had agreed to put him through the mill later in the day. If there was a file on Degroof or any of his children, it would surface. It was only a matter of time.

Pending further news, Van In first made some inquiries at the Records Office. He planned to contact Versavel and have him bring him up to speed on potential new developments.

The Records Office had been moved from the halls beneath the Belfort to the former courthouse on Burg Square a couple of years earlier. The Tourist Office was housed on the ground floor. Van In resigned himself to the pushing and shoving. After all, he had nothing to be nervous about.

When he showed his police ID to the Records Office clerk, he was allowed behind the counter. A girl in her early twenties wandering around with a tray even offered him a cup of watery coffee.

Laurent De Bock slowed the VW Golf he had hired the previous day in Blankenberge on Bishop Avenue and pulled over onto the grass verge. He opened his newspaper and looked up at regular intervals, focusing his binoculars on a whitewashed bungalow a couple of hundred yards down the street.

He waited a full forty-five minutes and was about to drive off for fear that people might get suspicious when a boy appeared on his bicycle coming from the opposite direction.

Laurent carefully folded his newspaper and kept a close eye on the lad. He must have been thirteen or thereabouts. He slowed down at the bungalow and cycled around the back of the house via a gravel path. Less than five minutes later, two boys cycled onto the road via the same gravel path. Laurent started the car and drove toward them.

Beside him on the passenger seat there was a photo of Bertrand, the only son of Patrick Delahaye and Charlotte Degroof.

He recognized the blond athletic boy as he drove past.

Bertrand was on a brown mountain bike. He had a linen rucksack with leather straps on his back. His friend had attached his roller-skates underneath with one of the straps.

Laurent heaved a sigh of relief. His information was correct. Bertrand still went skating every Thursday and Saturday. He drove to the end of Bishop Avenue, turned the car, and followed the boys as far as Boudewijn Park.

After they disappeared inside, he waited for five minutes and then installed himself with a cup of coffee in the cafeteria next to the ice rink that served as a roller-skating rink in the summer months.

Van In was back home and in the garden, poring over the information he had picked up from the Records Office.

Ludovic Degroof had married Elisa, baroness Heytens de Puyenbroucke, in 1942. They had five children: Aurelie, Ghislain, Charlotte, Benedicta, and Nathalie. Their address in all those years hadn't changed: Spinola Street 58 in Bruges.

Ludovic had a doctorate in law and a master's in economics. The baroness had studied history.

Nothing unusual at first sight, Van In thought, scratching the back of his ear. He read the information for a second time. He hadn't really been expecting much. If the Degroof family had something to hide, data from the Records Office wasn't going to be a great deal of help.

The first child, Aurelie, was born less than a year after they married. The other children were born after the war: Ghislain in 1948, Charlotte in 1950, Benedicta in 1951, and Nathalie in

1960. Nathalie had probably been an accident. Elisa de Puyenbroucke was already forty years old in 1960, and in those
days that was far too old to be having children. Only Ghislain
and Charlotte still lived in Bruges. Aurelie was domiciled in
Loppem, Benedicta in Marche-les-Dames, and Nathalie in
De Panne.

Van In decided to concentrate first on Aurelie. Loppem
wasn't far, but it was difficult to reach by bus or train so he
needed a car. He called Hannelore. This was an opportunity
to find out how far she was willing to go.

"Hello, Hannelore, Pieter Van In here."

"Hoi, Pieter. What can I do for you?"

He brought her up to speed and quickly explained his plan.
To his surprise, she didn't hesitate for a second.

"I'll be with you in ten."

She sounded enthusiastic, but Van In only realized the risk
he was taking when he put the phone down. If Degroof got
wind of this, he'd be pounding a beat before the year was out.

The same was true for Hannelore, of course. If the public
prosecutor tumbled to her insubordination, she could bury her
career under six feet of sand.

Or was she naïve enough to believe that politicians always
kept their promises? *Someone must have promised her something*,
he figured, *otherwise she wouldn't be sticking her neck out like this*.

And why was he going along with it all? Was he trying
to impress her, or was he fed up being kicked around? If the
women's magazines were anything to go by, men were capable
of the strangest things when they reached forty.

He turned everything over in his head as he closed the door
behind him and walked under the Vette Vispoort into Moer
Street. He only had to wait a couple of minutes.

"You don't let the grass grow, do you?" she said as he got
into the car.

"And you aren't afraid of risks," he answered in a reasonably relaxed tone.

Van In inspected her with an approving eye. He had never seen a Deputy in a miniskirt before. *That must have slowed down traffic in the courthouse,* he thought. He wanted to give her a compliment, but kept it to himself on second thought. They had only met a couple of days ago, and God alone knew how the case was going to evolve.

"Loppem, Commissioner?" she grinned.

"Loppem, ma'am."

The atmosphere was excellent from the get-go. She steered the Twingo like the captain of a ferryboat: practiced, no frills.

"So we're journalists," she laughed. "I hope you have a camera. You know what women are like."

When she noticed Van In turn to her with surprise all over his face, she shrugged her shoulders and said: "Okay. No camera. You do the talking and I'll take notes."

She navigated the car through a series of traffic hold-ups without losing a minute.

She stopped by the church in Loppem and asked directions from the obligatory old-man-on-the-village-square. It wasn't far. The man shook his head at her stupidity. The Twingo's front wheels were already in the street she was looking for. *I'll never understand those city folks,* he muttered under his breath.

Number eleven was a typical example of a nineteenth-century country house. It was a mixture of rural and urban building styles, and was surrounded by an overgrown and neglected walled garden. Hannelore parked her car in front of a rusty wrought-iron gate.

"Magnificent house, don't you think?"

"Not bad," Van In admitted. "But why are the rich so bad at looking after their property?"

The gate squeaked and was stiff. Van In had to put his shoulder to it to open it. They walked up the drive. The enormous country house was shrouded in silence.

"No one around," said Hannelore. She walked ahead, certain she would distract Pieter's attention. There wasn't a man in the world who could ignore her legs.

"Apparently," Van In muttered in his confusion.

They made their way to the front door. The lace curtains behind the window frames were gray with dust and the paint was flaking from the shutters and sills. Van In pulled the bell, which clattered like a tin can full of pebbles.

"Are you sure she still lives here?"

Hannelore adjusted her mini. Van In nodded. He was sure. He yanked the greening copper bell-pull with a little too much enthusiasm and felt something give. The dreadful noise ended abruptly.

"Intentionally damaging private property is a punishable offence," she said, half serious, as Van In stared in bewilderment at the broken bell-pull in his hand.

"Journalists get away with murder," he mumbled. Hannelore pressed her nose against one of the windows.

"See anything?" Van In asked. He stood beside her and tried to peep under the lace curtains. There wasn't enough light inside to make anything out.

"Looks pretty empty," Hannelore concluded with a sigh. "And what there is doesn't look as if it's been used for years."

Van In tried another window. But beyond a couple of dilapidated armchairs and a rickety display cabinet, there wasn't much to see.

"Let's have a look around the back," Hannelore suggested.

The back garden was a jungle, with shoulder-high grass and grotesque overgrown fruit trees. All the windows were boarded up with crooked shutters riddled with mold and woodworm. *No wonder it's so dark inside*, he thought. Eighty percent of the courtyard's sagging floor was overrun with weeds.

"If one of Degroof's daughters lives here, I'll ask the public prosecutor to marry me next time we meet," Hannelore jested.

And why not me? Van In wanted to say.

"Mysteries and riddles galore," he said instead. "I suggest we ask around in the neighborhood."

"As a journalist or a police commissioner?' she asked. Van In hesitated.

"Country folk are more likely to talk to a policeman than a journalist," he concluded. "The way things are looking, we're going to have to take more risks. And if we keep it up long enough, either De Kee or Degroof is going to hear about it."

"You're the boss, Pieter," she said, feigning subordination.

Every time she said "Pieter," he got goose bumps.

"Do you mean it?" he asked dryly.

"Of course I mean it," she laughed.

The local ironmonger lived a couple of houses further, next to his store. Stoves, garden tools, and an insane collection of absurd bric-a-brac filled the window.

Van In pushed open the heavy wrought-iron door and they stepped inside. It took the best part of two minutes before a heavy-set woman appeared behind the counter. Hannelore inspected a kitsch biscuit figurine of a shepherdess leaning against a tree trunk.

"Afternoon, can I help you?" asked the woman with a broad smile. Van In showed her his ID, which made the innocent soul visibly nervous.

"Just a couple of questions," said Van In reassuringly.

Hannelore lifted another figurine, this time a shepherd blowing on some pipes. She pretended she had no interest in the conversation whatsoever. Luckily Van In managed to ignore her.

"It's about number eleven."

"Finally," said the ironmonger's wife. "It's time someone made that place their business. The neighbors have been complaining about it for years. But the mayor refuses to do any more than have the weeds cleared once in a while. You wouldn't believe what goes on up there at night, officer," she rattled in a single breath, clearly relieved that the police visit was about the Degroof place.

"You can't move due to the bikers that come up and take the place over on the weekends. Young guys. You know the type. God knows the filth they must get up to," the woman complained. "It's high time someone put an end to it."

"So no one lives there," said Hannelore in an unexpectedly professional tone. She returned the shepherd with the pipes to the display. This was the Hannelore he had come to know, cool and out of reach, just as she had been on Sunday when they had met for the first time.

"Oh," the woman yelped. "We've been living here for twenty years. A young lady, she came up from time to time at the beginning, but we haven't seen hide nor hair of her in the last ten."

"Was she alone?" Hannelore inquired. Background note taker wasn't her thing.

"Sometimes the daughter and her husband would come, with what's his name . . . little Bertrand. Mr. Delahaye worked in the garden a lot. You should have seen it back then, young lady, it was a jewel."

"Delahaye? Isn't that—"

"Mr. Degroof senior's son-in-law," said the woman, eagerly completed Hannelore's sentence. "Mrs. Charlotte's an eye surgeon. She fixed my father's cataract. She's very good . . . the best around these parts. And I should know."

"So apart from Mr. and Mrs. Delahaye, nobody ever made use of the house," Hannelore interrupted.

"Not that I'm aware of," said the woman. "If they had, we would have known, eh?" she said with a wink.

"Of course you would," Van In nodded. It's hard to keep secrets in the country.

"Would you like me to call my husband?" asked the woman obligingly. "Not that he'll have anything else to tell you."

"Thank you, but there's no need. You've been most helpful. We'll do what has to be done," Van In lied.

"Thanks and have a nice day," Hannelore echoed affably.

"A propos," said Van In with the door handle in his hand. "Is the local Records Office here in Loppem, or do we need to go to Zedelgem?"

"Fortunately not, it's just round the corner. A visit to the town hall used to be easy, but now most of the services are in Zedelgem."

Since the administrative fusion with Zedelgem, only three people still worked at Loppem's charming town hall.

A young man in his early thirties stopped what he was doing when Van In and Hannelore walked in. He opened a drawer in his metallic desk and tucked away his book of crossword puzzles without them noticing.

"Can I be of service?" he asked with a genuine smile. A pair of cheerful eyes sparkled from behind a pair of round turtleshell glasses.

Van In introduced himself, but unlike the ironmonger's wife the young clerk didn't flinch.

"The Degroof house," the young man drawled. "There hasn't been a murder, has there?"

"No, not at all," said Van In. "Can I count on your discretion?"

"Of course, Commissioner." The young clerk was all ears.

"A certain Aurelie Degroof recently took up residence in the center of Bruges and she gave Rijsel Street 11 as her last address. Turns out the place has been empty for years. So we wondered if you might be able to help."

The healthy red glow on the young man's cheeks quickly paled. He was now clearly nervous and looked anxiously left and right. Hannelore treated him to an appealing smile.

"You are from the police, aren't you?" he asked. "The real police?

"Do you have any reason to doubt?" asked Hannelore in a juicy West Flemish accent.

Van In produced his police ID card and showed it to the deathly pale clerk. He seemed convinced.

"I think someone gave you the wrong information," he drawled. "Aurelie Degroof was locked up in psychiatric hospital more than twenty years ago. In Sint-Michiels."

"Are you sure?" asked Hannelore pointedly.

"If we're talking about Ludovic Degroof's eldest daughter, then I'm quite certain," said the young man resolutely. "My father talks about her from time to time. She used to come here sometimes in the summer. My father did some work in the house and the garden in those days, and my mother cooked if she had visitors."

"You mean she's been crazy for more than twenty years?"

The young man bit his bottom lip. He was clearly having a hard time.

"They had her locked up against her will," he reluctantly admitted. "My father says it was all rigged. He's warned me more than once to be careful of the Degroofs. They're a powerful family. Degroof senior enjoys breaking people and ruining careers. According to my father, he had Aurelie's child taken from her and she tried to kill him, but I can't be sure of it."

He seemed to chicken out all of a sudden.

"There were so many stories doing the rounds back then. I'm not sure if anyone knows the truth anymore."

Hannelore adjusted her bra strap. This was music to her ears. A father who had his daughter locked up in a mental institution and then tried to keep the entire affair under wraps was just the kind of thing Van der Eyck was looking for. It fitted his strategy like a glove.

Silently jubilant, Van In reassured the young man that the information would be treated in the strictest confidentiality and that he could sleep easy.

"So what do you think?" Hannelore beamed when she got into the car.

"A couple of rumors, that's all," said Van In level-headedly. "And don't forget, it was all such a long time ago."

But he also had to admit that tragedies of the sort they had just heard often led to obstinate family feuds. He could see the dissolution of Degroof's gold having its place in such a feud. The absurdity of the crime went hand in hand with the freakish and illogical patterns people who were dead set on revenge often followed.

"Van der Eyck didn't set this up, did he?" asked Van In abruptly.

Hannelore turned to him, wrinkled her forehead, and glared at him in astonishment.

"What kind of nonsense is that, commissioner?"

"Why not?" he responded calmly. "I don't have to lecture *you* on how far people will go to fulfill their ambitions."

She clearly wasn't impressed. She indignantly straightened her neck and stared grim-faced at the windshield. It took a couple of seconds before she could come up with an argument that could screw his hypothesis into the ground.

"Van der Eyck wouldn't leave one or other note with a cryptic Latin message behind," she snorted. "And don't forget: I told him about the Degroof case first, *then* he came up with the idea. Timing!"

"That's what you said. . . . So you put the idea into his head from you."

"Exactly," she snapped. "I based myself on your conclusion. Revenge looked like a logical motive."

"So you immediately assumed there had to be some unsavory secret in Degroof's past behind the attack, a scandal perhaps, something your 'promoter' could use to his own advantage."

Hannelore didn't react. She continued to scowl at the windshield. Van In was worried he had gone too far.

"But you're probably right," he said, putting a good face on it. "It's a bit far-fetched to think that Van der Eyck would get up to this kind of trickery. But you have to understand . . . I can't leave any stone unturned. Anyway, everybody knows that cops can get a bit paranoid now and again."

Hannelore sat behind the wheel like a window dummy. The unpleasant silence was getting on Van In's nerves.

"So it's time to pay Aurelie Degroof a visit, I guess?" Van In felt helpless. Why did women always make him nervous? Maybe she was really vulnerable and that was why she pretended to be unnaturally macho every now and then. When he was with Sonja, it took an eternity for him to take the first step after an argument. That gave minor disagreements the time to escalate into major rows. And once they had reached the major row stage, even words of reconciliation were often taken the wrong way.

"Sorry," he said hesitantly. "What I just said about ambition wasn't intended to be personal, Hannelore."

Van In found "sorry" extremely hard to say. As far as he could remember, it was the first time he had succeeded. She eased off, turned to look at him, and twisted the left corner of her mouth into a smile. "Tut tut. . . ." She paused, "Okay, let's call it quits," she said in a not unfriendly tone. The skin on her cheekbones was like polished ivory. "But on one condition. In the hospital *you* play *my* assistant!"

Van In nodded in agreement. He actually didn't care who took the lead.

It took a while before someone came to the door at Our Lady's Psychiatric Hospital in Sint-Michiels.

Hannelore introduced herself to the nurse in her spotless white uniform. She was in her early thirties, slenderly built, and seemed anything but naïve. People who work in psychiatric hospitals are often inclined to assess the mental health of the people they meet with a single look. It's hard for them to resist the temptation.

Hannelore explained their visit. The nurse listened carefully but didn't react to the name Aurelie Degroof. It had been less than a year ago that a couple of men disguised as nurses had tried to kidnap their friend.

"Please walk this way," she said emotionlessly.

They followed her along what felt like an endless series of corridors until they arrived in a small waiting room.

"I'll be back in a jiffy," she said as she closed the door behind her.

Van In knew that the word "jiffy" mostly meant half an hour or more in hospitals. He took a seat and rummaged through a pile of rumpled magazines in search of something to read.

Hannelore refused to sit.

"What's keeping her?' she said after ten minutes.

"Pretend you're in court," he grinned.

Every now and then they heard hurried footsteps in the corridor, but no one stopped at their door.

"I can't imagine being in a place like this for more than a day," she sighed. "The place alone would drive a person crazy."

"Maybe magistrates should be required to do an internship here for a couple of weeks," said Van In. He couldn't help it. It was out before he realized it.

"Also not to be taken personally," she snarled.

"I wouldn't dare, ma'am."

Just as they both collapsed in hysterics, the door flew open. A tall thin man in a doctor's coat watched them in amusement.

"So you like it here?" he asked tongue-in-cheek.

Van In couldn't disagree. He would have thought the same thing if he'd found a Deputy public prosecutor in his office laughing her head off. Luckily Hannelore managed to pull herself together.

"Hannelore Martens, Doctor. I'm here about one of your patients," she said with instant and exemplary gravity, as if everything was normal.

"I'm Doctor De Boever, chief psychiatrist. May I ask why you want to speak to Mrs. Degroof?"

The nurse had clearly filled him in on the reason for their visit. Van In felt fortunate that he didn't have to answer the question. He studied one of the framed artworks that filled the walls.

Hannelore had anticipated the question. She had to think of a pretext for being there. Officially she didn't have a leg to stand on.

"There are claims that Aurelie Degroof was placed here without good reason," she blurted.

Van In held his breath. She was skating on very thin ice.

"I've been commissioned to determine whether there are grounds to review the procedure."

Doctor De Boever scratched cautiously behind his ear. *If this works*, Van In thought, *I'll paint my house bright blue.*

But De Boever was a seasoned expert and had spent a career listening to the weirdest stories. Some of which also turned out to be true, nonetheless.

"Aren't there, shall we say, more official channels for this sort of thing?" he suggested.

"Of course, Doctor. But I presume you know the Degroof family. And if I tell you that the person asking for a revision of Aurelie's involuntary internment is a member of the same family, then I'm sure you'll understand why I prefer to follow a less official route in the given circumstances. If her doctor's advice is negative, then I'll inform the complainant and the case will be dismissed without a word being committed to paper. The person in question also made his request in the context of a spoken interview."

She didn't bat an eyelid during her peroration. She deployed the same breezy, authoritarian tone she had used the previous Sunday.

"Extremely wise, Ms. Martens," said De Boever.

Van In left the abstract watercolor for what it was and took his place next to Hannelore. She had done the necessary dirty work with considerable cunning.

"But I fear I'm not going to be much use to you," said De Boever flatly. "Medical information is strictly confidential. I can only speak if I'm summoned as an expert in a court of law."

"I understand completely, Doctor," Hannelore concurred. "But I'm not asking for medical information. I would simply like to speak with Aurelie; under supervision, of course."

"I fear I'm going to have to disappoint you there too, Ms. Martens. Aurelie Degroof is extremely weak, and in her condition emotions can be damaging. She's been here for more than twenty-six years. False hope of release would bring her endless suffering. I'm not even sure she would understand what it meant, to be honest."

"But would it be possible just to see her for ten minutes?" Hannelore pushed the envelope. "An eyehole in the door would be enough."

De Boever was aware that he couldn't refuse every request.

"If you insist," he said, clearly reluctant. He couldn't see what good it would do. But if he let her have her way, she might leave them in peace.

"Aurelie's in the recreation room for the moment. If you promise not to attempt contact with her, I can let you see her, but only briefly."

They followed De Boever through another series of black-and-white-tiled corridors. The occasional patient shuffled past, their eyes dull and vacant. As they climbed a flight of stairs Hannelore jabbed Van In in the ribs. He almost missed the following step. He figured from the expression on her face that she wanted to know what he was thinking. He ran his finger across his throat. She grinned and stuck her tongue out at De Boever.

A number of older women were sitting in easy chairs in a spacious room on the first floor. The majority stared into space or busied themselves with some kind of useless occupational therapy. A tall blond woman in her mid-forties piled wooden blocks on top of each other until the tower she had made came crashing down with a terrible din. She started anew. Another wiped the leaves of the indoor plants with a moist sponge.

De Boever signaled with his head toward the window where a woman was calmly knitting. The sun engulfed her in a yellowish aureole. The clicking of her knitting needles seemed to devour time like a clock. She looked up for a moment and smiled at the newcomers.

Aurelie was the only patient to react to their presence. She was almost fifty-one, but her skin was still as smooth as silk. She had a fashionable hairdo and, in contrast to the others, she wasn't wearing a nightdress or dressing gown. She was elegantly dressed and her bearing was dignified. Her sharp jawline suggested a certain intelligence. But her eyes didn't fit the picture. Hannelore sensed a sea of sadness in them. After a couple of minutes, De Boever indicated that their time was up, and five minutes later they were standing outside.

"I wouldn't be surprised if our young friend at the town hall in Loppem was right," said Hannelore, visibly shaken. "Did you see what she was knitting?"

Van In hadn't paid any attention. Men never do.

"Baby clothes," she said.

"Really," said Van In. "Situations like that used to be common enough in the better circles. Problem kids were dumped in institutions without much fuss. It was safe and respectable, and it protected the family name."

"So you share my opinion," she asked rhetorically.

"I think so. Behind every big name there's often a huge pile of dirty linen."

"Shall I drop you off at home?" asked Hannelore as she drove under the viaduct on the outskirts of Bruges. He nodded, and she stopped at Saint James's Church, not far from the Vette Vispoort.

"Are you coming in?" asked Van In, hoping she would say yes.

"Sorry, Pieter, but I have an appointment at the courthouse at five-thirty."

"Then you're seriously late," he said. "It's five past six."

"I know, I know. But a Deputy's allowed to be late," she laughed.

"I'll call if there's news."

"Do that," she shouted through the open window. "But now I really have to get a move on."

Deep in thought, he sauntered through the Vette Vispoort. After so many years of dry routine and restrained obedience, the excitement of breaking the rules was surprisingly refreshing.

He suddenly felt like whistling, and he would have done so now if he had ever learned to.

11

HANNELORE CALLED VAN IN ON Friday morning at seven forty-five, startling him, but fortunately he was at least awake.

"Hello, Pieter. It's me. Hope I didn't wake you." She sounded excited. "I can't say much on the phone. Somebody passed me an important tip yesterday. I'm following it up as we speak. I'll see you tonight."

"What do you mean?" asked Van In, astonished.

"Sorry, Pieter, this is one I have to take care of on my own. Trust me. Bye!"

"That's nice," he grumbled as he hung up the phone. *I should have seen this coming*, he groaned. It wasn't the first time he had been dumped. Deep in thought, he grabbed a Duvel from the refrigerator despite the early hour and installed himself outside in his garden chair.

The grass was wet and cold, but he hated wearing slippers. All sorts of strange ideas lurched through his mind.

Had he allowed himself to be taken in by an ambition-crazed magistrate? Was the conspiracy real or imagined? And if it was real, wasn't it all a bit far-fetched? Why was Degroof senior so afraid of an investigation? What was he trying to hide? If he had let the investigation run its course, no one would have paid the slightest attention to what happened with his son, but his meddling had raised a huge red flag. Did the one have anything to do with the other? Did Degroof expect further actions? Three Duvels and a hundred questions later, Van In dozed off in his garden chair. The sun caressed him like a satisfied baby and he had a Robin Hood-themed dream. He was Friar Tuck, waiting on the bank of a fast-flowing stream for his merry-men brothers, in the company of a hogshead of ice-cold Rhine wine.

Hannelore sipped a Campari-and-soda. A young woman sat opposite her mechanically stirring a cup of coffee. She had classical elongated features and her hennaed hair was tied up in a bun. Her skin was deep brown and she was wearing a short beach dress without a bra. She wasn't particularly pretty, but she had so little on that most passing men couldn't resist a stealthy peek.

"No one gets on with my father," she said in a toneless voice. "He dominates everyone. That's why I ran away. My mother doesn't have a life. I hate my father." The bluntness of her words did not mask the rawness of her emotions.

She placed her spoon on a napkin and took several hasty sips of coffee.

Hannelore smiled gently but didn't interrupt her.

"No wonder my sister entered a convent. She couldn't take any more. Charlotte . . . she was the lucky one. She was a good student so my mother sent her to boarding school. When she was

studying in Leuven she came home three or four times a year, no
more. Otherwise he would probably have taken her too."

"Are you saying that your father mistreated Benedicta?"

Nathalie lifted her head and sparks of hatred flashed in her
gathering tears.

"He tried to rape her," she sobbed.

"And did he succeed?" Hannelore asked.

"She claims he didn't. Aurelie protected her."

"Did he rape Aurelie?"

Nathalie lifted her cup but returned it immediately to its
saucer. Her hand shook as if she had just spent an hour with a
pneumatic drill.

"He came to her room three times a week. That was the
price she had to pay for Charlotte and Benedicta."

"And did he get her pregnant?"

"God, no. He was too smart for that. And there are plenty
of ways to avoid getting pregnant. . . ."

Hannelore felt sorry for the young woman sitting in front
of her. She reached out and took her hand.

"My sister-in-law was next in line," Nathalie sobbed. "But
at least she made him pay."

"You mean Anne-Marie?" asked Hannelore, surprised.

Nathalie nodded.

"He slept with everyone. And if there weren't enough victims, he would hire a whore."

"Did your father arrange the marriage between Ghislain
and Anne-Marie?"

"What do you think?" Nathalie snorted. "Ghislain is gay.
My father never dealt with it." She spoke at speed, as if she
wanted to shake it all from her shoulders in a single breath.

"But he didn't get me," she said with sudden solemnity. "I
got out in time. Men only want one thing and I've known what
that is for a very long time. I hate men. Haven't you seen them

gawping?" she said, gesturing toward the street. "Innocent family men, yeah, right. I wear suggestive clothes on purpose. At least I know it makes them feel awkward or lines them up for a row with their little wives when they catch hubby darling driveling at my tits."

Hannelore thought of Van In. Nathalie's bitter testimony left her confused. She hadn't had a lot of experience with men, and Nathalie's story was hardly a selling one.

She lit a cigarette and offered the pack to Nathalie.

"No, thanks," she said. "I don't smoke tobacco."

"Are you still in touch with your mother?"

"She sends me money now and then."

"A lot of money?"

Nathalie didn't answer. Hannelore wasn't sure if she was being impolite.

"A thousand francs, ten thousand francs?"

The information she had received from Van der Eyck had been correct thus far. That was why she had to keep pushing on the money.

"My mother understands me," Nathalie rasped.

"How much is a gram of heroin these days?"

Nathalie shook her head and grabbed her bag.

"If you walk now, you can forget the twenty thousand I have in my pocket for you. Has your mother stopped sending you money?"

Nathalie's eyes filled with hatred. Hannelore had taken a calculated risk and it had paid off. Nathalie let go of her bag.

"Were you planning to blackmail your family because your mother didn't send enough money?"

A couple of passersby stared angrily in their direction when Nathalie burst into hysterical laughter.

"Me? Blackmail my family? My father wouldn't pay a cent. Who would believe a junkie? Would you believe a junkie?"

"Even if you threatened to turn to the press?" Hannelore whispered. "Your father is a prominent Catholic, a knight in the Order of Malta, a Prolife benefactor. What would be left of his reputation if it went public that he was sleeping with one of his daughters?"

"Don't you think I've thought about it?" said Nathalie grimfaced. "And by the way, do you think I don't know you work for the public prosecutor's office?"

Hannelore was taken aback.

"Next time you pretend to be a journalist, you should at least invent a false name. There's only one Hannelore Martens in the phone book and she happened to be a Deputy to the public prosecutor. It's printed in bold after your name.

"Okay," Hannelore sighed. "I'm a Deputy. I just wanted to help you."

"There's only one way you can help me," Nathalie snapped. "Give me the cash you promised and leave me alone."

Hannelore nodded.

"A promise is a promise. But tell me one last thing. How did Aurelie end up back at home after her marriage and why did your father have her locked up in an institution?"

"You'll have to ask my sisters. I was only seven when it happened."

"Did they ever talk about it?"

Nathalie shook her head.

"No, not a single word."

Hannelore had the impression she was telling the truth. It was clear enough that she had had nothing to do with the strange incident in her brother's shop, but that wasn't the problem. Her revelations about Degroof were much more important than some melted jewelry and precisely what Van der Eyck was after.

"And don't think for one minute that I'll ever repeat any of this in a court of law," said Nathalie, abruptly interrupting Hannelore's train of thought. "My mother wouldn't survive a court case. Anyway, it wouldn't make much of a difference. There isn't a judge in the country who would even think of convicting my father, and I doubt whether any of my sisters would testify against him."

Hannelore wasn't of a mind to explain that a professionally spread rumor usually did more damage than a court case.

Nathalie crossed her legs provocatively.

"If you've no more questions, Deputy Martens ma'am, then pay me for my services; otherwise I'll bug off out of here."

"Can I contact you again if I have new information?" Hannelore asked.

"If there's money in it, you can contact me as often as you like," Nathalie snorted.

Hannelore fished the envelope from her handbag and slipped it across the table. Nathalie Degroof swiped the bills from the envelope without counting, got to her feet, and made a beeline for the door and the dunes outside.

Hannelore called the waiter and ordered another Campari soda. She could feel the sun on her thighs and decided to extend her visit to the coast by a couple of hours. Van In wasn't expecting her until evening.

Leo Vanmaele called at one-thirty and woke Van In from his slumbers. It took an age for him get to the phone. He staggered through the open patio doors into the living room, cursing under his breath. His mouth was dry as cork and his head was full of fuzz from snoring.

"Pieter, Leo here. I've got something on Degroof. He had his daughter locked up in an institution in 1968. Nothing illegal, of course, but it might come in handy."

"Leo, my friend. Kind of you to think of me. But I found out about it yesterday, by coincidence," said Van In, stifling a yawn, his voice weary.

"On the bottle again?" said Vanmaele sarcastically. "We were busy well into the night digging up information. You could have let me know."

"Sorry, Leo. But I'm calling it quits."

"What?!"

"I don't trust her anymore. She thinks too much of herself," Van In mumbled.

"Blah blah blah."

"De Kee's right. I'm booking a vacation on Monday. Tenerife, here I come. I've had it up to here."

Leo and Van In had been friends for the best part of twenty years. It wasn't rare to find him in the pits for some futility or other, but he usually got over it quick enough. Van In was irrepressible in that regard. After every short depression, he rose from the ashes like a phoenix.

"Shall I stop by later?"

"Do that," said Van In without much enthusiasm.

Shortly after five, Hannelore stepped into her Twingo and drove back to Bruges, avoiding the freeway.

Her plan was to report to Van der Eyck first and then bring Van In up to speed. She thought it was a shame that they hadn't been able to interview Nathalie together, but Nathalie had insisted on her being alone and Van In would understand, she figured.

Leo hurried over to the Vette Vispoort after finishing work. He was a bachelor and didn't have to keep anyone informed of his comings and goings. Since the split between Sonja and Pieter, the two men had sought each other's company on a regular basis.

He parked his yellow monster on Moer Street, close to the rectory, and left again five minutes later with Van In.

Celine, who ran Café Vlissinghe, welcomed Van In and Vanmaele by their first names. As the two headed for a quiet table in the corner, she took a couple of Duvel glasses from the rack above the bar and started to shine them.

"You sounded far from happy this afternoon," Leo grinned. "Don't tell me you've really fallen for that stuck-up hussy."

Van In pulled an ugly face.

"What gave you that idea? Once is enough, friend. I'm no jackass," he said, trying to sound macho.

"So what's wrong then?"

Celine waltzed over with the Duvels humming a tune. She had bought a new car the day before and it had made her week.

"Throw in a couple of cheese sandwiches, Slien," said Leo. I haven't eaten a thing since early this morning."

"Idem ditto," said Van In.

"So are you going to tell me what's bugging you, or are we going to sit here guzzling Duvels the whole night like a pair of dummies?" Leo repeated after Celine had gone.

"Okay, okay," Van In growled. "If it'll stop you whining."

He told him about the smear campaign the opposition was planning and the strange discovery he had made the day before together with Hannelore.

"And Tallulah calls this morning to say she's got an important tip and has to check it out on her own."

"And you don't believe her?"

"Would you?"

Leo caressed the curves of his Duvel glass.

"Does Tallulah—as you call her—have anything to do with Van der Eyck?" he asked. Leo noticed Van In pale slightly.

"You're in a bad way, buddy," he teased.

"Jesus H. Christ. Give it a rest."

Leo nodded his head. "I was just trying to cheer you up. Surely you can take a joke," he grinned. "Ah, there's our Slien with the reinforcements. Let's eat first. Food makes everybody happy."

Celine had done her best. She had buttered half a brown loaf and thickly sliced at least a pound of cheese.

"Did you win the lottery?" Leo beamed as he inspected the generous rations with hungry eyes.

Celine leaned over.

"I bought a new car yesterday," she whispered.

"The New Car!" Leo yelped.

"The New Car," she concurred with a glow.

"Ooh-la-la, did you hear that, Pieter? Slien finally bought the Espace. And we paid for at least half of the bastard. True, Slien, eh?"

"Why do you think I'm treating my best customers to cheese sandwiches?" she asked with a smile.

A young couple had come in while they were talking, and Celine hurried to the bar to serve them. She hummed all evening.

Leo got stuck on the sandwiches. Van In confined himself to his Duvel for the time being.

"You suggested just then that Hannelore might have something to do with Van der Eyck," said Van In glumly.

Leo had prepared a second sandwich with an ample portion of cheese and was about to sink his teeth into it.

"But that was a joke! Although anything's possible," Leo grinned. "Martens told you herself that she was ambitious. Do you still believe in the integrity of the judiciary and clean-hands politics?"

Van In lit the cigarette he had been fiddling with for the best part of ten minutes.

"Of course I don't," he said cheerlessly. "But there are still a couple of things I can't figure."

"Out with it. Open the vent," Leo urged.

"Well, on Sunday I blabbed that the thing with Ghislain's gold might be the first of a series of actions against Degroof senior. I mentioned the same hypothesis in my report."

Leo listened attentively as he devoured his second sandwich.

"An inexperienced Deputy passes on my intuitive conclusion to a politician who's probably offering her protection and promotion. Two days later, a secret meeting is organized during which the political landscape is redrawn, apparently on the basis of a trivial incident and a couple of empty presuppositions. It's too much for me to swallow," said Van In decisively. "If you ask me, Van der Eyck knows more about the affair than he's letting on, and he's certain that the actions against Degroof are set to escalate. It's usually worth capitalizing on such situations just before an election, drag your opponents through the dirt, you know the score."

Leo took a deep breath. He washed down his third double sandwich with a mouthful of beer. "You don't mean that . . ."

"I imagine one of the perpetrators had already put Van der Eyck in the picture before the event because they shared the same goal: eliminating Degroof via an orchestrated witch-hunt in the press. Don't forget that Degroof only started to boil over after I got Radio Contact involved."

"But wouldn't it have been easier just to hand over the file on Degroof to the press or one of his political opponents? Why in God's name would you set up such a complicated operation? To attract attention? You have to admit, it's a pretty roundabout way of getting something done," Leo observed.

"That's what I thought at first," Van In continued hot on Leo's heels. "But if the file on Degroof is so explosive that no newspaper would be willing to open it without serious evidence, then the complicated approach might have its advantages. And even if the press were willing to publish its contents, there's every chance Degroof would be able to muzzle them. They say he can handle the local press. And don't forget, the general public isn't stupid. If a scandal erupts around a highly placed individual just before an election, their suspicions are doubled. It wouldn't be the first time the voter took sides with the victim, the underdog. Think about Clinton. His mistress's public confessions immediately before the election didn't stop him from getting re-elected. But if you make sure someone gets into the news indirectly, the chances of getting what you want are much greater."

"But then you have to keep him in the news," said Leo. It was slowly beginning to dawn on him where Van In wanted to go.

"Exactly," Van In winked. "You have to build up the tension, work up a crescendo. You have to make sure the newsworthiness of your diversion is big enough to attract national and even international attention. And if something else leaks out between the lines, its effects will be irreversible."

"But if you put it that way, you might just as well argue that Degroof knows who's got him in a corner," said Leo. "Maybe there's something about the Templars' Square and he's the only one who's figured it out. Maybe the perpetrators have his back against the wall and he's desperately trying to scupper the investigation and the potential publicity surrounding it."

"Possible," said Van In. "Then again, we might both just be paranoid."

"Do you think Martens knows more than we do?"

Van In shrugged his shoulders. "Nah. Maybe I was too quick to judge her this morning. She explicitly asked me to trust her."

"You won't hear a bad word said about her, will you?" Leo teased.

"Spare me the drivel," Van In snorted, "and eat another sandwich. You'll be hallucinating from the hunger next."

Leo took him literally and set about the plate. His appetite was legendary.

"You can always demand an explanation," he said between bites.

Van In fidgeted with the corner of a beer-soaked coaster. He had the impression that the people at the next table had been nervously listening in. The café had filled up in the course of their conversation.

"I think waiting is the safer option," he said in a hushed tone. "But one thing is sure: for the rest of today and tomorrow, the Degroof case can go to hell."

"A moment ago you wanted to stop altogether," Leo smirked.

"Did I say that?"

Leo raised his left eyebrow, amused.

"I meant stop for today," said Van In, reluctantly backing down.

"Pleased to hear it," muttered Leo.

Yet another depression had been suppressed. Leo raised his hand.

"Slien, sweetheart, another couple of Duvels, and throw in a couple of sandwiches for Van In. The loser's almost starved to death."

12

"*O FORTUNA, VELUT LUNA, STATU VARIABILIS.*"

Carl Orff's magisterial *Carmina Burana* shook the old house to its foundations. The volume control on the dated Sansui amplifier was at its max and Van In was stretched out on the couch, completely overwhelmed by his favorite music.

As far as he was concerned, Orff's music had to be played loud to be heard at its best. His eyes were closed and his head swayed to the irresistible rhythm. He wallowed in the heavenly warmth the music generated in his chest and the tingling between his shoulders.

As a result, it took a while before he was able to distinguish the sound of someone banging at the front door from Orff's overpowering percussion. He made a face and hoisted himself from the couch. He hated turning the volume down; but when he finally did, the sledgehammer blows to his front door took him aback.

"What the f . . . Jesus . . . where's the fire?" he roared.

The door wrecker suddenly stopped thumping.

"Pieter! Pieter!"

He recognized the voice immediately. Hannelore gasped from the exertion.

"Did you forget your cigarettes?" he quipped as he opened the door. Even in jeans and a white blouse, she was capable of making Miss Belgium look like a spruced-up scarecrow.

"They kidnapped Degroof's grandson," she screamed in an effort to be heard above the blistering music. The volume was still at fifty percent. "Your hypothesis was right, Pieter. You were right."

"Is that so?" he said, smelling a rat.

"And Degroof has a dirty secret as you suspected. But you weren't at home yesterday. I waited for the best part of an hour," she panted. "I promised to give you a report, didn't I?"

"Bad news for Degroof," said Van In indifferently. There was no longer any need for enthusiasm. "A real pity, but I'm on vacation. Come inside, let me make some coffee. You look as if you could use a cup."

"Your vacation has been cancelled," she retorted belligerently. "De Kee called the public prosecutor. He wants you to take over the kidnapping case from Deleu."

Van In was having a hard time controlling his impatience.

"Deleu, hmm. That's a surprise. Is De Kee worried his son-in-law will screw up, or is he looking for another scapegoat to blame if the case goes crooked on him?"

"Good God, man, get your act together. I'll tell you the rest in the car."

Van In continued to feign reluctance, but his heart was pounding.

He was right and they needed him, he thought victoriously. To hell with the doubts and the brooding! This time he would see it through to the bitter end.

"So Van der Eyck got what he wanted after all," he sneered as the climbed into the Twingo.

"You've got two more guesses," she snapped.

"The Minister of the Interior, then."

Van In tried in vain to fasten his seatbelt and in the process he accidentally touched her thigh. The sensation was exceptionally pleasant.

"No, not the Minister of the Interior."

She tore through the residential part of Moer Street at fifty per hour.

"Tell me. I give up."

"You had *two* guesses, Pieter."

On the corner of Wulfhage Street and Noordzand Street she forced a departing bus to slam on the brakes. The driver was furious, and the teenagers snogging on the back seat were left with blood on their lips.

"Not the king, surely," said Van In, pretending indignation.

Hannelore didn't find it funny. She didn't understand why he was being so infantile.

"Degroof senior is insisting that you take the case," she said.

"Fuck me."

"What happened to Jesus H. Christ?" she responded quick-wittedly. She turned her head and grinned from ear to ear.

"Look out," Van In shouted as she narrowly missed a delivery van.

Filip De Leeuw had just entered the tunnel under Zand Square on his motorcycle when he saw the Twingo cut in front of the delivery van. The driver of the delivery van shook his fist in a rage. De Leeuw calmly adjusted the speed of his BMW, accelerating from fifty to seventy with a minor movement of the wrist. The distance between the Twingo and his bike barely decreased. He then switched on his blue rotating light and siren. He managed to stop the maniac close to the Ezelpoort.

The Twingo was stuck at the lights, trembling like a wound-up spring. De Leeuw thumped the windscreen with his leather-clad fist.

"See what you get," Van In smiled when he caught sight of De Leeuw's purple face. Hannelore stared at the police officer in disbelief.

"Well, do something, then," she yelled in horror.

Van In leaned forward with a sigh to allow De Leeuw to recognize him. Hannelore obligingly rolled down the window.

"Excellent chase, Filip," he said affably. "But the Deputy here is in a serious hurry. She's in the middle of a kidnapping."

De Leeuw gasped for air, managing to swallow a couple of extremely unfriendly words just in time. The cacophony of car horns behind them indicated that the lights had changed to green.

"Far to go?" asked De Leeuw.

"Bishop Avenue," said Van In.

De Leeuw turned and put an end to the hooting with a gesture of authority.

"Follow me," he shouted.

Hannelore rubbed her hands together and hit the floor with the gas pedal.

"You've got talent," said Van In in amazement. "I don't know many who can keep up with De Leeuw."

Mr. and Mrs. Delahaye-Degroof's white bungalow was halfway along Bishop Avenue.

"When did they discover the kidnapping?" Van In asked as they turned into the broad tree-lined street. She was happy he had finally come to the point. His fooling around was beginning to get on her nerves.

"A couple of hours ago. The boy goes skating every Thursday and Saturday in Boudewijn Park."

"Is that where they grabbed him?"

"Probably. We still don't have a lot of details."

She parked the Twingo a good sixty yards from the bungalow. There were dozens of cars in front of the house, including police cars and a white truck with a satellite dish on its roof towering above the rest.

"They don't waste any time," said Hannelore when she caught sight of the commercial TV van with the satellite dish.

"What do you expect? Flanders is the size of a bedspread. They use local correspondents to listen in to the police frequencies 24/7."

De Kee's son-in-law, Deleu, had an olive green Saab Turbo. Van In frowned when he saw it parked close to the house immediately behind a Mercedes 500 SEL, a stately old-timer with the matte bodywork. A young man with a chauffeur's hat was smoking a cigarette in his shirtsleeves. A truly remarkable scene. When they got closer, they saw a group of policemen, about six in total, trying to keep a growing group of curious onlookers at a distance. Half the population appeared to be listening in to the police frequencies. Disaster tourists often arrived on the scene before the emergency services.

A couple of local cops had been posted by the door. They recognized Van In, but still insisted that he and Hannelore show their ID. They were allowed to go inside.

The front door of the bungalow was open. When Van In crossed the threshold, he felt an unpleasant chill glide over his shoulders, as if the house sensed that its occupants had been confronted with a dreadful tragedy.

The bungalow was bright and spacious, but the atmosphere was oppressive. The house had been built in a "U"-form around an open rear garden in Japanese style. The horizontal segment of the "U" was enormous and included the dining room, lounge, and kitchen. None of the connecting walls impeded the outside view.

Hannelore's attention was immediately drawn to the magnificent paintings gracing the walls. She recognized Magritte and Permeke, although she had always thought that the work of such artists could only be seen in museums.

Van In concentrated on the people. He counted ten in total. Versavel was standing next to Deleu in front of the enormous glass wall that ran the entire length of the house and subtly divided the interior from the garden. When Versavel caught sight of Van In and Hannelore, he abandoned Deleu and headed toward them. Van In shook his massive hand. Deleu cast a surreptitious glance in their direction but stayed where he was. To give the impression that he was doing something important, he joined a young police captain who had just been on the radio to technical services for assistance.

Versavel looked like a Chippendale in uniform and smelled of Sunlight soap.

"A pleasure to meet you again," he said to Hannelore when she held out her hand.

"The pleasure's mine, Sergeant Watson."

Versavel accepted the compliment with a macho grin.

"I thought you were on vacation," he said, turning to Van In.

"Was," Van In concurred.

"Vacation or not, I'm glad you're here. Deleu is a nonstarter. If I'm not mistaken, Degroof gave him the brush-off."

"Senior?"

"Yup," Versavel sighed. "Senior arrived half an hour ago with his chauffeur and seems to be lining himself up to take charge."

"Someone will have to make him think otherwise, eh, Pieter?" Hannelore jested.

"You're telling me," said Van In, raring to go. "But let's first introduce ourselves to the infamous Mr. Degroof."

Ludovic Degroof was in the garden on the other side of the patio doors. From a distance he had the allure of a bronze statue. He was at least six feet tall and he conversed with broad gestures.

Patrick Delahaye was a short nervous man who listened to what his father-in-law was saying without appearing to take much in.

Degroof spoke French, but switched seamlessly to a sort of civilized West Flemish when Van In and Hannelore introduced themselves.

"Aha, so you are Commissaire Van In," he said jovially. "I've heard a lot about you."

Van In understood the penetrating gaze and the coercive voice. This was a man who was used to being obeyed without question.

I've heard a lot about you too, he wanted to say, but he considered it inappropriate in the circumstances.

Delahaye remained in the background. His eyes were vacant and there was a hint of a smile on his face, a sad smile. Van In noticed the glint in Degroof senior's eyes when he shook Hannelore's hand.

"Have the kidnappers contacted you?" Van In asked, not beating about the bush.

Van In had addressed the question to Delahaye, but Degroof cut in.

"My son received this fax at ten past four." He fumbled in his inside pocket and handed a copy to Van In.

"I had it copied in the car," he added when he saw the surprise in Van In's eyes. "Patrick thought it was some kind of misplaced joke at first. But fortunately I managed to convince him otherwise. A kidnapping should always be taken seriously. Am I right, Commissaire?"

Van In nodded absent-mindedly. He read the fax together with Hannelore.

Your son was kidnapped one hour ago.
You will be informed of the nature of the ransom later today together with the conditions to which you will be expected to adhere.

```
R O T A S
O P E R A
T E N E T
A R E P O
S A T O R
```

"Is that it?"

Van In didn't say a word about the Templars' Square, nor did Degroof.

"The local police are doing their level best to put a tap on the phone and the fax. According to Captain D'Hondt, they'll be done in thirty minutes," said Degroof. "All we can do is wait until the bastards contact us again. Whatever they ask, we've decided to pay. My grandson's wellbeing is to be given absolute priority. My daughter and my son-in-law are in full agreement, n'est-ce pas, Patrick?"

Delahaye nodded vacantly. Van In had the impression that the man was on the verge of collapse.

"I should be with Charlotte. Please excuse me."

If someone's back could express sadness and dismay, then Delahaye's back was irrefutable in its eloquence. His shoulders stooped, he dragged himself toward the west wing of the house where the bedrooms were located.

"I'm expecting the public prosecutor at any minute. And someone will also have to speak to the press."

Hannelore found it difficult to believe how Degroof could be so impersonal in such circumstances.

"Perhaps you should do that yourself, Mr. Degroof," Van In suggested. "An appeal by a family member can sometimes make an impression on the kidnappers. I'll have a word with Commissioner Deleu, and then we can put together a tentative plan of action."

"Excellent," said Degroof.

"I imagine Captain D'Hondt is the man to talk to if you want to organize a press conference."

Degroof didn't argue. On the contrary, he even seemed grateful. He lurched across the room to the local police captain, who was watching a couple of technicians install a tape recorder.

"That's him out of the way," whispered Van In with satisfaction.

"The man makes my skin crawl. Did you see the way he looked at me?"

Van In growled something that could have meant both yes and no. If Degroof's lustful eyes were a hindrance, he only hoped she had no idea what was going on in *his* head. Then again, he didn't know what Hannelore knew.

"Where's Deleu when you need him?"

"He's gone out for a pack of cigarettes," a familiar voice smirked.

"Jesus, Versavel. I'd almost forgotten you were here. You disappeared a moment ago and I figured . . ."

"You know the score," he laughed. "Big boys move in, Versavel moves out."

"Did you come with Deleu?"

"No. I was here first, with Pol Verscheure. He's still outside."

"A stroke of luck, Sergeant. Are you on duty day and night?" said Hannelore.

"You only get to rest on your laurels after they promote you to inspector, ma'am," was Versavel's caustic response.

"Give it a break, guys," said Van In. "This is a kidnapping. Let's get down to business."

Versavel fished his notebook from the breast pocket of his neatly laundered shirt and gave his report telegram-style.

"Call from Mrs. Delahaye at 4:51 P.M."

"So late," Hannelore observed. "The fax came in at 4:10 P.M."

"We can ask her later. Continue, Guido."

"Sergeant Versavel and Officer Verscheure on scene 5:01 P.M. Request assistance after basic questioning. Assistance arrives at 5:34 P.M. led by Commissioner Deleu. Commissioner Deleu informs the local police. Captain D'Hondt arrives at 5:48 P.M., Ludovic Degroof at almost the same time. Assistant Commissioner Van In and Deputy Martens arrive at 6:13 P.M."

"Is that it?" Van In cursed.

Versavel snapped his notebook shut.

"In cases like this, no one's interested in the opinion of a mere sergeant," he snorted.

"Okay, then it's time we started to coordinate things. Guido, try to keep the press and the public at bay outside. Ask the technical guys to set up crowd barriers and seal the place off. If anyone questions your authority, send him to me. By the way, was anyone dispatched to Boudewijn Park?"

"Captain D'Hondt sent half his force," said Versavel enviously. "Watch out. There goes all the glory."

"Now I understand why De Kee was so adamant that we come here," said Hannelore: "to balance forces."

"And I thought Degroof wanted *me* on the case."

"That's what De Kee said, but do we have to believe him?" she said with a roguish smile.

"Tease."

She raised her eyebrows.

"Why didn't he come himself? The cameras will be rolling here before long and everybody knows how much he loves the cameras."

"Come," said Van In to Hannelore. "Let's pay a visit to mummy."

As they were heading to the bedroom wing—Versavel had slipped him a hastily drawn plan of the house—he heard someone call his name. Captain D'Hondt hurried toward him.

"Mr. Degroof tells me you're taking over," he said with a clear hint of suspicion in his voice.

Van In confirmed the captain's statement with an unassuming nod. Cooperation between the local police and special investigations was a delicate matter. In the last analysis, it was the public prosecutor who decided who was to lead an investigation, but the way D'Hondt had spoken to him was proof that the captain was aware of links between public prosecutor Lootens and Ludovic Degroof.

"For the time being," he added diplomatically. "I've just been told that your men are combing Boudewijn Park and its surroundings. That's fine by me. It saves me some manpower." D'Hondt seemed happy with the response. He was "new school" and hated inefficiency. Deleu was a windbag and he preferred to steer clear of him. Van In was another story, if the rumors circulating about him were anything to go by.

"The men from the telephone company have fitted a tap to the phone and fax line. If the kidnappers contact us again, we'll have their location in thirty seconds. And by the way, they found the boy's bicycle five minutes ago."

"Nearby?" asked Van In.

D'Hondt moistened his lips.

"Not exactly. A couple of colleagues from the Oostkamp division came across it by accident on Kuipen Street, a country road between Oostkamp and Loppem. I had already issued a police alert, so they called in their find immediately."

One-nil, thought Hannelore, who had been following the conversation with degree of malicious delight. Versavel had underestimated the young captain.

"We presume the kidnappers dumped the bike. Mr. Degroof is certain it belongs to his grandson. The model matches, as does the Greenpeace sticker on the mudguard. But we'll be able to confirm things in fifteen minutes. The bicycle is on its way here."

"Thanks for the information, Captain. We'll catch up later."

D'Hondt turned and made his way back to Degroof, who was waiting by the fax machine. The captain's face had been saved. He could now get on with his work undisturbed.

"Friendly guy, our captain," she teased. Van In didn't fall for it. "You're learning fast, Pieter Van In," she said with a laugh when he didn't react. "I still owe you a report, by the way, from yesterday. And if your behavior on the way over here is anything to go by, my little outing yesterday is still bothering you."

"Don't worry. I'm over it. From now on, I believe everything you say."

"Aha," she crowed. "So you thought I'd pulled a fast one on you and was off padding my own wallet."

Van In bowed his head. "It'll never happen again, Hannelore."

"Fine. Then I'll fill you in later at home, as long as you have enough Duvels in the refrigerator."

"We have a deal, if we escape at a reasonable hour. But first Charlotte Degroof."

The house was built in such a way that all the rooms on both wings gave out onto the garden, just like Roman villas in antiquity. The architect had clearly been inspired by Pompeii itself. All the rooms were accessible via a corridor on the inside of the exterior wall.

When Van In knocked on the first door, he heard Delahaye shout "enter" from the neighboring room. They moved on to the second door and thus arrived at the master bedroom.

Charlotte Degroof was lying on the bed and her husband was staring out of the window. He spent most of his free time in the garden, but now it seemed completely unimportant.

"Excuse us," said Van In. "But I fear we're going to need your help."

Charlotte was about to get up, but Van In stopped her.

"There's no need, ma'am."

Charlotte Degroof was a very beautiful woman. Her short haircut gave her a particularly youthful look. Van In found it hard to believe she was forty-six.

"You called the police," he said by way of introduction.

"We thought it was a joke at first," Delahaye answered in her stead. "Bertrand has given us a couple of scares in the past."

"So you questioned the authenticity of the fax."

Van In now knew why they had waited so long before they called the police.

"Last year he gave his friends a card saying it was time he saw something of the world," said Charlotte in a gentle voice. "His friends mailed it from Rome, while we thought he was camping with the scouts."

The anecdote made her smile.

"His father panicked and drove to Lanaken. And there he was, with the scouts."

"What made you finally decide this one wasn't a joke?"

"When I called Daddy and read him the text. He made us swear we would inform the police. He also insisted that you be put in charge of the investigation. Do you know Daddy, perhaps?"

"Yes, we know each other," Van In lied.

"Then there was that Latin text. Have you any idea what it meant?" asked Delahaye.

"We found the same text at your brother-in-law's store, Mr. Delahaye," said Van In in a neutral tone.

"So there's a connection between that ridiculous robbery and Bertrand's abduction?"

Van In nodded.

"We haven't been able to decipher the precise meaning of the text, unfortunately. But one thing is clear: the presence of the Latin puzzle proves that we're not dealing with one of your son's practical jokes."

Van In thus dismissed any remaining doubts and Delahaye felt strangely reassured. He sat on the bed next to Charlotte and took her hand.

At that moment someone knocked on the door. It was Deleu, and he didn't look happy.

"The public prosecutor wants to speak with you urgently, Van In," he said in an authoritarian tone.

"Surely not?" Van In replied feigning disbelief.

Deleu gasped for air.

"Why don't you finish taking Mr. and Mrs. Delahaye's statement? I'll be back as soon as I'm free."

Van In and Hannelore headed back to the lounge, leaving Deleu juddering like a blocked volcano. *Just you wait*, he thought to himself, seething with pent-up rage.

Public Prosecutor Lootens was roughly the same height as Ludovic Degroof. Both men were standing with Captain D'Hondt on the covered patio.

"The public prosecutor wants to speak with Van In, what an honor," Hannelore jeered.

Van In shrugged his shoulders, but behind his indifferent façade his heart was racing.

After the obligatory exchange of politenesses, everyone turned to the public prosecutor. Hannelore had told Van In that Lootens was part of the Degroof clique: rich, right-wing, and Roman Catholic, in that order.

"Captain D'Hondt has just informed me of the measures that have already been taken," said Lootens in a penetrating nasal voice. "I have decided to extend the police alert to the national level."

It was almost seven, and the kidnapping was four hours old. The kidnappers had had plenty of time to seek the safety of their hideaway. At this stage, a national police alert was about as useful as a bucket of water at a nuclear meltdown.

"Witness statements will be available later, no doubt," said Lootens with the self-assurance typical of senior civil servants. "In cooperation with the special investigations, the local police are questioning everyone, as we speak, who may have witnessed the abduction in one way or another."

His sentence structure would have made even Cicero's hair stand on end.

"But I fear there's little we can do until the kidnappers seek further contact."

It all sounded grave and consequential.

Degroof stared vacantly into space. The swollen artery on his forehead throbbed visibly and his jaws were clenched tight. No one could really estimate just how much suffering the abduction of his grandson was causing him.

"The best we can do now is proceed with practical matters," Lootens continued in the same meaningless tone. "It is vital that we coordinate our efforts."

He looked at his watch with an exaggerated gesture of the arm.

"In an hour's time I'm expecting Professor Beheyt from the Faculty of Applied Psychology at the University of Ghent."

Van In knew Beheyt. He had made a useful contribution a couple of years earlier after the kidnapping of the son of a West Flemish textile baron.

The Belgian authorities had little experience with kidnappings, but Beheyt had fended admirably for himself.

"You'll be working closely with the professor," said Lootens, pointing to Van In and Hannelore. "Captain D'Hondt here will maintain contact with the Ministry of Internal Affairs and will be responsible for interventions at the national level should they prove necessary. It goes without saying that I will be supervising this task force (he pronounced it as if it was French—*tasque-fors*). None of you is permitted to speak with the press unless he has my permission, and no one takes decisions on their own. Is that understood?"

"Yes, sir," said Hannelore, consciously defiant.

Lootens fortunately paid no attention to the tone of her response. He didn't give a damn about emancipation. He belonged to the generation of magistrates who hoped they would never see the appointment of a female public prosecutor. Van In tried to distract Lootens's attention nevertheless.

"If I may, sir," he said with a nervous gut. "According to the information Deputy Martens and myself have gathered, it's more than likely that the kidnappers are the same two men who burgled Ghislain Degroof's jewelry store last Sunday. And we have a detailed description of both men."

Van In's observation knocked Lootens off his stride for a second.

The outrage on Ludovic Degroof's face was a picture to behold. "Precisely why, Commissaire Van In, we have entrusted the investigation to you. The incident last Sunday at my son's shop was a waste of energy, don't you think, far too banal. A kidnapping is something else, I'm sure you will agree."

Van In got the picture. Degroof had to have a serious reason for keeping the two cases apart.

D'Hondt, who didn't appear to be aware of the burglary, kept his emotions in check as one would expect of a police captain.

"Of course," Van In concurred, resuming his deferential stance. He studied the expression on Degroof senior's face, but it was much the same as trying to penetrate the mask of a sphinx.

"So I can take it for granted that we all know what's expected of us?"

When no one responded, Lootens turned his back and started a conversation with Degroof in fluent French.

"I'll ask Versavel to organize some sandwiches and a case of beer," said Van In. "Can I get you something too, Captain D'Hondt?"

D'Hondt was glued to the spot, disconcerted by Van In's apparent friendliness.

"A Coke will suffice," he said humorlessly.

"Good, a Coke for Captain D'Hondt then. Let's see what Deleu has been up to," said Van In with a wink at Hannelore.

They could see through the window that the crowd outside was swelling by the minute, but the barriers appeared to be doing their job.

Versavel saw Van In give a sign and came dutifully running. Van In saw three or four camera crews keeping a close eye on the house. Twenty or so police officers made sure they didn't reach the front door. The assembled masses had been informed in the meantime that the public prosecutor would be giving a press conference at seven forty-five and not at seven fifteen as Ludovic Degroof had announced earlier.

The commercial TV reporter lit one cigarette after the other. He was in permanent contact with the news studio via his car phone. In spite of his pleas, the police held their ground. No one was allowed inside the barriers until seven thirty. At moments like this, Versavel was the right man in the right place.

A journalist from the state-run channel took a surreptitious sip from his hip flask. He was sitting pretty, no matter what. The state channel was set to broadcast exclusive pictures of the kidnapping to every household in the country in the middle of the evening news.

13

WHILE DANIEL VERHAEGHE WAS SENDING his first fax at ten past four, Laurent was parking the white Ford Transit in front of the chalet on the outskirts of Namur.

Bertrand Delahaye was lying on the floor of the van covered with a checkered travel blanket. The chloroform was beginning to wear off, and the boy groaned as Laurent dragged him to the loading platform. It wasn't going to be easy to carry him inside in this limp state. Laurent could feel the blood coursing through his veins. He was afraid he might black out, so he decided to rest a little first.

There were no prying eyes to worry about. The chalet was located at the end of a private road and was obscured from view by a forest of pine trees. He sat on the edge of the platform and waited until the dizziness had passed. He then made his way to the driver's compartment and fetched a linen bag containing a box of syringes and a vial of haloperidol. He filled a syringe with a double dose of the tranquilizing concoction and injected it into Bertrand's upper arm, his hands trembling with every move. The boy was half conscious but made no effort to resist when Laurent dragged him inside the chalet, a chore that took him the best part of ten minutes. He placed the boy on a bed, reluctantly handcuffing him, and carefully locked the door of the room. Panting and drenched in sweat, he collapsed into an old and musty armchair.

He was determined not to set a foot outside until their demands were met. They had stocked up on provisions for a week, and he could always call Daniel if anything unexpected happened. He considered their chances of being detected negligible. The chalet was his own property, and if everything went according to plan, the entire affair would be over by Monday.

He muttered a prayer and tried to imagine what Degroof must be feeling at that moment.

An hour before his daughter called and reported the abduction, Ludovic Degroof had been sitting alone at the kitchen table in his dreary canal house on Spinola Street. His gray eyes followed the cognac waltzing in the snifter he had just filled.

Like Eichmann on trial in Tel Aviv, locked inside a glass cage, he realized that his time was at hand.

He had received a letter two weeks earlier warning him that he was going to suffer for his misdeeds, but he hadn't let it worry him much. The letter had been anonymous, but he knew who had sent it. He and his friend—well, former friend—Aquilin Verheye had spent nights on end talking about the Templars' Square.

After more than fifty years, Degroof was in little doubt that the square at the bottom of the letter was the signature of Aquilin himself.

He also knew why Aquilin wanted him to suffer. The only thing he didn't understand was why it had to happen now. They were both old, and fifty years was enough to heal any wound, wasn't it?

While he hadn't let the letter worry him, he still took its contents seriously.

No police. Otherwise everything would be forced into the open. And because Degroof was used to paddling his own canoe, he hired a private detective to track Aquilin down, a routine assignment the man accepted with pleasure.

Degroof was unable to estimate what Aquilin knew and how he would use his knowledge to avenge himself. If the private detective found him, Degroof planned to pay him a visit and try to buy his silence. If that didn't work, he would have him eliminated. He had the necessary contacts and money was absolutely no obstacle.

Why did the old fool sign his letter with the Templars' Square? he asked himself. *Why be so stupid? He must have known I would have made the connection.*

The ridiculous incident at Ghislain's store had made Degroof nervous, leading him to presume that Aquilin was deliberately looking for press attention. He then pulled rank with De Kee and insisted on having the investigation shut down. After all, it was only a question of time before the detective located Aquilin. And Degroof was determined to keep his past a closed book. He didn't want anyone sniffing through its pages.

He had been drinking for the best part of twenty-four hours. The private detective's report had left him at a complete loss. If somehow the man threatening him *wasn't* Aquilin Verheye, then he was in serious shit.

Daniel Verhaeghe waited until nine o'clock before going to the public fax next door to the Vienna Tearoom on Vlaming

Street. The tearoom was relatively busy and there were dozens of shoppers eagerly perusing the windows in the snug new shopping arcade. Daniel punched in Delahaye's number and slipped a sheet of paper into the machine.

Sergeant Lobelle was manning the switchboard in the company of an official from the telephone company and keeping a close eye on Delahaye's line. He reacted immediately.

"How much time do we need?" he snarled.

"It depends," said the nervous official as his fingers danced across his computer keyboard.

Lobelle radioed in to his colleagues on Bishop Avenue.

"We've got him," the official screamed after twenty seconds or so. "Vlaming Street. The public fax in the new shopping arcade."

A relaxed Daniel Verhaeghe strolled across Market Square as a slew of police cars with wailing sirens honed in on Vlaming Street from every direction. Just before the impressive army of police hermetically sealed the entire block, Daniel dipped his handkerchief in the fountain on Zand Square. The tension excited him, and the wet handkerchief almost sizzled when it touched his forehead.

Captain D'Hondt read the incoming fax line by line as it rolled out of the machine. He had seen some crazy things in his career, but this topped them all.

Van In and Hannelore were in the lounge trying to cheer Mr. and Mrs. Delahaye. They hurried to the fax machine, followed by Degroof senior. Public Prosecutor Lootens had already left. He had excused himself shortly after the press conference and handed Van In the number of De Karmeliet, a three star restaurant on Long Street where he had an urgent appointment. At least that's what he said.

"Has to be a bunch of jokers," said D'Hondt in an effort to calm everyone down. "Here, read this."

He handed the fax to Van In. But before Van In read the first line, he caught sight of the small square at the bottom of the page.

"Forget it," Van In snarled.

"Oh, my God," Charlotte sobbed. Patrick Delahaye stood beside her and took her hand. Hannelore read the fax over Van In's shoulder.

> *Your son is alive and well. If you carefully follow the instructions below, the boy will be left unharmed. One thing should be clear: there will be no negotiation on the ransom. Any attempt to delay the procedure can have potentially fatal results for Bertrand.*
>
> *If you wish to see Bertrand again and in good health, you must do the following: on Monday July 8 at 8 a.m. precisely you must bring the paintings listed below to Zand Square . . .*

A list of paintings followed, each with the name of the artist.

> *. . . at 9 a.m. Patrick Delahaye must remove a strip of paint at least four inches wide from each of the paintings with a scraper. This must take place on Zand Square in front of the cameras. The paintings are then to be piled up in front of the fountain and set alight.*
>
> *The public are to be informed about this event via radio and television. On the day of the burning, the public must be given free access to Zand Square, and the distance between the first row of people and Patrick Delahaye is to be no more than six feet. During the burning, however, the distance may be increased to thirty feet.*
>
> *Should this procedure not be followed to the letter, or in the absence of public or media interest, Bertrand will be killed. There will be no further communication.*

The Templars' Square served as a signature.

"Jesus H. Christ," Van In muttered.

No one paid any attention to his exclamation. He passed the fax to Delahaye. The color drained from Patrick's face as he read, and he leaned for support on Charlotte, who was head and shoulders taller.

Van In had noticed the paintings, of course, but hadn't realized they were by painters like Delvaux, Permeke, Mondriaan, Peire, Magritte, Appel. There was even a work by Gustave Klimt, on its own worth tens of millions of francs.

"This can't be true," Delahaye screamed. "Charlotte, tell me it's some kind of wicked prank."

The man was beside himself and Charlotte put a reassuring arm around his shoulder.

"If I may, Mr. Delahaye," said D'Hondt, his tone resolute. "I don't think we have to take this seriously. No kidnapper in his right mind would insist on burning a fortune in paintings."

He sounded so self-assured that Delahaye raised his head. Was there a glimmer of hope? A tentative smile appeared under the policeman's obligatory moustache.

"Forget it," said Van In for a second time. "I'm sorry, but this *is* from the kidnappers. There's no doubt about it."

Van In hadn't found it necessary to fill D'Hondt in on the background. The captain glared at him.

"Is that right?" he sneered.

"Commissaire Van In is completely right."

Everyone recognized Ludovic Degroof's authoritarian voice. "Captain D'Hondt is probably not aware of all the facts of the case, otherwise he would never defend such a hypothesis."

D'Hondt stood his ground, but inside his ego withered like a deflating balloon.

"What makes you so certain?" Delahaye asked, clinging to the last straw.

"Just take it from me, my boy," said Degroof, trying to sound sympathetic. "Paintings can be replaced."

Van In spotted Hannelore whispering something in Charlotte Degroof's ear.

"Excuse me." Everyone turned to the front door. Van In recognized the short, dusty man immediately.

"Professor Beheyt, perfect timing. The kidnappers have just made contact."

Versavel had opened the door for Beheyt and now joined him with the others.

Adelbrecht Beheyt looked as if he had walked out of a comic strip. He was wearing an ill-fitting, old-fashioned three-piece suit and kept one hand tucked upright in his vest pocket, a pose that afforded him a certain degree of dignity. He was in his early sixties and small of stature, but a pair of intelligent boyish eyes sparkled behind his horn-rimmed glasses. Many a student could testify to his fiery character and his exaggerated sense of honor, but outside the classroom he was an affable man.

"I was a little late, so I decided to book a room in a hotel first."

Making him even later, thought Hannelore, unable to follow his crooked logic.

Beheyt spoke with a warm voice, and anyone could tell that he had spent more than ten years teaching at a Dutch university in Leiden.

"There was no need for that, Professor. You would have been most welcome chez moi." Ludovic Degroof's reaction was closer to that of a concerned host than a grandfather at his wits' end.

"That's most kind of you, Mr. . . ."

"Degroof, Ludovic Degroof, grandfather of the kidnapped boy."

It took a good five minutes before everyone was introduced according to the rules of etiquette.

Van In took it upon himself to bring Beheyt up to speed. The professor listened attentively, and when Van In was done his only request was to see the fax. Charlotte handed it over and Beheyt took a moment to study the kidnappers' demands. He was intelligent enough, however, not to draw any immediate conclusions.

There was an unearthly silence in the room as he read. The arrival of an expert always kindled a spark of hope.

"I suggest we sit down for a moment," he said, "take time to talk things through and put together a strategy."

His approach seemed to work. Even Patrick Delahaye breathed a little more freely.

"Shall I make a pot of coffee?" Charlotte suggested.

In contrast to an hour earlier, she appeared relieved. For her, it was an open–and–shut case. They would bring the paintings to Zand Square on Monday and burn them. Then Bertrand would be set free.

"With cognac perhaps?" she asked halfway between the lounge and the kitchen. Van In said yes on everyone's behalf.

The lounge was in proportion to the rest of the house and took up the space of an ordinary room. There were enough armchairs for everyone. Since no one had dismissed him, Versavel likewise took a seat. He was in the mood for coffee.

"I think the time has come to collect all the available information."

Van In took the floor, and it pleased him that Beheyt spontaneously concurred. This time he provided a comprehensive report of what had happened between Sunday and the present. He intentionally omitted a couple of details, notably the pressure Degroof had been applying to have the investigation buried. He didn't fail to observe that Degroof had nodded approvingly in his direction every now and then. He figured the old fox must have stuck his neck out. By insisting that the public prosecutor and De Kee assign Van In to the case, he had limited the spread of a potential scandal.

"Extraordinary," said Beheyt when Van In had had his say. "At first sight I'm inclined to agree with Commissioner Van In's conviction that we're dealing with a personal vendetta. The demands of the kidnappers suggest revenge rather than material gain."

Captain D'Hondt was boiling with rage because Van In had failed to mention the information he had now provided. Hannelore considered throwing what she had discovered that Friday into the pot, but Van In had been silent about their visit to Loppem and she presumed he had his reasons.

At that moment Charlotte marched in from the kitchen carrying a wooden tray with coffee, cookies, and a bottle of Otard cognac. She had been away for the best part of twenty minutes. Hannelore saw from her eyes that she had been crying.

When everyone had been served coffee and cognac, Beheyt continued.

"The Templars' Square points in all probability in the direction of a romantic run amok. The style and language of the fax leads me to presume that whoever wrote it is well educated. If you ask me, he's not young either, and that would appear to tally with what I've just heard from the commissioner. The combination of an old man working with a young accomplice is a curious one. When an old man seeks revenge, it's usually for something that happened a long time ago. Perhaps the young man somehow engendered his actions."

Captain D'Hondt busily took notes. The oppressive silence reinstated itself.

"What struck me," said Charlotte completely out of the blue, "was that the young man used eye drops when he was at my brother's store. Isn't that what you said this afternoon, Commissioner?"

As an eye doctor, it was logical that such a detail would draw her attention.

"He was also exceptionally tall. All the witnesses seem to agree on that point."

Everyone turned to her in surprise.

"You have a good memory, ma'am," said Van In, sounding like a teacher giving a gold star to his best student. She understood that he didn't wish to be unkind when he asked her to explain the connection between the two observations.

"Indeed," she said with a feeble laugh, "perhaps it does sound absurd, but if I'm not mistaken there's a rare eye condition that combines both features."

"Is that so, Charlotte?"

Ludovic Degroof sat on the edge of his chair.

"And how rare is rare?" Van In inquired.

"Pretty rare," said Charlotte, scouring the deepest caverns of her memory in search of the condition's name. "It's a syndrome . . . something syndrome . . ."

She ran through the letters of the alphabet in her mind, hoping that one of them would jolt her memory. They left her to think for a while.

"Please, just ignore me," she said when she realized everyone had fallen silent. "It'll come to me. And it's probably not that important. Please continue . . ."

"I suggest we follow Mrs. Delahaye's example and do some brain-racking. We need to bring all the evidence together, search for a connection," said Beheyt, still grave.

Hannelore looked at Van In, but his lips remained sealed.

"We're pretty sure the culprits used a dark Mercedes station wagon. Isn't that something we've overlooked?" said Charlotte.

"Have you any idea how many Mercedes station wagons there are on the roads in Belgium?" Van In sighed. His tone was ill-chosen and he immediately sensed Charlotte's glare.

"But you're right," he resumed, correcting himself. "I believe Captain D'Hondt is exploring that line of inquiry."

D'Hondt placed his cup on a nearby side table, taking care not to let anyone see that his hand was shaking.

"That's news to me," he said, his voice subdued. "Thus far the local police have not had access to the statements and official reports surrounding the Ghislain Degroof case. In the present case, however, there are no witnesses. We can't be sure that the boy was taken in a Mercedes. But there's no reason why we shouldn't include this element in our description," he said, raising his voice slightly.

"The captain is completely right." Van In took a wicked delight in kicking, then comforting. "Let's not forget that the perpetrators will be holed up somewhere safe by this time. The vehicle used to kidnap the boy isn't likely to be parked at their front door."

It had started to rain. The outside broadcast units of the national and commercial TV stations had acquired the backup of a modest Renault Espace belonging to a local TV station. A Dutch broadcasting team had joined the assemblage an hour earlier.

One thing was clear: if the kidnappers' demands went public, Bishop Avenue would be awash. A kidnapping alone was a stroke of luck, but a kidnapping with a ransom note demanding that a bonfire be made of an art collection worth millions was enough to attract even CNN's attention.

Versavel had sent the majority of the police home, and the two remaining officers on duty had sought the shelter of their police vehicle. The handful of curious onlookers who had remained obediently respected the barriers, and there was nothing new to excite the press. The occasional passerby peered and pointed at the bungalow's lit windows out of curiosity.

No one paid the least attention to the scrawny young man sauntering past the bungalow. Neither the police nor the reporters gathered in deliberation noticed the derisive smile on his face as he stopped for a moment in front of the house. Daniel Verhaeghe relished the tension. He felt the adrenaline pump through his fragile aorta. Mocking death, with whom he had made friends long ago, sent him into ecstasy.

Five minutes before he went on the air, a journalist spotted an envelope taped to the door of the national TV station's Mercedes.

Halfway through the news, the Delahayes' telephone rang. Captain D'Hondt was the first to reach the phone and he switched on the Nagra tape recorder before lifting the receiver. Charlotte closed her eyes in nervous expectation while the others gathered in a circle around D'Hondt.

Van In saw the police captain's adam's apple bounce up and down as he gulped. There was no need to wait for the end of the conversation. The public prosecutor's voice was loud and clear enough for everyone to hear.

"What in God's name is going on, D'Hondt? Which fucking idiot informed the press, and why didn't Van In call me? Is he there?"

D'Hondt handed him the receiver with a nasty smile. Van In couldn't blame him. It was his own fault. He had completely forgotten to call Lootens when the fax with the kidnappers' demands was received.

"Good evening, sir."

"Haven't you been watching the national news?" Lootens bellowed.

Hannelore raced to the lounge and switched on the TV just in time to hear the newsreader say: ". . . the ransom note is said to be demanding the public burning of twenty-five valuable paintings from the collection of Patrick Delahaye, the father of the kidnapped boy. Those were this evening's headlines."

Lootens rattled on in his rage. Van In was saved by Degroof, who indicated that he would speak to Lootens and calm him down.

"I'm passing you to Mr. Ludovic, sir."

Van In grabbed his mobile phone and sounded the alarm. Five minutes later, half of West Flanders was in a state of uproar, while Bruges witnessed the launch of the biggest manhunt the city had ever seen.

Ten minutes later, the local police closed every road leading out of the city.

Before the first patrol headed out, Daniel Verhaeghe was already safely ensconced in the Park Hotel on Zand Square, only sixty yards from the police station. The swirling blue lights of dozens of departing police cars gave his room the appeal of a discotheque.

That's the last place they'll check, Laurent had said. *No one suspects the disabled, and no one looks next door.* Daniel gave the wheelchair in which he had just rolled into the hotel a shove and lined himself up by the window.

The reporter was still holding the envelope with the statement he had just sent out live on the air when Van In stormed up to him. The other journalists formed a protective cordon around their diminutive colleague.

"Where in God's name did you get that information?" Van In snorted. "And why didn't you inform us?"

"No one was allowed through, police orders," the journalist aptly retorted. Even the Dutch reporters had trouble suppressing their laughter.

"The envelope was taped to the door of the van."

"When did you find it? Who was here? Did anyone notice anything?"

Van In fired question after question like a multiple rocket launcher.

"Those two didn't see anything either." One of the Dutch journalists pointed at the two officers, who had just left their car and were on their way over, completely unaware of what had happened. The laughter was unrestrained.

Van In thought his head was about to explode. But he realized in the nick of time that he would be making a complete fool of himself if he lost his cool.

A sharp-eyed cameraman from the commercial station was about to film the scene, but Versavel stopped him, grabbing the lens with his massive hand and pushing the struggling cameraman aside with the other.

"I could easily break your arm and say it was an accident," he hissed. There wasn't even a hint of anger in his face. He was smiling. Versavel was an avid power trainer, weekly sessions. He grabbed the cameraman's fragile arm with both hands as if it was a stick of wood.

"Okay, gentlemen. Your attention please."

Van In tried to stem the flow of adrenaline. Information was now more important than bickering.

"Did anyone see an elderly man in the last hour, or a younger guy, lanky, overgrown?"

"What did he say?" one of the Dutchmen asked his neighbor.

"He wants to know if anyone spotted an old guy or someone younger, tall and thin," he answered with a drawl.

"What about the guy who was here half an hour ago? He must have been well over six feet. He hung around for a couple of minutes, staring at the house, and then walked on. Didn't you see him, Rien?"

Rien furrowed the sea of wrinkles on his forehead and fiddled with his earlobe.

"Nope, didn't see him. But if you say so . . ."

The two Dutchmen were on the verge of starting an endless discussion.

"So you didn't see anyone near the BRTN van?" Van In interrupted impatiently.

"I had just sat down for a cup of coffee," Rien said in a what-else-do-you-expect tone of voice.

"My colleague will be along in a minute to take a statement," said Van In when he realized the Dutchman had nothing else to say. "Thanks, in any event."

"Pleasure. Cheers."

If the Dutchman's timing was accurate, the lumbering beanpole couldn't have gotten far. Van In trotted back to the house and had a word with D'Hondt. He had received confirmation by radio that a ten-mile cordon had been set up around Bruges. Every vehicle entering or leaving the city was being thoroughly searched.

"If he doesn't have a car, then he has to be in the city," said Van In. "We've deployed all our available manpower. If he's wandering around, we have to find him."

"Unless he's got a safe house somewhere," D'Hondt suggested.

"He's got balls, you have to give him that," said Hannelore.

"The worst of it is that we're sitting here wasting our time, for Christ's sake," Van In grumbled. "If only we had a clue to follow, one goddamn clue!"

Beheyt had stayed in the lounge, adjusting his profile of the perpetrators in his typically jagged scrawl. The compulsion of one of the kidnappers to hang around the scene of the crime had given him food for thought.

"Rash behavior to say the least," said Beheyt when Van In joined him and tossed back a mouthful of cognac.

"If we take it as given that there are only two people involved, then we also have to assume that Bertrand is being held by the elderly man on his own," said Beheyt. "They have to be pretty sure of themselves to take such a risk. The younger man's presence here in Bruges seems totally pointless."

"Nothing is coincidental or pointless in this affair," said Van In, his voice toneless, "it only appears that way. And to be honest, I'm not particularly worried about the boy's safety. The kidnapping itself isn't their real goal."

"And do you have any idea what that might be, Commissioner?"

"Perhaps," said Van In, cursing himself for his indiscretion. "But we'll talk about it later."

"We're supposed to be working as a team, Commissioner, I presume you realize that," said Beheyt pointedly.

"Of course, Professor. But please don't pay too much attention to the meanderings of a policeman's mind, especially when he's worn out."

Beheyt's expression softened, a sign that he had accepted Van In's excuse. Van In breathed an inner sigh of relief.

"Another cup of coffee, Professor?"

Hannelore had perfect timing. Van In wanted to throw his arms round her.

"Please," said Beheyt. "In the meantime, I'll finish my profile. We can run through it in the morning when we've all had some sleep."

"According to Captain D'Hondt, there are five hundred policemen working on the case, and according to the latest reports Bruges is like a city under siege. I wonder if they'll catch him," she said, upbeat.

"I doubt it," said Van In. He poured himself another glass and lit his first cigarette. He suddenly realized that Deleu had made himself scarce. In all the commotion, no one had noticed that he had returned to the police station.

Van In racked his brains trying to think of his next move. He was just about to light his second cigarette when something came to him. He jumped to his feet and headed toward D'Hondt, who was standing by the telephone. Hannelore was right behind him.

"Get me the bus company," he said, "someone in charge of scheduling."

D'Hondt didn't ask questions. He radioed his people and requested details of the bus company's regional director. He needed the man's telephone number ASAP. The local police could be arrogant bastards, but their professional qualities were never in question.

Van In had the information he was looking for in less than three minutes. When D'Hondt had the regional director on the phone, he spoke with concision and with a persuasiveness worthy of Van In's envy. Within five minutes, he had the name and number of the scheduling department.

Marc Ballegeer new the names of more or less all of the drivers by heart and was immediately able to identify Michel Devos as the driver of the Bruges-Courtrai bus.

"Has he been up to something?" asked Ballegeer, genuinely concerned. Devos was an excellent colleague . . . they got on like a house on fire.

"Nothing untoward," D'Hondt assured him. "But we need some information from him and it's urgent."

"Thank God for that," Ballegeer sighed.

Michel Devos remembered the tall young man getting on the bus at Oostkamp around three thirty. How could he forget?

D'Hondt used a sort of self-invented shorthand to take note of the details Devos spewed out at high speed.

The guy was way over six feet. He bumped his head on the automatic doors, spoke with a Bruges accent but as if he hadn't lived in Bruges for a long time, was extremely thin, was wearing glasses with thick lenses, faded jeans and a greenish T-shirt with an open denim jacket in top. Devos had kept an eye on him in his rearview mirror. There was no one else on the bus. He put drops in his eyes just before he got off at the train station.

D'Hondt thanked the observant driver and asked if he would stop by the following morning to make an official statement.

"I'll arrange time off with Ballegeer," Van In heard him conclude as he hung up the phone.

"Not bad, Commissioner," said D'Hondt. "I should have thought of that one myself. Bertrand's bike was found in Oost-kamp and you figured our man didn't have a vehicle. Sharp thinking."

D'Hondt spread the bus driver's accurate description over the radio as Van In made his way to the kitchen. Three pairs of eyes stared at him in anticipation.

"Good news?" asked Delahaye, a shadow of the man Van In had met only seven hours earlier.

Van In briefed them, but insisted at the same time that they shouldn't cherish false hopes.

"The only thing we're certain of is that the younger of the two men is in Bruges at this moment. With a bit of luck we should be able to track him down before Monday. I'll give my men orders to keep searching, but I'm afraid there's little more we can do here for the time being."

Degroof senior was about to protest, but his daughter put her hand on his shoulder.

"Mr. Van In is right, Daddy. I think it would help if we all got a little rest."

Charlotte was a strong woman. She had come to terms with the news of her son's abduction. She was clearly the practical type, just like her father.

"A patrol will stand guard by the door throughout the night and one of the local police will keep an eye on the phone."

Van In arranged to meet Beheyt and D'Hondt at the police station at seven A.M. sharp. He would call them if there was news in the meantime.

He was surprised that no one objected. But why should they? No one had any experience with kidnappings. Beheyt had been called in as an expert, but in reality he had only negotiated once in a kidnap case. And the way things were looking, there probably wouldn't be much to negotiate. The tight schedule and the bizarre demand to destroy the paintings only made the case all the more peculiar.

Van In had consulted the literature. Most kidnappings were settled when the ransom money was handed over, but this was a different kettle of fish. None of them knew what to expect.

"Dare I ask for a lift, ma'am?" said Van In when they left the house.

"At your command, Sherlock," she quipped.

14

"WHY DIDN'T YOU SAY SOMETHING about Aurelie?" asked Hannelore as Van In poured them both a Duvel in his kitchen back at home.

He made a pouty face. "And I thought *you* were the one with the news. But no, Deputy Hannelore Martens had to follow up on an important tip all by herself on Friday, no onlookers allowed."

Hannelore felt her cheeks redden. "I had no alternative, Pieter. She insisted that I come alone."

"And I'm expected to believe that."

"Believe what you want."

"Then again," said Van In, "why should I care?"

He pulled open the sliding door and popped his head outside.

"The rain's stopped. We might as well sit outside. Then you can tell me the whole story at your leisure."

Hannelore was too tired to bicker, and she was sure he hadn't set out to hurt her.

"Go on, then. I don't see us getting much sleep." Van In grabbed a kitchen towel and dried a couple of chairs.

"Van der Eyck called me on Thursday," she said as they settled at the garden table. "He was the one who gave me the idea."

"What idea?"

"To contact Nathalie Degroof. Van der Eyck knew that she had run away from home when she was seventeen."

"He just knew. Divine inspiration?"

"Sorry, Pieter. I should start from the beginning. Can you spare a cigarette?"

Van In slid his lighter and cigarettes across the table.

"You too?"

Van In shook his head.

"I'm trying to cut down. I get pains in my chest sometimes climbing the stairs. And you know how much men my age love hospitals."

Hannelore took a stiff drag, inhaled deeply, exhaled a cloud of smoke, and began. "Van der Eyck has spent months looking for a scandal he can use to eliminate one of the Christian Democrat heavyweights before the election. The Italians managed it last year just before their local elections, so why not in Belgium, he figured. And as we know, reality has caught up with him. The Socialists have been decapitated in a major bribery scandal, and if they dig any deeper there won't be any Socialist representatives left."

"All rise for Judge Véronique Ancia, politician slayer. Or should it be Judge Hannelore Martens?" Van In jeered.

"Don't mock, Pieter Van In," she snorted. "Give me the name of a police division that isn't corrupt and I'll sleep with all of them."

"You'll what?" said Van In, his eyebrow raised. "I prefer to keep you to myself."

"Men! Jesus! Do you ever think of anything else?"

"Sorry, but you provoked me."

"That's what they all say," she protested.

"No more interruptions," he promised. "I'm not in the mood for feminist indignation."

Hannelore sighed. "Where was I?"

"Van der Eyck and his quest for a scandal."

"The man is captivated by power. He'd give his left arm for the mayor's job," Hannelore continued. "I met him at a New Year's reception. I was a lawyer without work, a recently gradu-ated working-class girl with a passion to restore some balance to the scales of justice. I'd had a couple of glasses of bubbly and we were chatting, you know, this and that. After fifteen minutes he hinted that he might be able to arrange something for me."

"And the same guy's looking for a scandal to screw the opposition," said Van In, but the sarcasm in his voice wasn't intentional. He had also been expected to pull a few stunts before he was appointed assistant commissioner.

"He called me three months later. There were plans to appoint a new Deputy. It was up to the Liberals to suggest a candidate, and I was fed up doing crossword puzzles."

"Nobody's perfect," said Van In philosophically.

He kicked off his shoes and rested his feet on a garden chair. "That's what happens when old age starts to set in," he said, pulling off his right sock and starting to massage his painful foot.

"You're probably wondering why I'm telling you all this."

Van In was happy he was rubbing his foot. It meant he didn't have to look her in the eye.

"When I met you last Sunday for the first time, I felt a . . . how should I put it . . ."

"A kinship?"

"Exactly," she said, relieved. "You too?"

"You could call it that," he muttered though his teeth.

"What I meant to say was . . ."

She hesitated and grabbed a cigarette. Van In held his breath. He could hardly believe his ears.

"I like you, Pieter Van In. And don't be thinking I say that to every man I meet."

"Thank God for that," said Van In awkwardly.

"Come, let me have a go at that foot." She pulled her chair closer and rested his swollen foot on her lap.

"Work at the courthouse isn't what you'd think. The men just want to chat you up, and if they don't get their way they spit you out like old gum."

"Wow! Man, that feels good," Van In groaned. "You know what you're doing."

"Picked it up as a student. I had to do *something* to pay for my tuition."

"You don't mean you . . ."

He jumped to his feet. Hannelore couldn't control her laughter.

"Take it easy, Van In. It was all aboveboard, quite classy really, next to a gym. Most of the customers were sportspeople and I always wore long pants, you know, like a nurse's uniform."

"See-through blouse? Ouch, that hurt, Jesus!" he screamed when she pressed the swollen part of his foot with both thumbs.

"That'll teach you to be jealous."

Van In felt exhaustion make way for tingling bliss. He thought about Sonja and the sensations he had missed for so many years.

"A policeman chumming it up with the public prosecutor's office . . . people will talk," he said, half serious.

"Then we keep it a secret."

"Right, secrecy, stirring stuff! Why didn't I think of that?"
He took a swig of beer. Duvel had never tasted so good.

"But before we get romantic, you have a story to finish."
She stopped abruptly. His foot massage was over.

"Jesus H. Christ, I almost forgot," she smirked.

"One moment, miss, but it's hard to listen properly when you have a sore foot."

Hannelore grabbed his foot and diligently resumed her massage.

"Men!"

Van In listened carefully to Hannelore's accurate reconstruction of her conversation with Nathalie.

"The dirty old bugger," he snorted when she had finished her story. "But we still don't know for sure if the two cases are related. That's why I thought it better not to say anything about Aurelie earlier. We can pursue that separately once Bertrand is recovered. Most families have a skeleton in the closet, but they always put up such fancy façades. They need a place to hide their dirt."

"What's the next step?"

She caressed his foot with one hand and held her glass in the other. Van In had no plans to protest as long as his foot could stay on her lap.

"I think it's time to confront Ludovic Degroof with the facts. Face to face, that is."

Hannelore bit her lip.

"Don't misunderstand me. I think it's safer if Degroof thinks only one person knows about his past. In his eyes, I'm just an insignificant police officer. If he lets something slip in the middle of a conversation, he knows he's safe, that whatever he says can't be used against him in a court of law."

She nodded, reassured.

"If someone else is with me, he'll close up, I'm sure of it, especially if it happens to be a Deputy public prosecutor."

"Sounds logical. But do you think there's a connection between Degroof's incest and the abduction of his grandson?"

"I still don't get a couple of things. That absurd incident at Ghislain's store bothered me from the start. That's why I suggested the entire operation might be geared against the Degroofs as a family and not Ghislain Degroof alone. If the perpetrators aren't crazy, their only motive has to be revenge. But revenge for what? Aurelie? Something else? At first I thought the key was in the Latin text, but now I'm having serious doubts."

"An intentional red herring?"

"Yes and no. The text itself is open to interpretation, but I'm more inclined to see the so-called Templars' Square as a sort of signature."

"A signature only Degroof senior would understand. Are you suggesting he knows who did this?"

"I think he does," said Van In. "That was another reason to say nothing. The public prosecutor wouldn't have believed me, ditto D'Hondt and Beheyt. I can imagine you're not finding it easy yourself."

"Not easy, indeed," she grinned. "No one's stopping you from trying to convince me. But if Degroof knows who's doing this, why doesn't he say so, for Christ's sake. They've kidnapped his grandson and they're threatening to kill him."

"Maybe he thinks it'll all work out if he pays the ransom, or should I say sets it on fire. I really don't know. If you ask me, Degroof senior's their target and they're using the same tactics as Van der Eyck. But I think any connection between the two is coincidental. It was your patron's maneuvers that gave me the idea, by the way."

"But if they have incriminating evidence, why don't they go to the press?"

"I thought the same thing. I discussed the matter with Leo the day before yesterday. Why doesn't Van der Eyck just go to the press? But there's logic at work here. The world's infested with scandals. They're served up on a daily basis, and we forget them just as fast. You have to warm up your public, get them ready. The stunt with the gold was to focus attention on the name Degroof. The abduction, less than a week later, was intended for the international press. Their timing is perfect: soup, starter, and main course all in one week. The press will be begging for a follow-up."

"Just what Van der Eyck had in mind. If someone hangs out the dirty laundry about the daughter, Degroof is finished, a lamb to the slaughter."

"That's why I thought Van der Eyck was also in on the plot, or at least knew what was going to happen."

"But then he would've had no need for us, as I already said," Hannelore responded. "Van der Eyck's just lucky that someone else is doing his dirty work. Aren't you getting tired, Pieter?"

"Maybe so," Van In admitted. "But there's more. The perpetrators have an accomplice within the family. I'd stake my life on it."

"Perhaps you're right. I can't make heads or tails of it anymore. Maybe we're way off beam."

"You're right," said Van In. "It's high time we talked about something else."

"You took the words right out of my mouth," she said. "Maybe you could start by giving me a tour of this lovely house of yours."

"Try to get some sleep, honey. Fretting won't help. You know that."

"Can you sleep?" asked Patrick Delahaye bad-temperedly.

"Shall I make some hot milk?" Charlotte leaned on her elbow and groped around for the lamp.

"He's compensating you for the paintings. Why keep worrying about it? In five years' time, you can show off your brand-new collection."

"It's not about new collections, Charlotte," he grumbled. "Why didn't they just ask for money? Where's the profit in watching me burn a bunch of paintings? And don't forget, we have no guarantee they'll—"

"Stop this right now," Charlotte interrupted him angrily. "No postponement, no delaying tactics. I won't listen. This is about your son, for Christ's sake."

Patrick Delahaye blinked when his wife switched on the other lamps. He rubbed his day-old beard disapprovingly. He hadn't shaved that evening, something he always did before going to bed.

"I'm sorry, Lotte. You're right and I'm being stupid. Looking for alternatives makes no sense. But why make me do it myself? The very idea . . ."

Charlotte blew him a kiss from the edge of the bed. She was wearing nothing but an old T-shirt, a habit from her student days.

"Put a shot of whiskey in it," he called as she left the room.

The T-shirt had been laundered so often it had shrunk, and as she walked out the door he suddenly felt a desire to huddle up beside her when she got back to bed. It had been months since he last noticed her thighs. Maybe it would help calm his nerves. It had been the perfect remedy in the past.

Charlotte filled a pan with milk and flicked on the gas burner. They refused to have a microwave in the house. She hated them. She found a bottle of Teacher's Highland Cream in the drinks cabinet and splashed a generous measure into the large flowery cup. She remembered that she still had some marzipan left from a bar she had bought for charity the week before. The sugar would do her good. She hadn't eaten since lunch the previous day.

Patrick gulped greedily at his cup of grog. There had been so much whiskey in the cup that the boiling milk had more or less cooled. Charlotte blew over her hot milk and nibbled a portion of marzipan.

"Want a bite?"

She sat facing him on the bed with her legs crossed.

"It's the middle of the night. What are you eating?"

"Marzipan. I'm hungry. Aren't you?"

"I'll pass, thanks."

"Wait a minute. Marzipan! What made me think of marzipan?"

"What?" he asked.

"Marzipan. Marfan syndrome. One of the kidnappers . . . they can trace him . . . there's a register," she stammered, not making much sense.

"What are you on about?" he asked in amazement. He could hardly remember a word of the previous day's conversations.

"The lanky guy, one of the kidnappers, the young man who took the bus from Oostkamp to Bruges and passed on the ransom demand to the press."

"Sorry, but I'm not getting it."

Whiskey on an empty stomach could have a surprisingly fast effect.

"Two witnesses described him as exceptionally tall. He wears glasses with thick lenses and is constantly pumping drops into his eyes. It's perfectly possible and it needs treatment. He might even have had a couple of operations. As far as I remember, Marfan syndrome is extremely rare. It *has* to be traceable," she squealed euphorically.

"And I thought you were a fervent opponent of doctors who diagnose patients without seeing them," Patrick observed, not particularly convinced.

"But it's a possibility, remote perhaps, but still a possibility. I'm calling Van In."

"Now? At two-thirty?"

"If they arrest the kidnappers, there won't be any need to burn your precious paintings," she snapped.

Van In and Hannelore were still outside in the back yard. He had talked about his divorce for a while and then showed her around the house.

Hannelore was particularly taken by the room above the cellar. She had to admit that Van In—or was it his ex—had good taste.

"After the divorce, Sonja took all the furniture. It was the only way I could keep the house."

So he does have taste, she thought to herself.

"I built the fireplace myself."

Hannelore felt completely at home. In contrast to the rest of the house, the room above the cellar was neat and orderly.

"What a beautiful piece," she said, pointing to a sensitively polished antique chest of drawers.

"Did you buy it?"

"Yes, from a divorced couple who couldn't agree on who got what."

"Oh, the irony," she laughed.

"Watch out for the step," Van In warned as they made their way toward the living room. Hannelore collapsed into one of the armchairs. It almost devoured her.

"Fortified foam rubber," he explained.

"Expensive?"

"Very. I can't help myself. I'm addicted to beautiful things."

A pair of miniature Bose speakers hung from the ceiling.

"Where's the rest?"

Van In pointed to a cabinet.

"I'll put on *Carmina Burana* for you in a minute."

She struggled free of the Ligne Roset armchair and made her way to the other side of the room. The entire wall opposite the music cabinet was taken up by a beechwood bookcase. She ran her finger along the spines.

"Art lover and intellectual all in one," she said in a slightly jeering tone. "Eco, Dante, Ruusbroec, Jung—what made you join the police?"

"Don't overdo it. I'm not one of the local boys. At least I can read and write."

They both laughed at the tired joke, and Van In suddenly realized how relaxed he felt in her company.

"Come, let's finish the tour."

He deliberately avoided the bedroom and she didn't ask about it. He took her to the kitchen-dining room.

"Sorry for the mess. But you know how it goes with bachelors."

"I should care," she said. "I live alone too, by the way, and you should see my kitchen."

She stood in front of the enormous mirror above the mantelpiece. She turned sideways and looked at herself in profile just as Van In was inclined to do.

"Jesus, is that a Michel Martens mirror?"

"Do you know him?" asked Van In, surprised.

"I went to an exhibition last week. All I could afford was something small for my purse."

"Problem is . . ." he grouched, "you should see my overdraft."

"If that's the case, then you have to be corrupt."

"If only."

He took her hand.

"Dangerous stairs," he gave as an excuse.

They descended a spiral stairway built on to the outside of the house.

"I love the oval windows. Are they original?"

"It's all original. Wait until you see the cellar."

The stairwell gave out into the cellar. Another door led to the back yard.

"Are we now under the room I love so much?" asked Hannelore as she looked up at the whitewashed barrel vaulting. "Looks fifteenth century, no?"

"Probably. The Vette Vispoort dates back to 1434. The five houses on the right are old almshouses and my house is on the left."

"Surely this isn't an almshouse," she said taken aback.

"No, absolutely not," he hastened to add. "No one's sure why they built this place opposite the almshouses. They say it was commissioned by a fish merchant."

"Logical, I suppose . . . Vette Vispoort . . . Oily Fish Street . . . smelly!"

"But the historians don't buy it. Too obvious. They need evidence."

"So do we," she grinned.

They left the cellar and took the door into the back yard, which was no more than a long, narrow strip between the old canal wall and the back of the house.

The silence of the summer night, the stars glistening in the sky, and the water of the canal gently murmuring in the background transformed the otherwise empty yard into an idyllic oasis. *Morning can wait*, Hannelore thought.

"I didn't know the house backed onto the canal. But it fits the picture. Wherever you find water, you find people fishing."

"Not really. There wasn't a lot of fish to catch in those days. The canal was used more for transporting fish from elsewhere. At least that's what I've read. This part runs along the old city wall dating back to 1127, which means—"

They both froze at the sound of the telephone.

"Thank God we're still awake," she jested. But Van In paid no attention to her remark and raced upstairs. She followed at his heels.

"Call all the hospitals?" she heard him ask when she arrived in the living room.

Before he had the chance to say: *do you know how many hospitals there are in Belgium*, Charlotte said: "Start with the university hospitals, and if they can't help we can try the general hospitals."

"Presuming, of course, that the young man actually suffers from Marchand syndrome," Van In responded, unconvinced.

"Marfan, with an 'f',' she corrected.

Van In realized he couldn't openly ignore her request.

"I'll get my men onto it at seven. If need be, we can ask the ministry to involve the local police, have them call the hospitals in their region. Yes, you're right . . . no stone unturned. I'll do my best," he said. "And try to get a couple of hours sleep yourself. We still have a pile of work ahead of us tomorrow . . . I mean later."

Hannelore looked at him questioningly when he returned the receiver to its cradle.

"It only gets really tricky when the parents start playing detective," he sighed.

He brought her up to speed in a few words.

"Do you think there's anything in it?"

Van In shrugged his shoulders.

"The country's crawling with tall guys wearing glasses."

Bertrand Delahaye woke up with a throbbing headache. In all the excitement, Laurent had given him too much sedative.

The first thing he saw through the unsightly dormer window was a twinkling starlit sky. He was lying on a bed and it wasn't his own, he thought. It wasn't even his own room.

Bertrand wanted to jump up, but a physical stupor overpowered him. He heard something jingle. It was as if he was being sucked onto the mattress. It took him three tries before he was able to stand, and only then with difficulty. He took a few unsteady steps, but was suddenly held back by an invisible hand. His arm was attached to something and his wrist hurt. He felt helpless and couldn't make up his mind whether to return to the bed or stay where he was.

Something was making it difficult to think, although it also seemed to stop him from panicking. He had a vague awareness that something bad had happened to him, but he didn't really care. If only the pounding in his head would go away.

The chain was firmly attached to the wall. He tugged at it a few times, but it only aggravated his headache. He sat on the edge of the bed, resigned to his situation.

His eyes got used to the darkness and he squinted around the room. It was empty apart from the bed. The walls were made of wood and there was a rectangular carpet on the floor. When he stood up again and walked around the bed, he bumped into a chemical toilet. His parents brought something similar when they went camping; that's why he recognized it immediately.

His head began to spin and he had to sit. He recorded everything in his mind without thinking about it. He had no idea what time it was and just sat there staring listlessly into space. A strip of light under the door suddenly caught his attention. He heard someone shuffle along the corridor on the other side. He heard a key turning in the lock. Strangely enough, he wasn't afraid.

"I've brought you some cookies and lemonade," said Laurent in a gentle tone when he walked into the room. "You have to stay here for a couple of days, but don't worry; your parents have been informed."

Laurent placed the bottle and the cookies on the floor within Bertrand's reach.

"There's no need to be afraid. Nothing's going to happen to you."

"Can you put the light on?" asked Bertrand. "It's so dark in here."

Laurent groped for the light switch. The bare forty-watt light bulb was still enough to make him blink.

Bertrand got to his feet and shuffled toward the lemonade and cookies. The bald old man didn't look dangerous.

"If you want, we could play a game of checkers or chess," Laurent suggested. "Unless you want to get some more rest."

Bertrand was surprised by the strange suggestion, and it confused him.

"You kidnapped me. You were in the police van. I recognize you."

He snatched the cookies and lemonade as he spoke and then pulled back onto the bed.

Laurent didn't move a muscle, but simply looked on as Bertrand gobbled up the cookies and guzzled down the lemonade.

The pounding in his head slowed down as he ate. The haloperidol was wearing off, and the first emotion to surface was rage, blind rage.

"Let me out of here," he screamed. "You've no right to keep me locked up like this."

He grabbed the bottle and held it threateningly in the air.

"It's the only bottle of lemonade I have," said Laurent calmly. "If you smash it, you'll have to drink water all day long."

"Why didn't you buy more bottles, then?" Bertrand yelled. He lowered the bottle. Besides, it had a French label and it tasted a lot better than the lemonade at home.

"I've got chocolate too," said Laurent. "If you're still hungry, I can get you some."

Bertrand placed the bottle on the floor close to the bed. The old man's friendliness was irritating him. Was this an abduction, or what?

"Is it Cote d'Or?" he asked in an arrogant tone of voice.

"It is, actually," the old man smiled. "Wait, I'll be right back."

While Laurent made his way to the kitchen, Bertrand checked the handcuff. A protective strip of foam had been taped around his wrist before they cuffed him. The chain was roughly seven feet long and was attached to a wrought-iron ring built in to the exterior wall, which, unlike the others, was made of stone. The ring and the chain combined were easily strong enough to hold a bull in check.

When the old man returned, he had more than chocolate with him. The chessboard was under his arm.

"I brought the chessboard just in case," he said almost apologetically.

"How did you know I played chess?" asked Bertrand suspicious.

Laurent shrugged his shoulders.

"I just did," he said. "But if you don't want to play, I'll leave you in peace."

If Bertrand agreed to a game, he would at least have some company. But if he said no, the old man would leave and that would give him a chance to get rid of the foam under the handcuff and try to wriggle his hand out of the thing. The old man didn't look strong. Without the chain, he figured he had a good chance of overpowering him and freeing himself.

Bertrand checked the cuff. Laurent saw him but paid no attention. He knew the boy would never be able to break loose.

"You're sure I'll be home in two days?" Bertrand asked hesitatingly.

"Absolutely, my boy."

"Go on, then, but I play white."

"Fine by me. Do you mind if I sit beside you? Otherwise I'll have to fetch a table and a stool, and I have problems with my back."

Laurent had almost given himself a hernia dragging Bertrand from the van.

Bertrand took the chessboard and the pieces. Laurent sat down on the bed. The joint in his left knee cracked like a dry twig.

15

VAN IN RACED UP THE stairs to his office on Sunday morning
at five past seven to be greeted by Beheyt, D'Hondt, and
Hannelore. She had had just as late a night as he, but she looked
sprightly and awake nevertheless.

"Good morning," he said in an upbeat tone.

Beheyt barely looked up. He had a hefty pile of paperwork
in front of him on the table, through which he was nervously
browsing. D'Hondt was standing at the window and responded
to Van In's greetings with an indefinable gesture.

"A splendid day, Commissioner, don't you think?" said
Hannelore in the best of spirits.

"Any news on the precise location of the abduction?" asked
Van In when no one appeared to have anything to say.

"We're guessing somewhere near Boudewijn Park. A couple
of the boy's friends saw him at the roller-skating rink around

one-thirty," said Beheyt without lifting his head. "There's been no reaction to the appeal we broadcast on the radio. BRTN and VTM have promised a breaking news broadcast this morning at eight."

"You never know," said D'Hondt indifferently.

On the floor above, De Kee was on the phone with the district commandant of the local police. The man was far from happy about Assistant Commissioner Van In and the way he had been leading the investigation.

De Kee listened with patience to the enraged commandant. Everyone knew that the local police had much more experience and know-how and that serious crimes like kidnapping were always assigned to them and the judicial police.

It took the man a couple of minutes to say what he had to say. De Kee then tried to calm him down.

"I'm afraid the decision was made at a higher level, Jacques," he said mealy-mouthed. "Public Prosecutor Lootens appointed the taskforce in person. It was the public prosecutor himself who assigned Van In to head up the investigation. And if it's any comfort, he didn't appoint an investigating magistrate."

"That doesn't surprise me," the district commandant grumbled. "Everyone knows that Lootens and investigating magistrate Creytens can't stand the sight of one another."

De Kee grinned. Gossiping about magistrates was a favorite police pastime.

"I can only advise you to contact Public Prosecutor Lootens. I'm told he's spending the day in Knokke. But there's nothing stopping you from joining us here. We have an evaluation lined up for eight. You're welcome to be part of it."

De Kee returned the receiver to its cradle with a bogus smile.

The phone started to ring before he had let it go.

"Your lordship, always a delight to hear from the mayor's office."

De Kee leaned back in his chair and enjoyed the warmth of the sun's first rays.

Minutes later, Van In was developing the impression that he was talking to the wall.

"I just heard from Sergeant Versavel that no one in the neighborhood of Boudewijn Park noticed anything unusual. If my information is correct, the local police interviewed no fewer than four hundred people."

D'Hondt nervously rearranged his tie and released his adam's apple from his pinching collar.

"And they're still interviewing," he said. "Someone has to have seen something, surely!"

"If we assume that the boy was kidnapped near Boudewijn Park," Hannelore observed matter-of-factly, "then what about the bicycle?"

"Mr. Vanmaele took it apart to the last bolt. Nothing, zero. All we know for sure is that it's the boy's bike. And we questioned people near Oostkamp where it was found," D'Hondt added despondently. "I presume efforts to hunt down the young kidnapper also failed to produce results," he scoffed.

"That's what I was trying to explain yesterday, Captain."

Van In was, by now, tired and highly combustible. "On the face of it, the kidnappers have taken a number of incredible risks. If we presume they're not being protected by some kind of magic force, then we have to face the fact that the entire operation has been prepared with precision. Long-legs is safe and sound, believe you me. We shouldn't underestimate the brain behind all this."

"I wholeheartedly agree." Beheyt suddenly woke up. "According to my profile, based among other things on the two faxes, the older kidnapper must certainly have enjoyed a university education. If you ask me, he's an engineer or a mathematician. I wouldn't be surprised if he specialized in probability calculus or statistics. I also think we're looking for someone who has spent several years as a sort of recluse, living well outside the city. It would surprise me if he was actually capable of violence."

Van In nodded in agreement. D'Hondt didn't quite understand where Beheyt was getting all this information.

"I don't have a crystal ball," said Beheyt. "We imported profiling from the States. The FBI organizes an annual course for foreign police agencies. I've just completed such a course and I can assure you, I was just as surprised as you at first."

"To what extent is such a profile reliable?" Van In was curious to know.

"In a lot of cases the broad lines are amazingly accurate, although we have to account for the fact that we're dealing with Americans. Europeans tend to be a little less predictable."

"So what makes you think that the older man is a mathematician or a statistician?" Hannelore asked. "If you're right, and we presume the man is older than seventy, then we only have to call a couple of universities. I can't imagine there were too many math or statistics graduates in the nineteen forties."

"That sounds like an excellent idea, Miss," said Beheyt. "But let me answer your question. The entire procedure followed in both the attack on the jeweler and the abduction suggests that what we would call risks are in fact measured and deliberate steps in their plan. If I'm wrong, then according to the laws of probability they would have to have made at least one mistake, perhaps more. Take the attack on the jeweler. They went to work before midnight in a brightly lit space. They had to have known that someone would see them." Beheyt rummaged through his papers and pulled out a couple of pages.

"The Dutch couple and the other witness described the older man in very different ways, but the only thing they agreed on was his long gray hair. Everyone knows that the majority of men over seventy have short hair or are either balding or bald. The long gray hair is far too conspicuous. I'm pretty certain it was part of a disguise. We can also say the same about the young man's beard, another point on which the witnesses were agreed."

Beheyt peered around the room with a look of victory on his face.

"And there's plenty more where that came from. Commissioner Van In should be congratulated for anticipating a number of my conclusions intuitively."

"Thank you, Professor."

Van In decided to thoroughly revise his opinion of the professor. Hannelore beamed and D'Hondt bit his nails.

"I'll order my men to call the universities immediately," said Van In with enthusiasm.

"And if he lives in the countryside, it might make sense to check if any remote properties have been rented out short-term in the last couple of weeks," D'Hondt said, determined to show that he had a contribution to make.

"The professor said he's been living in the countryside for some time. If he's holding the boy in his own home, we haven't got a snowball's chance of locating the place unless we identify the man first," said Van In in what came close to an arrogant tone. "And don't forget, he's alone with the boy. He'll probably stay holed up for the next few days. If the house looks occupied, no one will suspect anything."

"But no one knows if he's alone. There might be other people involved."

D'Hondt was nervous, and nervous people say stupid things.

"Out of the question," said Beheyt, flatly putting an end to the discussion.

Now it was Van In's turn to explain Charlotte Degroof's hypothetical diagnosis to the others.

"Versavel and his men are calling round the university hospitals. A five-man team has taken responsibility for the other major hospitals."

"How long have you known this?" D'Hondt snorted.

"Since last night, Captain."

"And you waited until now to tell us. I thought we had agreed to contact one another if there were new developments."

"I have a couple of photocopies to make," said Beheyt, not interested in witnessing an exchange of words between Van In and D'Hondt.

The situation frustrated him enormously. As an expert, all he could do was draft a hypothetical profile of the perpetrators and wait. Maybe he had been a little too quick to draw conclusions. No further negotiations were planned with the kidnappers. His job was done, more or less. The rest was in the hands of the detectives.

If he had had to choose between the orthodox Van In and the proud local police captain, he would have opted for Van In, no competition.

"Have you scheduled a visit with the parents later?" asked Hannelore. She sensed that D'Hondt was about to explode, and she wanted to alleviate some of the tension. D'Hondt got the hint and reluctantly made himself scarce.

"Deleu's with them right now," she added.

"Then they'll be in need of a visit," Van In grinned. "Poor bastards are having a hard enough time as it is."

Beheyt bumped into Versavel in the corridor. The sergeant almost knocked him over.

"A new tip has come in," he shouted before the door was fully open.

Versavel pointed to the phone. "We have a potential witness to the abduction on the line. You can take the call here."

Van In lunged at the telephone on his desk.

The witness told his story for the second time in less than fifteen minutes.

The day before around two P.M., he was driving on the ring road near Bruges's windmills. A couple of hundred yards before the traffic lights he noticed a Ford Transit belonging to the local police parked on the cycle path. He slowed down, thinking it was a speed trap. To his surprise, he saw a policeman rip off the reflective orange strip running along the side of the vehicle. It was only then that he realized that there was no light bar on top of the van and there was no sign of the police logo or the emergency number usually found on the sides. He thought it was a bit strange, so he checked in his rearview mirror after driving past.

The van had pulled onto the road, and he had seen an elderly man in civilian clothes at the wheel. The Ford Transit overtook him just after the lights.

"Was the policeman wearing glasses?" Van In asked.

"Yes."

"And he was taller than most," Van In repeated as the witness provided a reasonably good description of Daniel Verhaeghe. *Beheyt will be pleased*, he thought to himself. *The alleged policeman had no beard.*

The witness hadn't noted the vehicle's plates, but when Van In asked if there was anyone else in the Transit his answer was formal.

"No, just the old guy and the cop," he said with conviction.

Van In thanked the man and turned to the others.

"Now we know when and where."

"If what the witness saw had anything to do with the kidnapping," said D'Hondt.

Van In wanted to punch him. Why was the bastard so contrary?

"Shouldn't take long to check, Captain," Van In barked. "Or is it normal for bona fide policemen to screw around with their vehicles when they're on duty?"

"Listen here, Van In," D'Hondt hissed. "The way you've been handling this case is unprofessional, to say the least. But good, I can live with that. What I don't have to put up with are insults directed against me and my men."

"Insults," Van In snorted. "Everyone knows you need a lot more shit to mold one of your men than one of mine."

D'Hondt gritted his teeth and said nothing. Hannelore expected him to burst into flames at any minute. His face was bright red.

"Gentlemen, gentlemen. A little respect, if you don't mind."

De Kee was standing in the doorway dressed in a loose-fitting pinstriped suit. He looked as if he had just walked out of *The Untouchables*.

"Don't we have other fish to fry?"

Van In looked at Hannelore, and when she glanced furtively at De Kee he couldn't help smiling.

D'Hondt backed down with a stiff nod of the head.

"That's much better," said De Kee in a cheerful tone.

Beheyt reappeared with a pile of photocopies under his arm and chirped: "Are we having the meeting here?"

"Why not," said De Kee. "The public prosecutor sends his apologies and Colonel Verriest should have been here by now."

Van In sighed. He hated meetings. Everything had already been said, as far as he was concerned.

"Let's take a seat then, shall we," he suggested apathetically.

Fortunately, the discussion passed without incident. D'Hondt wisely kept his options open. Van In repeated his report of the events of the preceding week on De Kee's explicit request. He then suggested that a description of Long-legs should be given to the press. "Long-legs" had now been accepted by everyone concerned as the younger kidnapper's nickname.

"We can be reasonably certain that he'll be present at tomorrow's spectacle," Van In concluded.

Everyone appeared to agree, and Van In was happy that the most tiresome part of his day was behind him.

"Excellent," Beheyt concurred. "But allow me to add a final observation. In my opinion, the young man commissioner Van In has appropriately styled 'Long-legs' is suffering from depression and is exceptionally unbalanced. One might almost be inclined to think that the older man set up the abduction as a sort of 'live cinema' just to assuage Long-legs's volatile personality."

De Kee ran his fingers through his hair and D'Hondt scratched his head. Only Van In seemed surprised.

"Who knows, Professor Beheyt. Anything is possible in a case like this. But even if we manage to arrest Long-legs before tomorrow, it's not likely to change anything. The kidnapper's demands will remain the same."

"I'll have the Ford Transit checked out just to be sure," said D'Hondt decisively. The pig-headed policeman still didn't understand that his traditional approach wasn't going to produce results.

Van In wasn't in the mood for explaining things yet again. He wished everyone a fine morning and headed toward the door.

In the corridor he bumped into Versavel.

"Any news from the university hospitals?" he asked in passing.

"It's Sunday, and the doctors we've managed to speak to have all pulled the professional confidentiality card. They're only willing to cooperate if we provide a name."

"And the other hospitals?"

Versavel shook his head.

"Do you really think this is going to get us anywhere?"

"Probably not, Guido, but keep trying all the same and don't forget to put it all down on paper."

Versavel nodded understandingly. He knew from experience that policemen always surrounded themselves with mountains of paperwork if a case was in danger of unraveling.

"What's your next step?"

"A visit to the parents. There's still a pile of work to be done before tomorrow's bonfire and I want to have another word with Degroof senior," said Van In with a secretive smile. "And don't forget they're still saddled with Deleu."

"As if they didn't have enough problems," Versavel laughed.

"One last thing, Guido." Van In turned. "Keep an eye on D'Hondt, will you? Tell him he's responsible for keeping order tomorrow on Zand Square."

"Your word is my command."

Van In raised his hand and went on his way.

"Hey, Commissioner. Aren't you forgetting someone?" he heard Versavel call from behind.

Hannelore came shuffling along the corridor, her tight miniskirt forcing her to take short steps.

"That's a new one! Commissioner Van In wants to take off on his own." Hannelore grumbled. "Couldn't you wait just a minute? Or don't you want my company?"

"Secrecy," he whispered with his finger on his lips. "Didn't we agree to act normally in public?" he grinned.

"I'm following you for professional reasons," she snorted. "Don't read anything into it."

"Okay, but let's make a move before D'Hondt gets the same idea."

When they arrived at the scene, Van In had to ask a motor officer to ride ahead of him down Bishop Avenue. As he had predicted, the chic neighborhood was crawling with outside broadcast units, satellite dishes, camera crews, and photographers. Curious onlookers had also formed a serious crowd to contend with.

Degroof's neighbors had become world-famous overnight, their testimony being the only thing worth broadcasting at that moment in time. On Professor Beheyt's advice, Patrick and Charlotte Delahaye had decided not to speak to the press.

When Van In and Hannelore finally reached the bungalow and stepped out of their car, they were immediately surrounded by a swarm of microphone-carrying mosquitoes.

"They'll be offering you a contract next," Van In teased. "You're just as good-looking as Judge Ancia."

"Just as good-looking," she sneered. "You can't be serious. Anyway, maintaining professional standards has nothing to do with looks. Véronique Ancia is a career woman, and so am I!" she huffed.

They elbowed their way through a forest of cameras and padded microphones. Once they were behind the barriers, Van In heaved a sigh of relief. He didn't envy the celebrities who had to deal with this sort of craziness every day of their lives.

"I wonder what it's going to be like tomorrow," said Hannelore. In contrast to Van In, she appeared to be enjoying the circus, if only a little.

Charlotte had seen them arrive and had opened the door for them.

"Come inside, Commissioner. And you too, Ms. Martens," she said as if they were expected for dinner. She looked gaunt and pale. Her carelessly applied makeup failed to conceal the inner chaos. She was like a zombie.

"My husband will join us soon. He's resting," she said mechanically. The house was bathed in an impersonal emptiness, as if desperation had taken material form. Today the designer interior looked like a bargain-basement version of a page out of *Better Homes and Gardens*.

"I'm afraid there's not much to report, ma'am," said Van In once inside the house.

"The hospitals?" she asked, her voice wavering. She had clamped on to her hypothesis like a baby gorilla to its mother.

"We're making the calls, ma'am, but try not to build your hopes up. The bastards haven't given us enough time for an in-depth inquiry."

There was no sense in pulling the wool over her eyes. Poor coordination had cost them a great deal of time endlessly ruminating over the same limited evidence.

"Is Commissioner Deleu still here?" Van In deliberately changed the subject.

"He's with Daddy in the garden. I was just about to make a pot of coffee. Can I tempt you?"

"You certainly can, ma'am."

Van In felt sorry for Charlotte Degroof, but he also admired her for the grace with which she carried her burden. Beheyt had explained to him that the parents of kidnapped children often experienced an unnatural sort of high in the first twenty-four hours after an abduction. The real pain came much later. He compared the situation with a man who has accidentally cut off his finger. First there's blood everywhere, then he realizes he's cut off his finger, and only then does he feel the pain.

"There's still some cognac left over from yesterday," Charlotte added with a melancholic smile.

"And why not, ma'am," Van In quipped.

As she made her way to the kitchen area, Van In noticed she wasn't wearing a bra. He cursed himself for noticing and staring against his will.

"Mrs. Delahaye!"

"Yes, Commissioner?"

"Has your father been here long?"

"Daddy spent the night here."

She sounded surprised at his question. Hannelore wondered why he wanted to know.

The sliding doors that gave out onto the terrace and the back yard were wide open. A gentle breeze stirred the curtains. The unmistakable smell of freshly mown grass mixed with kerosene drifted into the room. Delahaye had gotten up that morning at five-thirty to mow the lawn, and none of the neighbors had complained about the noise.

As they made their way out onto the terrace, Patrick Delahaye slid open the bedroom window. In contrast to the day before, he was wearing threadbare jogging pants and a T-shirt with the logo of the company of which he was a director and a shareholder. He was unshaven and his eyes were sunken and dull. He came to meet them barefoot.

Van In shook the man's limp and listless hand. He seemed to be on the verge of a nervous breakdown. It wouldn't be long before the protective elation Beheyt had told him about disappeared. He was going to need the professor's help. Without it he was never going to be in a fit state to "pay" his son's ransom the following day.

Degroof senior was sitting on a stool, his back straight, his tie knotted flawlessly.

"Commissaire, Madame," he said with a sparing nod of the head.

Deleu was scribbling enthusiastically and barely made the effort to say hello.

Van In had no idea what he was writing so frenetically. He sat down next to Degroof and pensively rubbed his nose trying to figure out his opening line. He had to admit yet again that the Bruges special investigations department had no experience with this sort of case.

The public tended to believe that some ingenious system swung into action when there were crimes to be solved. In the soaps and the movies, criminals always left conspicuous clues behind; either that or some star witness appeared at the last minute. Reality, of course, was quite different. The majority of crimes were solved by accident or after months of detailed and methodical detective work. Van In had been given no more than forty-eight hours, almost half of which had now expired.

Success in kidnap cases often depends on a tip from the criminal underworld. The procedure is simple. The police carry out arbitrary raids until someone gets fed up and makes an anonymous phone call. There are two reasons for this: real criminals don't like kidnappings, and raids in gambling joints and brothels are bad for business. Money in their world is more important that solidarity.

But Van In had no evidence at his disposal that could demonstrate a link between the abduction and organized crime. The kidnappers were working alone. That was the only thing he was sure about.

"Are Mr. and Mrs. Delahaye's statements ready?" he asked, suddenly authoritarian. Even Degroof momentarily raised his eyebrows. Deleu watched him like a hyena waiting for its prey to give up the ghost.

"Can I please have a look?" Van In insisted when Deleu didn't respond to his question. He enjoyed making a fool of Deleu, but this time it was a delaying tactic. He still wasn't sure how to approach Degroof senior.

Hannelore could feel Degroof looking at her. The sun's slanting rays filled the room, and she was aware that they made her blouse almost see-through.

Deleu muttered an incomprehensible curse and reached for his expensive briefcase.

"Your silence leads me to presume there has been no progress," Degroof snapped.

Jesus H. Christ, Van In thought. He's on to me. Deleu handed him a pile of papers.

"I'm afraid I can't deny it, Mr. Degroof. That's why I'm here. I think it makes sense to deal with the question of the ransom first. If something new surfaces between now and tomorrow, we can always adjust our plans."

"Fine," Degroof snorted. "So what do you propose?"

Van In glanced at the first lines of the official report on which Deleu—as usual—had wasted so much time and effort.

"Mrs. Delahaye will be here in a moment. I prefer both parents to be present."

Degroof winced like a diver being stung by an electric eel. Delahaye could hardly believe his eyes. His father-in-law wasn't used to being put in his place.

But Van In couldn't back off. He had made a major decision that night. If he was right, Degroof senior would soon be changing his tune. And if he was wrong, he could look forward to a new career as a parking attendant.

A chilly silence settled on the terrace as Van In leafed through the report. Deleu's pompous prose didn't make him any wiser. He hadn't expected it to.

During the holidays, Bertrand went skating on Thursdays and Saturdays at the Boudewijn Park ice rink. In the month of July he was forced to use roller-skates because the management considered it too expensive to keep the ice rink functional in hot weather. On Thursday afternoons he always went with a friend, but on Saturday mornings he went alone. He usually got back at two in the afternoon. He would stay later on occasion, but neither of his parents had let it worry them. The remainder of the report described events from the reception of the first fax to the arrival of the police. The hypothesis that Bertrand was prone to a practical joke now and then and may have set up the whole thing to needle his parents had been undermined by the testimony of the driver who spotted the camouflaged patrol van and provided a detailed description of Long-legs.

Bertrand lay on his bed. It was stifling hot in the chalet and he had taken off his T-shirt. The old man had gone to get a bottle of lemonade. He had been gone ten minutes, and Bertrand was beginning to wonder what had happened to him.

They had played three games, and his opponent had turned out to be exceptionally strong. He stared at the pieces on the board. As the man was now playing, he was going to need four moves at most to beat him, and Bertrand smelled a rat. Was he letting him win on purpose? He rehearsed his strategy. Whatever the old man tried, he could checkmate him in four moves and that was too good to be true.

The chessboard occupied his attention for the best part of fifteen minutes. It was only then that he started to feel uneasy.

He yanked at the chain out of sheer frustration. The protective foam under the handcuff began to irritate him. His wrist had swollen in the heat. He threw himself on the bed in desperation and stared at a passing cloud through the dormer window with tears in his eyes.

The last thing he needed was to panic. He decided to count to a hundred and then start to scream.

He listened carefully to the sounds in the house as he counted. Maybe the old man had fallen asleep. Maybe the lemonade was gone and he'd gone to the store for more. By why hadn't he said anything?

In the distance Bertrand heard a truck struggling to accelerate. The wind rustled in the bushes outside and a couple of sparrows chirped in the roof gutter. But inside the house there was an eerie silence: no shuffling footsteps, no creaking hinges, no clatter of cups and plates. Bertrand emptied the lukewarm bottle of lemonade. It tasted awful. He gave up the count at 78, stood in the middle of the room as close to the door as he could, formed a bullhorn round his mouth with his hands, and started to yell.

"Hello, mister, wake up, mister . . . wake up!" He waited for a moment and then repeated the same thing every thirty seconds.

But there was no reaction, not even after the hundredth time.

Bertrand was soaked in sweat. His throat was sore from shouting and all he could manage was a hoarse whisper. Trembling with rage, he jumped onto the bed and started to yank at the chain until he gasped for breath and fell forward, hurting his head on the wall. He sobbed and buried his face in the pillow.

When he had cried himself out, he sat upright on the bed. Bertrand had his mother's character. No matter what the problem, there was always an answer, she had told him often enough. But if you lose heart you don't stand a chance. He tried to think, to stay calm. He looked at his watch and jumped. It was only ten to nine. The house was probably far from civilization. Kidnappers always choose a lonely place to hold their victims.

Victims, brrr, what a scary word. The house had to be far from the main road, otherwise they would have gagged him.

Bertrand kept his head up until the middle of the afternoon.

Panic, like fear, hits you unawares. It engulfs you like a wave and can reduce even the single-minded to a jabbering miserable wreck. The relative calm of the first hours of his abduction had been due to the haloperidol, but Bertrand was unaware of the fact. The old man had left him behind and God alone knew when he'd be back. Maybe he had wanted to punish him for his insolent behavior. Or for beating him at chess. The boy concocted the weirdest explanations.

In the afternoon he had trouble with dizziness. His dry tongue felt like sandpaper on his chapped lips. The temperature in the room was unbearable. The foam around his wrist had caused an irritating rash. In desperation he tried to sleep, but the tears filled his eyes once again and all he could do was repeat the word "mommy" under his breath.

Charlotte served coffee without a word, placed the bottle of Otard next to Van In, and sat down.

"What if we had photographs made of the paintings?" Deleu suggested. "We could have them printed on canvas and use the original frames. No one would notice the difference."

"Out of the question," Charlotte snapped. She glared first at Deleu and then at Van In, as if she expected him to put Deleu in his place.

"The kidnappers are a step ahead of us on that," said Van In. "Why do you think they insisted that Mr. Delahaye scratch a strip of paint from each canvas?"

Deleu was stupid, but for some strange reason it didn't bother Van In that day. He had in fact had the same idea himself.

"If there had been more time we could perhaps have had copies made," he said.

Delahaye scratched nervously at his unshaven chin. Van In was right. The kidnappers had left them no choice. He had worried himself sick the night before, trying to come up with an alternative.

"I think we should first arrange matters for tomorrow," said Van In. "But in the meantime I have a question. What do we do if we manage to arrest Long-legs before the bonfire?"

"What do you mean, Commissioner?" asked Delahaye, in spite of the fact that he understood Van In perfectly.

"Do we continue, or do we wait?"

"No waiting," Charlotte whispered, her voice hoarse. This time, the rage in her eyes was intended for Van In.

"Relax, sweetheart," said Delahaye. "The commissioner is convinced they won't touch a hair on Bertrand's head, even if we don't hand over the paintings." He used the expression "hand over" because he couldn't bring himself to say "burn."

"I'm sorry, Mr. Delahaye, but that's not what I said. I told you I was convinced they wouldn't carry out their threats.

Professor Beheyt agrees with me on the question, but we can never be one hundred percent certain. There's always a possibility they might panic."

"Enough! I refuse to allow my grandson to be put at the slightest risk," Degroof cut in, sparks flying from his eyes. Hannelore could see that he was ready to skin his son-in-law alive. Delahaye's questionable attitude left her at a loss. *Jesus,* she thought, *we're talking about your own son!*

"Okay."

Van In slammed the table with the flat of his hand.

"Whatever happens, we don't call off the bonfire, unless young Bertrand is found before then and brought to safety. All agreed?"

"Of course we all agree," Charlotte snarled.

"Good. Then here's the procedure. Tomorrow at seven A.M., four men will come and collect the paintings in an armored vehicle. Mr. Delahaye will accompany them. They're expecting a serious crowd on Zand Square and we have to be sure he gets through."

Van In poured himself a drop of cognac and lit his first cigarette of the day.

"I presume the paintings are ready for transport."

"I put them all in the guest bedroom earlier this morning. I didn't need to wrap them, did I?"

Her words were close to comical. But only one thing mattered as far as Charlotte was concerned: the safe return of her son.

Van In smoked another three or four cigarettes as they discussed the details. Hannelore kept a close eye on him. It was only when Degroof got to his feet and announced that he had a couple of things to take care of at home that Van In made his move.

"There might be one other way to get the young man free before tomorrow," he said abruptly.

Delahaye's jaw dropped and Charlotte almost knocked over her cup. Deleu, who was on the point of going to the toilet, was glued to the spot.

"I hope this isn't some kind of tasteless joke," said Degroof, his tone frosty.

"Nothing of the sort, Mr. Degroof. As a matter of fact, the success of my plan depends entirely on your cooperation."

Degroof turned pale around his nose, and Van In realized there was no turning back.

"Don't be a fool, man," Degroof snorted. "Of course you have my cooperation, although I've no idea what I can do to help you. But you only have to ask."

Van In emptied his glass in a single gulp.

"In that case, Mr. Degroof, I would like to have a word with you in private."

Charlotte was on the point of tears, and a sparkle of hope glistened in Delahaye's eyes.

"Perfect timing, Commissioner," Degroof snapped. "Let me have my chauffeur collect us. We can talk at my place."

16

THE AIR-CONDITIONING IN DEGROOF'S LIMOUSINE was working perfectly. With the assistance of a motor officer, his chauffeur piloted the Mercedes deftly around the vehicles parked criss-cross the length of the street. In spite of the low temperature, Degroof dabbed his forehead with a paper handkerchief.

Van In knew he had the upper hand.

He lit a cigarette without asking and peered out of the window. Degroof understood that Van In didn't want the chauffeur listening to their conversation. During the short journey, he used up half a pack of tissues, crumpling a fresh one every few seconds and tossing it on the floor.

The house on Spinola Street, a tasteless neo-renaissance edifice, looked neglected on the outside.

"Is your wife at home?" asked Van In when they reached the front door. Degroof jammed the key in the keyhole and turned it with an angry gesture.

"My wife has nothing to do with this affair. She's severely handicapped. I would appreciate it if you would keep her out of it."

"Was it for her that you came home?" In normal circumstances, he wouldn't have dared ask such a question.

Degroof muttered something incomprehensible that was meant to pass for a yes, but didn't react in the slightest to Van In's indiscreet curiosity.

"Come inside, Commissioner," was all he said.

The black-and-white tiled entrance was even colder than the air-conditioned Mercedes. There was an overpowering smell of musty clothes, brown soap, and cheap soup. Oval portraits of respectable gentlemen and white-powdered ladies lined the walls above the oak panelwork.

A colossal stairwell with a wrought-iron art deco banister led to the first floor. The two latticed windows that gave out onto Spinola Street allowed precious little light into the room. A Liege Louis XV grandfather clock towered between them.

Van In followed Degroof through a double door that was close to ten feet tall. The corridor behind it was even gloomier. There were three doors on either side, symmetrically apportioned along the length of the corridor. A threadbare runner graced the floor.

So this is where it all happened, Van In thought to himself and shivered.

Degroof opened the second door on the right and stepped back to allow Van In to enter first.

"Take a seat, Commissioner. I'll be right with you."

Degroof's departing footsteps sounded hollow and echoed down the long corridor. *He didn't walk on the carpet*, Van In observed unconsciously.

Degroof had shown him into the lounge, a room that was probably much the same as the others in the house. It was furnished with old-fashioned furniture and was almost as tall as it was broad, Van In figured. In several places, the obligatory stuccowork that often adorned the ceilings of such houses was damp and covered in mildew. The smell was worse than in the hallway.

Van In made his way instinctively to the fireplace, a hideous concoction of kitsch tiles, faded bas-reliefs, and bronze lion heads. But he was more interested in what was on the mantelpiece. Dozens of photos in ornate frames with Ghislain in a sailor suit, Charlotte on skis in front of an impressive mountain chalet, and Benedicta prostrate on the floor making her perpetual monastic vows. He did not see a picture of Aurelie or Nathalie.

Between the photos of the children he discovered Degroof's wedding photo. It was yellow with age but still crystal-clear. The young Baroness de Puyenbroucke was wearing a simple dress and a ridiculous voile turban. They were standing side by side, both stiff as a post. Degroof was clearly recognizable in his top hat and tails. His hair was now a little thinner and his cheeks now hung in fleshy crescent moons just below the corners of his mouth, but the years had been relatively kind to him. He had maintained his stiff demeanor together with his sharp jaw line and sparkling eyes. The baroness's head was turned to one side as if she was looking for a line of escape.

Van In tried to imagine her without the old-fashioned hat and in the tight outfit Hannelore had been wearing the first time she came to his house. There was little doubt that Elisa de Puyenbroucke had been an exceptionally beautiful woman.

"Sorry for keeping you waiting. My wife is very sick and I wanted to check in on her."

"And is she on the mend?"

Degroof stood beside him. In his own familiar surroundings he seemed a great deal more vulnerable.

"Her condition has been stable for the last few days. She knows nothing of the kidnapping, of course."

"I understand," said Van In.

Degroof took the photo of Benedicta from the mantelpiece and slowly shook his head.

"As you can see, I've had nothing but misfortune with my children."

Van In was taken aback by his spontaneous candidness.

"Misfortune?" he echoed.

"Yes, Commissaire, although it might not be so obvious at first sight. When we were in the car it suddenly became clear to me why you wanted to speak to me in private. I presume you've heard a thing or two about me in the last couple of weeks, things, shall we say, that can't bear the light of day."

Degroof appeared to be unashamed of his dirty secret.

"You might say that," said Van In, maintaining his cool.

"But before I continue, I would like to thank you for your discretion. You could have gone public with this information, but you didn't."

Van In nodded, not quite sure how to respond. He wasn't planning to tell the man that Hannelore Martens knew as much as he.

"Come."

Degroof gestured in the direction of the chesterfields with a stiff old-fashioned bow and a sweep of the hand. He fetched a couple of cognac snifters and a half-full bottle of Rémy Martin from a modern cabinet with interior lighting.

"You appreciate a good glass, if I'm not mistaken," he said with a limp smile. They sat opposite one another, and Degroof poured two generous measures.

"So, I presume you've spoken to my youngest daughter," he said cautiously.

"Yes," Van In lied.

"As I thought."

The old man waltzed his cognac.

"And do you believe the rumors she's been circulating?"

"I also visited your eldest daughter," said Van In evasively.

"Aurelie," Degroof sighed. "And you probably think I had her locked up because she refused to have an abortion."

"That's what people are saying," said Van In, taking a quick sip of cognac.

"Do you know that they even approached Benedicta in the monastery with their disgusting claims? She attempted suicide a couple of days ago. One of the sisters was concerned when she didn't appear in the chapel for daily mass and found her in the nick of time. She had almost bled to death."

There wasn't much left of Degroof's authoritarian voice. The man clearly had a lump in his throat.

"She's locked away in the monastery of Les Soeurs de Beth-léem in Marche-les-Dames, the strictest monastic order in the world. They're not allowed contact with the outside world. When someone enters the monastery, all family ties are severed. They remain in the monastery until they die."

The old man was clearly in difficulty. His voice faltered.

"It's quite exceptional for the monastery prioress to contact the family of one of the sisters. Even if one of them is terminally ill, they're not in the habit of informing the family. But when she found the letters in her cell, she broke the silence. I had my chauffeur collect them."

Degroof rummaged in his jacket pocket and handed Van In the letters from Daniel Verhaeghe.

"They had a priest at the monastery this week, a young man, tall with thick glasses," he explained. "Benedicta is an extremely sensitive girl, a little melancholic like her mother. The bastards took advantage of it."

Van In cast a quick eye over the letters and was inclined to agree with Degroof. This was the lowest of the low.

"But why did she try to commit suicide?" Van In asked in a tone that suggested he was convinced the letters were full of lies.

"Aurelie poisoned her mind long ago with a whole host of absurd stories. They were inseparable back then. Aurelie lived in a world of fantasy and she drew her sister into it. She also ran away from home as Nathalie did. Aurelie was sexually frustrated. She needed the company of young men, and I thought she was too young."

"Were you a strict father?"

"I think I was," Degroof mused. "But it was expected in those days. I raised Charlotte in precisely the same way. Does she resent it?"

He said nothing about Ghislain. Admitting that his son was gay must have been too much for him. He had probably never come to terms with the idea.

"Aurelie married the first loser she came across when she was twenty-one, and she did it to hurt me and nothing more."

"You couldn't prevent her marrying because she'd come of age."

"Precisely," said Degroof relieved. "I disinherited her and I would do the same again today."

"But it didn't take long before she came back to you looking for help?"

"You're well informed, Commissaire. Tant mieux. Elisa, my wife, begged me to take her back and I did, under certain conditions of course. As I had predicted, her marriage hit the rocks when her husband discovered she didn't have a penny to her name. She was covered in bruises when we took her back in. Everything went relatively well for six months, but then she reverted to her old lifestyle. She spent night after night in the bars, went to bed with whoever would have her, and ended up pregnant. I lost my temper and insisted she have an abortion. Aurelie became hysterical at that point. She ran into the kitchen, grabbed a breadknife, and attacked me."

Degroof unbuttoned his shirt and pulled up his undershirt. His wrinkled belly was covered with white scars.

"A doctor friend stitched me up. I told everyone I'd had my appendix removed. The last thing I wanted to do was report my own daughter to the police."

As Degroof senior continued his story, Van In sensed his original hypothesis crumble like a sandcastle at high tide.

"She fooled her sisters into believing that she had finally taken revenge on me, and made up a story about me raping her almost every day from her eleventh to her seventeenth."

Degroof took a serious mouthful of Rémy Martin.

"She drove a wedge between her sisters and me and assured them she had said nothing about her past in an effort to protect them. She told them they would have met the same fate if they had given anything away or hadn't accommodated my wishes."

Degroof looked Van In in the eye as if to say he was telling the truth.

"That's when I decided to have her committed, and the psychiatrists treating her agreed. They even accused me of waiting far too long. My wife was extremely upset by the entire tragedy. She's never been the same since. She pined away and started to neglect our youngest daughter. I was forced to look on in sadness as Nathalie went astray. I was abroad a lot in those days and couldn't devote time to her upbringing. She was an addict by the age of fifteen. She left two years later, calling me a disgusting bastard and assuring me I'd never get the chance to lay a hand on her. I could only guess who had filled her mind with such nonsense."

Van In heaved a heavy sigh. Degroof senior's story hadn't simplified matters by any stretch of the imagination. Van In had expected something completely different and no longer knew what to think of the dignified and unbending man in front of him.

"I presume you were told another story," said Degroof as he looked Van In in the eye once again.

"I wasn't planning to discuss that with you," said Van In evasively. "But I still think there's a connection between your past and the situation we're now in, albeit at a different level."

Degroof feigned surprise, but not very well.

"I'm all ears, Commissaire."

Van In cleared his throat.

"When your son fell victim last week to a rather bizarre break-in, I immediately thought of revenge. It also became clear soon enough that the perpetrators had been able to rely on the support of someone within the family."

Degroof listened without flinching. If he knew anything, he was certainly not letting it show.

"The burglars knew the code to the alarm, but they needed explosives to get into the safe."

"Yes," said Degroof.

"According to your son, the safe combination hasn't been changed in twenty years. Both you and your son knew it by heart. You had just turned sixty when the safe was installed. The alarm system, by contrast, was only fitted seven years ago or thereabouts, when you were seventy-three."

Degroof nodded.

"Ghislain knows I have difficulty remembering numbers. The older one gets, the quicker one forgets the simplest things. Ghislain suggested a code I would never be able to forget."

"Your date of birth?"

"Correct, Commissaire: nineteen zero five. I was born on May 19, 1914."

"Your son claims that you and he were the only ones who knew the combination of the safe. Is the same true of the code to the burglar alarm, Mr. Degroof?"

Degroof was visibly taken aback.

"Ghislain made the suggestion at a Christmas party. We had all been drinking and . . ."

"The entire family was gathered round the table," Van In completed his sentence.

"Precisely," said Degroof. "Everyone must have heard it, although there was rather a lot of noise."

"Is Nathalie still in touch with the family?"

"Commissaire, you're not trying to suggest that one of my children is responsible for this masquerade?"

"Your wife sends her money."

Degroof bowed his head.

"I know, Commissaire. But so does Charlotte, and apparently she and my daughter-in-law Anne-Marie go out together on occasion."

"So she had opportunity enough?"

"But I still find it hard to believe. Why would she do such a thing? She has nothing to gain from it, and Nathalie only needs one thing and that's money."

Degroof folded his arms and sat there for a couple of seconds looking like a punished schoolboy.

"Perhaps she sold the alarm code to the burglars," said Van In softly. "And I have a couple of questions to ask about them too."

The truth was out. If he screwed it up now, he was going to look like a complete idiot.

"I strongly suspect that you know the perpetrators. But what I don't understand is why you're covering for them."

Degroof didn't start to rant and rave. He froze.

"So I wasn't wrong about you after all, Commissaire."

Van In blinked. He had expected a completely different reaction.

"May I ask how you reached your conclusion, Commissaire?"

He was never going to forget the sense of victory that tore through his head like a rush of pure cocaine. Finally one of the untouchables was going to have to admit that he, Pieter Van In, was correct.

"The Templars' Square," he said, cool and poised. "I thought it was a cryptic message, that its solution might shed light on what motivated the perpetrators. But that wasn't it, was it? It was a signature, intended for you alone."

Degroof heaved himself out of his chair and filled the glasses.

"Your health, Commissaire."

He held out his glass and they clinked like old allies.

"I do indeed know the man. We studied together in Leuven and he was my closest friend. We were both fascinated by all things alchemical and esoteric. We spent nights on end discussing the writings of Blavatsky, Papus, De Guiata, Steiner, Crowley, the Egyptian mystery schools, the neo-Platonists, and the Templars. The Latin square was a shared secret. We swore an oath that we would never talk about it with anyone else. When I received a letter full of threats a couple of weeks ago, I realized right away it was from Aquilin Verheye."

"He warned you in advance," Van In noted. "And you paid no attention."

Degroof burst into a hoarse laugh.

"At the time I did, Commissaire. I took the letter very seriously indeed. You should know that when we were young, Aquilin and I fell in love with the same girl. She loved him infinitely more than she loved me, but the de Puyenbroucke family chose fortune over love. They had the name and my father had the money, a lot of money. Elisa, who had little choice in the matter, became Mrs. Degroof. Aquilin was distressed beyond words, and he swore he would avenge the injustice."

Van In shook his head. "But that was more than fifty years ago," he said, finding it hard to believe. "Your friend Aquilin must be roughly the same age as you."

"He's two days older," Degroof smirked. "But even if he was a hundred, I still wouldn't dare to underestimate him. And if I hadn't known him so well, I would indeed have paid no attention to that ridiculous threatening letter. Aquilin Verheye was a fanatic. Every student knew back then that he never went back on a promise and he never made empty threats. I could tell you a few stories, Commissaire. Your hair would stand on end."

Degroof had gotten to his feet and was pacing back and forth, his glass of cognac secure in his hand.

"I could have informed the police, of course, and had him prosecuted."

"But you didn't."

"No, I didn't, Commissaire. The Degroofs prefer to take care of their own problems. And don't forget, I had no substantial evidence."

"Did you ever hear from him prior to this?"

"No. I lost track of him after the wedding. I had no idea what had happened to him, so I hired a private detective to track him down."

"So that's why you didn't want to involve the police," Van In warbled. He now understood why he had at first fallen into Degroof's disfavor.

"Correct. When Ghislain called and told me what had happened, I immediately suspected Aquilin. Dissolving gold in aqua regis is just the kind of thing he would do. And because it all appeared so ludicrous, I wanted to contact him myself. Perhaps he had lost his mind, I thought; perhaps there was something I could do to help him."

"And did you succeed, Mr. Degroof?"

"Yes, I succeeded," said Degroof slowly. "The private detective delivered his report on Wednesday. Aquilin Verheye died two years ago. He's buried in a village in the Ardennes."

Degroof crossed to a dresser by the window and took a cardboard folder from one of the drawers.

"The detective was even kind enough to take a few photos of the grave."

Van In took the folder, which contained three large-format photos. The detective had first photographed the grave from a distance between the other graves, and had then made a couple of close-ups with a zoom lens. The text was perfectly legible: Aquilin Verheye. The dates of birth and death were a little less in focus, but the years were clear enough: 1914 and 1992. It was a simple bluestone memorial, probably the cheapest model.

"Do you now understand why I called in your help on Saturday?"

Van In wasn't sure if he should feel honored or fan the suspicion that was smoldering at the back of his mind.

"When my grandson was abducted and I knew that Aquilin had nothing to do with it, I wanted someone I could trust. I heard that you had given up part of your vacation to poke your nose into my family's past, and not without results it would seem."

"I can't see why my involvement would help avoid a potential scandal," said Van In, on his guard. He wasn't sure where Degroof senior was leading.

"Your discretion, Commissaire. Your discretion is what attracted me. It's a rare quality, Commissaire, one I rate highly and one I'm prepared to reward. You get my drift? Let's be frank, Commissaire, everyone likes a little luxury, a social life, a beautiful home. But not everyone can afford it."

Van In got his drift, all right. Degroof was a cunning old fox, and his offer was tempting. Shame Hannelore knew everything and was also involved.

"I've mixed with all sorts of people all my life, Commissaire, and many envy my ability to judge a person's character," said Degroof, his mood lighter.

"I don't doubt it, sir. But I fear my discretion won't be of much use to you. The identity of the letter-writer was my only clue thus far. I don't see how we can find a solution before morning. Our only hope is that our tall young friend will drop his guard, but even then it won't be enough to prevent the bonfire. And we might even be putting Bertrand's life at risk if we make an arrest."

"That's true, Commissaire. But what if he's spotted?"

"Then we'll shadow him discreetly," said Van In.

"Let's hope Bertrand is returned to us safe and sound," said Degroof. "Whatever happens, I insist that my grandson's safety be given the utmost priority. I'm counting on you for that, Commissaire. If you succeed, I'll be in your debt."

"We'll do our best," Van In grinned sheepishly.

"Another cognac, Commissaire?"

Van In checked his watch.

"Mmm. Why not," he said.

When someone knocked at his hotel room door, Daniel Verhaeghe jumped from the bed into his wheelchair.

"Come in," he shouted.

A spotlessly dressed waiter opened the door and wheeled the cart into the room.

"Would sir prefer to eat by the window?" he asked politely.

"If it's possible," said Daniel.

"Of course, sir."

The waiter pushed a table up against the window, leaving room for Daniel's wheelchair.

"Will that suffice, sir?"

Daniel nodded. The waiter draped a fine linen tablecloth over the table and arranged the silver-plated cutlery next to the plate. He made sure the bowls and dishes were close enough for Daniel to reach from his wheelchair.

"Enjoy your meal, sir, and if there's anything you need don't hesitate to call."

"I will. Thank you."

Daniel produced a one-hundred-franc note and slipped it to the waiter.

As soon as the man was gone, Daniel got to his feet and replaced the wheelchair with a normal chair. From his room on the hotel's third floor he had a magnificent view of Zand Square. He tucked in to a helping of smoked salmon while keeping a close eye on the various police vehicles turning into Hauwer Street. The manhunt continued unabated. The previous evening he had made his way from Bishop Avenue to Boeverie Street on his scooter. Boeverie Street ran parallel with the side of the Park Hotel where Laurent had reserved a room for him. The reporters had discovered his message at the appropriate moment and he was going to be just in time for the late evening news. He parked the scooter in front of the Franciscan friary and made his way to the dark blue Ford Transit parked nearby. He unloaded the electric wheelchair with the help of a plywood panel resting on the rear fender.

Laurent had informed the reception that the guest in room 306 was a wheelchair user and that he would be arriving late. The seat of the wheelchair had been lowered three inches so that Daniel's six feet ten inches would be less obvious. He also took off his glasses when he entered the hotel and waited until he was in his room before putting them on again.

A police patrol had called in at the hotel in the course of Sunday morning. Daniel had just parked himself in the hotel lounge, and he listened with bated breath as the receptionist informed the two officers that no one in the hotel matched their description.

Daniel thought back to the moment with an indescribable sense of euphoria. He poured himself a glass of Muscadet and replaced the empty plate of salmon with a plate of oysters.

Everything had gone like a house on fire thus far. Laurent had kept his promise. Daniel had been able to experience every phase of the plan at close quarters.

"The police will never find you," Laurent had assured him. "Unless they've read Edgar Allan Poe's *The Purloined Letter*. And even then they would never make the link between fiction and reality."

Laurent De Bock had a PhD in Applied Mathematics, defended on the basis of a dissertation titled *Methodological Complexity as Source of Inefficiency*. He had mathematically structured and scientifically analyzed what Poe had recounted in his intriguing story, and had succeeded in demonstrating that standard procedures were rarely successful when they were used to solve unique problems.

The apparent recklessness with which Laurent and Daniel operated had a single purpose: to confuse. The police were completely in the dark when it came to motive, making their actions against the Degroof family appear inexplicable. The only information the police had at their disposal was a vague description. Their investigations were focused on an exceptionally tall young man with glasses. But Laurent had in fact arranged it so to make it more exciting for Daniel.

When Daniel had finished his exquisite meal, he lit a cigarette and punched in the number of the chalet in Namur.

Bertrand heard the telephone ring. It was five-thirty. His eyes rolled in their sockets and his heart thumped visibly against his ribs. He screamed without making much noise and yanked hysterically at the chain. In spite of the foam, his wrist was badly cut. The sight of the blood made him nauseous.

He couldn't remember how long he had slept. The telephone had woken him with a start. His lips were chapped and his tongue blistered. *If someone doesn't let me out of here soon, I'm going to die of thirst*, he thought in a panic. The unnaturally high temperature in the room had left him soaked in sweat. He had once read that people rarely survived more than twenty-four hours in the desert without water. His situation was much the same. He had nothing to drink and was losing massive amounts of fluid.

Daniel let the phone ring for five minutes. Perhaps Laurent had gone to the bathroom or had ventured outside?

He smoked a couple of cigarettes and tried again.

By eight o'clock, he started to worry. Laurent had a weak heart. Maybe all this effort had been too much for him. A drive to Namur was too much of a risk, and Laurent himself had explicitly forbidden it.

"I've taken care of everything, my boy, down to the last detail. Nothing can go wrong. There's plenty of food and drink in the chalet," Laurent had insisted. "Whatever happens, stay in the hotel until I come and get you."

There must be something wrong with the phone, Daniel figured with naïve optimism. *If there's a problem with the line, it'll probably be Monday morning before it gets fixed*, he thought.

"I'll try again in the morning," he said, half out loud.

Hannelore had left half an hour before Degroof's chauffeur dropped Van In off at the bungalow. Bishop Avenue was a lot quieter. Most of the foreign TV crews had moved into hotels in the city and had relocated their hardware to Zand Square in readiness for the following morning's spectacle.

Van In looked worn out and Charlotte immediately offered
to make coffee. Only two policemen were still in attendance
outside, and when the coffee was ready she offered them a cup.

Van In installed himself in the garden. Charlotte joined him.

"Patrick's asleep," she whispered. "I gave him a couple of
sleeping pills; otherwise he won't make it through tomorrow."

"And what about you?"

Van In's tone was personal and intimate for a change, now
that he was no longer around the rest of the cops, and she didn't
appear to mind.

"I'm counting the minutes," she said, putting on a brave
face. "The only thing that worries me is the possibility that the
kidnappers are mentally disturbed, that they're playing a game
and have no intention of letting Bertrand go."

She raised her eyes to heaven. She didn't need tears to prove
her sadness.

A couple of hours earlier, Van In had assured her that there
was no need to worry about Bertrand being freed, but now he
was less certain. He drank his coffee. Their eyes met. She didn't
need to ask. Van In knew that he owed her an explanation.

"I'm afraid we haven't made much headway. I thought there
was an alternative way out," he said, taking his time.

She didn't ask what he had tried to do immediately, but
Van In could see the question in her eyes. A tear ran down her
cheek. She sobbed.

Then Van In did something he had never dared to do before:
he took her hand. He told her what he had discussed with her
father, and Charlotte listened without interrupting him.

"I had hoped I could persuade him to reveal the identity of
the perpetrator, but your father had already organized his own
investigation. The man he had suspected has been dead for two
years. He gave me photos of the gravestone."

Van In showed her the photos.

"Did your father ever abuse you sexually?" he asked, unexpectedly blunt.

She didn't jump at his question. Instead, she raised her head and wiped her tears.

"No," she said, without a flinch. This topic had been raised before, apparently.

"And your sisters?"

This time her answer took a little longer.

"I don't think so," she said with a sigh. "Everyone knows my father's a ladies' man, Commissioner. He even has a relationship going with my sister-in-law. My father arranged the marriage with Ghislain. That way, she was always around. But to be honest, I know nothing about Aurelie. She's never spoken to me about it. I was always away at boarding school."

"Did you know that Benedicta tried to commit suicide?"

This time she jumped.

"Did he tell you that?"

Van In nodded.

"One of the kidnappers, the younger of the two, managed to approach her in the monastery. Is it possible that she knew something?"

Charlotte was silent. Van In was overcome once again by an oppressive unease.

"Apparently the entire tragedy has to do with Aurelie. Your father claims she lost her mind when he forced her to have an abortion."

"Abortion? Aurelie never had an abortion! My father banished her to our country house in Loppem. That's where she had the baby. The local priest arranged for an adoptive family. She never forgave him for it. My father had her committed because her aggressiveness was getting out of control."

"Is this true?" asked Van In, barely able to control his excitement.

"Of course it's true!"

She sounded like a doctor refusing to back down after making a diagnosis.

"But what does it have to do with the abduction of Bertrand?"

There are moments when the solution to a problem presents itself in a flash and then turns gray all of a sudden before you have the chance to grasp its essence. Van In was familiar enough with the frustrating experience. He had to act quickly.

"I beg your pardon, ma'am, but I think we might finally have a tangible clue."

"Really, Commissioner?" was all Charlotte could manage.

She sat frozen to the spot as Van In rushed inside.

He called Hannelore, Public Prosecutor Lootens, and De Kee in that order.

In less than half an hour, the investigative machinery they had at their disposal was running flat out.

17

THE ELDERLY DOMESTIC ADMITTED VERSAVEL to the episcopal palace, astonishment written all over his face.

The bishop in person was waiting for him and brought him to the archives that had been housed for the last couple of years in refurbished stables at the back of the commanding mansion.

"The archivist is on his way," the bishop declared nervously. "Pity I can't be of personal assistance, but the archives are not my domain."

"No problem, your grace, I'll wait."

The archivist, a skeletal cathedral canon, arrived a couple of minutes later, puffing like a leaky bellows. He had run all the way from his home on High Street to the palace on Holy Ghost Street.

"1964," he wheezed. "Loppem. I don't have to check. Fernand Debrabandere was parish priest in Loppem from '63 to '72."

"Is he still alive?" asked Versavel, hoping for a positive answer.

"Let me think . . ."

The canon furrowed his brows and held his hand in front of his eyes. His memory was apparently not perfect. After a couple of seconds he rushed over to a metal filing cabinet and opened the bottom drawer.

"Debrabandere Georges, Debrabandere Adolf, Debrabandere Fernand."

He pulled the file from the drawer and opened it.

"Pastor in retirement since 1982. He lives with the Sisters of Mercy in Ruiselede," he crowed triumphantly.

The bishop produced a studied Pepsodent smile, the sort he saved for the faithful on feast days, and turned to Versavel with sparkling eyes. He hoped the media would appreciate the diocese's spontaneous cooperation after the successful resolution of the kidnapping.

Versavel contacted the station on Hauwer Street by radio and passed on the information.

"Perhaps your grace would be kind enough to contact the sisters in person."

Versavel caught himself striking an unctuous tone.

"Commissioner Van In insists that we question Father Debrabandere this evening. He's on his way to Ruiselede at this very moment in the company of Deputy Public Prosecutor Martens."

"But of course, Inspector."

"Sergeant, your grace," said Versavel. "I'm a sergeant."

Hannelore leaped at the telephone like a tiger when it rang that evening at seven-thirty.

She had spent the entire time moping over the stunt Van In had pulled with her. She found it hard to believe that the conversation with Degroof had lasted so long. If he had discovered something, why in God's name hadn't he called?

Van In was straining at the leash with impatience when she turned onto Bishop Avenue. The adrenaline pumped through his veins. He had never managed to force such a breakthrough in his entire career. But honesty also compelled him to add that he had never been confronted with a case of this magnitude in all his years in the Bruges police.

Van In felt reborn, liberated in one fell swoop from twenty years of routine. If he managed to successfully conclude the Degroof case, he could finally salvage some of his long-lost self-respect.

"Hi, Hannelore!" It was the most upbeat he had felt in years.

"Do you need a chauffeur, or am I allowed to join in properly this time?" she snarled, her mood an antidote to his good cheer.

Charlotte was taken aback by the way they interacted, but she didn't let it show. Van In was in such a euphoric mood that her sarcasm didn't bother him in the least.

"Let's call it a draw," he chirped. "Don't forget, you weaseled out on Friday in the interests of the inquiry."

Hannelore caught sight of Charlotte and bit her lip. They were acting like an old married couple.

"But at least I gave you a full report, Commissioner," she said, sounding a bit more formal.

"And you can expect the same from me, ma'am."

Charlotte accompanied them to the front door. The tempo of the investigation had picked up since earlier in the morning. Now she had the impression that something was actually happening.

"Don't wake your husband," said Van In. "Who knows, perhaps we'll have better news before morning."

Just before they walked out the door, Charlotte grabbed Van In by the arm and gave him a warm kiss on the cheek.

"Every success, Pieter. You can't imagine how much we'll be in your debt if you find our son alive and well."

Van In beamed, and he didn't fail to notice the short but nasty look from Hannelore.

"Ruiselede, and don't spare the horses," he said as Hannelore started the Twingo.

Versavel had just returned from his visit to the bishop and was waiting in the station's inner courtyard for them to pick him up. He had called Charlotte and knew they were on their way.

Sister Marie-Therese kept watch at the convent gate on mother superior's orders.

"Don't keep them waiting, whatever you do," the bishop had insisted. "The life of an innocent child may be at stake."

Hannelore steered her diminutive Renault at breakneck speed in the direction of Ruiselede, while listening carefully to Van In's slightly revised account of his meeting with Degroof. He made no mention of Degroof's bribe offer.

In the meantime, mother superior shepherded Father Debrabandere, the convent's spiritual director, with considerable urgency toward the front door. The poor man had already been in bed for an hour and she had had to push her powers of persuasion to their limits to convince the half-senile priest that the police visit was of exceptional importance.

"The bishop himself called," she had said when the stubborn clergyman protested. She deposited him in a chair in one of the parlors and hurried to join sister Marie-Therese at the gate. Five minutes and three Hail Maries later, Hannelore's Twingo tore around the corner into Pensionaat Street. The convent door swung open before she got out of the car.

"Walk this way," said the plain-spoken mother superior in what sounded like a cross between an order and a request.

"Father Debrabandere is still a little groggy. I think I should be present, given the circumstances . . . with your permission, of course," she added devoutly.

THE SQUARE OF REVENGE

Debrabandere was a quirky old clergyman. He had devoted his life to the Church, and as a priest he had instilled the faithful under his charge with awe. The simple among them had believed his every word, and the prominent among them had provided him with the necessary prestige.

He was now eighty-two. He had watched the Church slide from a mighty organization to a narrow-minded institution that had lost almost all of its credit.

Father Debrabandere had kept his promise of celibacy throughout his priestly life. But the whirlwind of renewal that had raged through the Church in recent years had ultimately driven him to the bottle. When the bishop concluded that he was no longer in control of his drinking, he banished him to the convent.

"I remember the incident well," said Debrabandere with a twinkle in his eye when Van In cautiously inquired about Aurelie Degroof's child. "Mr. Ludovic consulted me personally."

"And the child was probably placed with a family immediately after the birth? A Loppem family, I would imagine?"

Van In raised his voice. Mother superior had told him that the priest was hard of hearing.

"Absolutely," said Debrabandere. "I took care of it myself."

"And do you remember their name, Father?"

The elderly priest closed his eyes. Deep wrinkles appeared in the parchment skin of his forehead.

"Their name, Father," Van In insisted when the man remained silent.

Debrabandere's fleshy chin sagged to his chest.

"Don't fall asleep, Father. These people have come especially from Bruges. A boy has been kidnapped," said mother superior, shaking his shoulder. Debrabandere raised a single eyelid.

"Forgive me, sister," he mumbled. "My memory isn't what it was. But a good glass of Burgundy might help. I know that from experience."

Van In and Hannelore were perplexed and turned to mother superior. The sturdy sister was also at a loss.

"But Father," she protested. If Van In and Hannelore hadn't been there, she would have given him a good telling off, reminding him that the bishop's orders had been clear and unequivocal: no alcohol, not even on feast days.

"If a glass of wine can help, sister," said Hannelore impatiently.

"We urgently need this information," said Van In, piling up the pressure.

The sister was of two minds. The bishop's orders had indeed been clear, but he had also asked her to help the police in whatever way she could.

"All right, then," she sighed. "His grace will forgive me this once."

When she was gone, Debrabandere signaled that Van In and Hannelore should come closer.

"The family's name was Verhaeghe, Jan and Bea Verhaeghe. The lived on Station Street in Loppem back then. Jan was a teacher at the village school and Bea raised money for the missions. They were childless, but the Degroof child brought them enormous happiness," the elderly priest grinned.

"Are you sure?" asked Van In.

"Of course I'm sure. They left Loppem in 1966. The boy had health problems and they decided to move to the coast, De Panne if I'm not mistaken."

"De Panne?"

Debrabandere straightened his back, almost got to his feet, and raised a bony finger to Van In.

"Listen, young man. There's nothing wrong with my memory."

And your hearing's fine too, Hannelore thought to herself.

"The Verhaeghes live in De Panne," he snapped.

He collapsed back into his chair with a gasp. Van In was worried they might have pushed the old man too far. He wasn't to know that Debrabandere was worried too, that his harshness toward the police officer might have endangered his liquid reward.

"But do me a favor," the priest groaned endearingly. "Wait till she comes back with the wine."

Van In gave him the opportunity to empty two glasses, which the elderly priest managed in no time at all. Mother superior followed the drinking session with her eyes on stalks.

They thanked Debrabandere and mother superior accompanied them to the gate, her skirts in a flurry.

"I'm certain his grace would appreciate it if Father Debrabandere were to receive an appropriate reward for his assistance. Don't you think, Deputy Martens?" said Versavel.

"Absolutely," Hannelore concurred with a wink. "I think he earned every bit of his bottle of Burgundy. It stimulates the memory, my grandfather used to say. If I were you, I'd treat him to a couple of glasses every day."

"Is that true, ma'am?" mother superior asked, a little awe-struck.

"Of course. Who knows . . . that bottle of Burgundy may have saved an innocent child's life," said Van In.

They all burst out laughing in the car.

"To De Panne?" she asked rhetorically.

"There's a telephone box next to the church. Call Bruges and ask them to contact the local police."

"Can't we just look up their address in the telephone directory?"

"But what if there's more than one Verhaeghe in De Panne? It's a fairly common name. Let's not take any chances. And let's swing by the station in Hauwer Street first. I think it's time to switch to a police car."

"As long as I get to drive," said Hannelore. "And switch on the sirens," she added.

No one could accuse the De Panne police of not being fast and efficient.

"The Verhaeghes are on vacation," Versavel shouted as they stepped out of the car in the station's inner courtyard.

"One of the duty officers happened to know the family. They're driving around the south of France in a camper van for three weeks."

"Shit," Van In cursed. "That's all we needed."

Hannelore was bewildered.

"And the children? Do they know where they live?"

"They don't have their own children! Why else did they adopt Aurelie's child?"

"That's what I meant," said Van In, irked.

"We're working on it," said Versavel.

"Okay, let's go inside and have a coffee. Sorry, sweetheart, but I promise you can switch on the lights and siren next time."

"Is that a promise, Pieter?" she pouted.

Versavel pretended not to have heard. *Jesus . . . what are they like?* he thought. *A couple of schoolgirls . . .*

Van In grabbed the phone from a colleague.

"If they find the adopted son's address, they have to search the place right away. I presume you can convince them that they'll be covered by a warrant," he said to Hannelore.

"Hello, Van In here."

Inspector Simpelaere of the De Panne police greeted his Bruges colleague warmly. He was honored to have his men working on the Degroof case. At that moment, someone handed him a scrap of paper with Daniel Verhaeghe's address.

"I'll send round a couple of men on the double," said Simpelaere enthusiastically. Van In shrugged his shoulders. The chances that Daniel Verhaeghe would be at home were more or less zero.

"Do that," he said. "And make sure . . ."

"Nathalie lives in De Panne," Hannelore hissed while Van In was passing on his instructions. "Jesus, why didn't I make the connection?"

She tapped Van In on the shoulder and scribbled *Nathalie also lives in De Panne* on the white edge of a newspaper. Van In spun round with such force that he almost knocked the phone from the desk.

"Jesus H. Christ," he groaned.

"What was that?" said Inspector Simpelaere.

"You have to pick up Nathalie Degroof. Find her address and send your men round immediately. Arrest her and lock her up," he snarled. "We're on our way."

Inspector Simpelaere pulled a face when the connection was abruptly broken. To add to his troubles, the commissioner marched into his office with the mayor in his wake. *There they are*, he growled under his breath. All ready to take a pat on the back.

"Let's get a move on," said Van In to Hannelore and Versavel. "De Panne, top speed."

"Do we take the GTI?" asked Versavel.

"Whatever, as long as it's fast."

The sergeant grabbed the keys from the wall cupboard and ran ahead of them

"Sorry, Guido. I promised Hannelore she could drive."

"With lights and sirens," Versavel jeered.

He changed his tune when they were ripping down the freeway at one hundred twenty kilometers per hour. Versavel plainly had to admit that Deputy Martens could handle the GTI with some panache. He resigned himself to the nightmare journey, which took all of thirty-six minutes. The roar of the engine and the blaring sirens made it impossible to carry on a normal conversation. Versavel wasn't able to point out that no one had considered the possibility that Nathalie might not be at home.

But for once they were in luck.

When they stormed into the police station in De Panne, there was Nathalie parked red-eyed between two burly officers in the interrogation room.

"I'll get straight to the point, friend," said Van In. "We know that Daniel Verhaeghe is an accessory to the abduction of Bertrand Delahaye. And we also know that you're part of his little scheme," he gambled.

Nathalie's eyes were swollen. When they arrested her, she had started to cry from rage and frustration. She was going to miss a meet with her dealer. Her eyes shot flames at Hannelore.

"I've nothing to do with it. I don't even know Daniel Verhaeghe."

"We're talking abduction, sweetheart," said Van In softly. "The penalty for complicity is pretty scary."

"If you plan to accuse me of something, get on with it. Then I can call my lawyer."

In spite of the fact that her life was going down the drain, with some serious drug withdrawal to boot, Nathalie was still a Degroof: proud and arrogant.

"It's up to you. Keep up the denial and say farewell to your stuff for a while."

Hannelore drew herself up to her full height and stood in front of Nathalie, her legs wide apart.

"Never heard of the law of May 14, 1994?"

The question clearly threw her.

"In serious criminal cases such as murder and kidnapping, the public prosecutor is at liberty to have suspects held on remand indefinitely."

She gave Nathalie a moment to let her words sink in.

"A junkie like you wouldn't survive, would you? You'd either go crazy or you'd beg for permission to confess," she added, twisting the knife.

"Fucking bitch!"

Nathalie started to shake at the thought of being held for even more than twenty-four hours. Even Van In was shifting nervously in his chair. He'd never heard of the law of May 14, 1994. No one had heard of it.

"Come, come, ma'am, surely we can rule out indefinite detention. If Miss Degroof can tell us where we can find Daniel Verhaeghe, she'll be home in half an hour."

The oldest police trick in the book, good cop/bad cop, and it still worked like a dream in plenty of cases. But Nathalie had apparently read too many thrillers and watched too many detective series on TV.

"Give me some credit," she snarled. "And by the way, this interrogation is illegal. Deputy public prosecutors aren't allowed to be present during police questioning. You're not welcome, Deputy asshole."

Hannelore gulped, not because of Nathalie's insults but because she was right. It was extremely unusual for magistrates working for the public prosecutor's office to take part in a police interrogation. It may even have been against the law, as Nathalie had suggested.

They continued to question her in turns until four in the morning. The interrogation room was blue with smoke. Nathalie had cursed them, snapped at them, and provoked them. She had tried to escape a couple of time in a rage, but she continued to insist that she had nothing to do with the abduction of her nephew.

"Do you think she's lying?" asked Hannelore while Nathalie was cooling off in a police cell.

"No idea," said Van In. "But there's no point in continuing the interrogation. The bitch knows good and well that we're running out of time."

"What do you suggest?"

Van In mooched a cigarette from the duty sergeant and searched nervously in his pockets for his lighter.

"Back to square one . . ." he sighed, "and just in time to witness the spectacle. Mind you, I could do with a couple of hours sleep first."

The TV people had set up their equipment long before the crack of dawn. Swarms of technicians had worked through the night to get ready for the big moment. They had built towers and laid out miles of cable. Everything was ready for a live nine o'clock broadcast, and the world was about to hear about one of the weirdest kidnapping in history. The diehard curious who didn't want to miss any part of the spectacle had started to trickle into the city in search of the best vantage points.

With Versavel at the wheel, the drive from De Panne to Bruges was a lot calmer than the outward trip. The atmosphere in the car was one of defeat.

"The tracks run cold and the hunters lose heart," said Versavel philosophically.

A cheerless Van In stared into space.

"Who in God's name would want to get his own back on a man of eighty if not someone within the family?" said Hannelore. "It all seems so unlikely."

Van In was in the back, deep in thought. He didn't really register what Versavel and Hannelore had said. Something had been niggling him since the previous afternoon. It was like having a spot on your nose: it might be tiny and barely visible when you look in the mirror, but it's there and you can't stop looking at it.

Memory is a complex labyrinth, a living mishmash of memories, some registered, others wandering lost until they find a home. But if one such homeless memory, meaningless in itself, bumps into another and latches on to it, the encounter can sometimes spur the most original insights.

"I don't think Aquilin Verheye is dead," he said out of the blue.

Hannelore turned to look at him. She thought he had started to talk nonsense in a fit of insanity.

"I don't just think it, I know it."

Van In dug into his inside pocket and produced the photos of Verheye's grave.

"Pull over, Guido, and give me the flashlight."

Versavel asked no questions and parked the car on the shoulder.

"Here," said Van In. He handed Hannelore one of the photos. "Read the dates."

"15.10.1914," she said.

"And you, Guido."

Versavel reluctantly put on his glasses and carefully studied the photograph. It took a minute, but he also said: "15.10.1914."

"Jesus H. Christ. It's time I got myself one of those," Van In grumbled. "I should have thought of it earlier."

"Glasses . . . you need glasses? You shouldn't be so vain," Hannelore mocked.

"No, for Christ sake. The dates don't tally! Degroof told me that Verheye was two days older than him. And he was born on May 19, 1914."

"What the . . ." said Versavel. He hadn't a clue what Van In was talking about.

"But if Verheye isn't dead, who's lying in his grave?" asked Hannelore.

"No one, or someone else. But it shouldn't take long to find out."

While Van In radioed dispatching in Bruges, Hannelore and Versavel changed places.

"If it gets exciting, I get to drive," she beamed. She started the engine, stamped on the gas, and took off with sirens wailing.

Fleurus is a small community to the west of Namur. At four-fifteen, thirty-five minutes after Van In had called dispatch, the tranquil village's picturesque cemetery was hermetically sealed off from the outside world.

Thirty hurriedly assembled policemen were nervously awaiting further instructions.

Public Prosecutor Lootens had never made such a quick decision in his life. He had called his colleague in Namur, and the man had immediately given orders to have Verheye's alleged corpse exhumed.

Six men armed with shovels and pickaxes went to work without delay. They paid little attention to the damage they were causing to nearby graves.

Van In received a message at six precisely. The exhumation was complete and there was a corpse in the casket. The police physician, who had just arrived, confirmed that the casket contained an elderly man, but it was too early for further details.

"Fuck."

Van In thumped the desk with his fist. He was exhausted and his capacity to cope with setbacks was about as flexible as Versavel's baton. They were running out of time and every clue was a dead end. The entire Degroof affair was a succession of misjudged events and half-baked conclusions. Just as he had started to believe in his job again after so many years, his illusions started to disappear like the smoke from the cigarette he was holding between his trembling fingers.

"Surely the Records Office has to know something." Hannelore articulated the most obvious next step a fraction of a second before it entered Van In's mind.

"You're brilliant!"

Van In took her by the arm and pulled her inelegantly toward him. The resounding kiss on the cheek echoed through the scantily furnished room, and four pairs of eyes, including those of De Kee, watched the outpouring of affection open-mouthed.

"Records Office, here we come," he said to a speechless De Kee. "If the corpse isn't Verheye, then Verheye has taken on the identity of the dead man. It also wouldn't surprise me if he lives in the neighborhood, and if we find Verheye, we find the boy. Hannelore, bring your mobile. It's important that we keep in contact with everyone."

As they rushed downstairs, Van In collided face on with D'Hondt, who had hurried over from Zand Square. He had heard on the radio that there was a new evolution in the case.

"Sorry, buddy, but there's no room in the car," said Hannelore. She waved at the bewildered captain and chased after Van In.

She fastened her safety belt and before Van In had the chance to settle into his seat, she revved the Golf GTI's intimidating engine a couple of times. De Kee, Versavel, and D'Hondt watched from the window above.

"Those two think they're in a Western," De Kee observed dryly.

"Dogs in heat," D'Hondt sneered. "They'll probably stop on the way for a quick one," he added snidely.

Versavel wanted to tell him off but resisted just in time. D'Hondt was a captain, and insulting an officer wasn't good for your career.

Hannelore took off American style, with screeching tires and swaying rear axle. In the meantime, Van In tried to contact Fleurus. He succeeded as they tore past the church in Sint-Michiels, in the suburbs of Bruges.

The connection was bad, but the local police officer in charge of the investigation in Fleurus was more than willing to help. He immediately sent two men to the mayor's house with orders to have the Records Office clerk summoned ASAP.

"So you really think the corpse isn't Verheye," said Hannelore in a relaxed tone as she drove the car with wailing sirens onto the freeway.

"I don't just think so, I'm pretty sure."

"But how in God's name did he get away with it?"

"Ever read *The Day of the Jackal*?"

She glanced at him in bewilderment for a fraction of a second.

"Shame," said Van In. "It's a good read. Our friend must have used the same method. The Jackal is a hired killer who keeps changing his identity. Verheye must have done the same, Belgian style."

"Get to the point, Pieter, for God's sake. You're not trying to tell me that someone used the tricks from some novel to organize a crime."

"I wouldn't want to be responsible for all the crimes that were based on the plot of a film or a book, sweetheart. But people have written about *The Day of the Jackal,* and what Forsyth describes in the book is perfectly doable with the right amount of time and resources."

The car phone started to ring.

"Commandant Evrard here, 'allo?"

The Walloon policeman spoke more than reasonable Dutch.

"Hello, Van In here. Good morning, Commandant Evrard. We're on the road, just passing Aalter. ETA around 7:30. Is the Records Office clerk on hand?"

"Affirmative," was the professional reply.

"Does he have access to Aquilin Verheye's address and family situation?"

Commandant Evrard responded once again in the affirmative, although he had no idea why the information was so important.

"Did he live alone?"

It took thirty seconds before he received an answer to his question.

"The man was unmarried. He moved to Fleurus in 1990."

"Shit," Van In muttered under his breath, "another dead end!"

Hannelore, who was determined to cover the Aalter-Namur trajectory in less than thirty minutes, revved the engine once more. A police vehicle tearing past at that speed was guaranteed to give the region's well-behaved early commuters something to talk about when they arrived at their boring office jobs.

"Where did he live before that?" Van In snarled after a full minute's silence.

Commandant Evrard was fortunately a very patient man.

"One moment, Commissioner."

Van In would have given his right hand for an ice-cold Duvel.

"Schaarbeek," he said after a couple of seconds.

Van In now had no other option than to play his final trump. If he was wrong, Mr. Forsyth could expect an angry letter signed Van In.

"Can you check if Aquilin Verheye applied for a new identity card before he died?"

Commandant Evrard gulped.

"Start three months before he moved to Fleurus and if that draws a blank, then we'll have to check further back," said Van In.

"Do you realize what you're asking, Commissioner?"

Van In knew exactly what he was asking. And when he announced that he wanted the information within the hour, even Evrard started to lose his patience.

"Call in the Ministry of the Interior if need be, or the National Records Office."

"Okay, Commissioner, but I hope you're right."

Evrard ended the conversation and put his radio man to work.

"If I'm to be honest, Holmes, I'm finding it hard to follow your line of reasoning," said Hannelore. Her knuckles were white and the hair of her fringe was sticking to her forehead.

Van In stretched his legs, insofar as that was possible in the limited space, and breathed a deep sigh.

"I'm taking it for granted that he hatched his plan a long time ago. His obsession with getting his revenge on Degroof probably dates back to their student days. Verheye knew he needed a different identity to be sure that Degroof couldn't track him down. He planned it that Degroof would know from the outset who was responsible for this act of revenge, but would be left powerless and forced to look on as destiny unfolded in front of him. Don't forget, only the sower knows the burdens and vicissitudes of life. And if the sower is the one who devised the plan, then our Latin riddle suddenly becomes crystal-clear. Billen's explanation led me astray for a while. You remember, the concierge at the basilica."

"Do you think someone would take so much trouble just to exact revenge?"

Jesus Hanne, he thought to himself, *surely you're not that naïve.*

"For certain types of people, exacting revenge is a sacred task. They're like religious fanatics. It is their only goal, and no cost is too great."

"The way you describe him, our friend Verheye must be totally psycho," she said, still finding his explanation a little hard to take. "But good, I interrupted you. Continue."

"So he's faced with a question: what's the best way to 'legally' adopt a different identity?"

"And Forsyth had the answer?" she sniggered.

"I told you that Forsyth tested his ideas against reality. You can be sure that anyone with a bit of creativity would find a solid answer to such a question. And we can hardly accuse Verheye of not being creative."

"Fine," she said. "I believe you."

Van In lit another cigarette. The excitement of the preceding hours had taken its toll on his good intentions.

"I hope you do," he said.

"Go on. I'm listening."

Van In felt she was making a fool of him. After all, his chances of being wide of the mark yet again were pretty high.

"Surely you don't think I'm winding you up," said Hannelore, half serious. "For me you're the smartest detective on the force."

"If you say so. Try to picture it: Verheye befriends an old man in Schaarbeek, roughly his own age, unmarried and on his last legs. He discovers the man has no family. Major cities are awash with people like that. After a couple of months, he works his way into the man's life, becomes his prop and stay. He goes to the store, makes meals, keeps him company. On a given day—he's turned into a close confidant by this time—he informs the police that the old man has lost his ID card. Under normal circumstances, the person who lost the card has to take care of the formalities. But everyone knows that exceptions are made now and then for the elderly. The police provide him with a certificate and he takes the document to the Records Office. But instead of a photo of his elderly friend, he hands in a photo of himself. After a couple of weeks Verheye collects a genuine

ID card in his friend's name but with his photo. A while later he repeats the procedure, but this time the other way round. From then on Verheye takes the place of his elderly friend. Once that's done, he persuades his 'victim' to come and live with him in the Ardennes. Maybe he threatened to abandon the old man, who knows, but as we said, he's on his last legs, so he agrees to move to Fleurus. From that point on, all Verheye has to do is wait until his buddy dies. It wouldn't even surprise me if Verheye made over all his property to the old guy in his will before the exchange of identity. That way he would inherit it all back after the man's death."

"And you think you can get away with such an operation in Belgium," she said skeptically.

"Anything's possible in Belgium," Van In responded, sure of his answer.

"But something doesn't fit," she said hesitatingly.

"What doesn't fit?"

Hannelore bit her bottom lip. She found disappointing Van In painful.

"Even if Verheye managed to change his identity as you suggest, there's still a problem. I can believe he switched the photographs, but he would never have been able to change the other details held at the Records Office."

"Sorry, I'm not following," said Van In on edge.

She took a deep breath and placed her hand on his thigh.

"If Aquilin Verheye had the identity card of an unknown man at his disposal, the old man's details would also be on the card and vice versa," she said with a regretful smile. "The date of birth on the grave would have to correspond with that of the real Aquilin Verheye, namely 17.05.1914."

"And yet it reads 15.10.1914," Van In persisted.

"Unless . . ."

Hannelore grabbed the wheel with both hands. She beamed.

"Say Aquilin Verheye made a mistake," she said triumphantly. "Every criminal makes a mistake sooner or later. It's common knowledge . . ."

"Hannelore, you're trying my patience," Van In groaned.

"Okay," she said with a hint of caution, "let's say your theory is right."

Van In nodded eagerly.

"The old man who has to pass for Verheye dies. He has no family. Who takes care of the funeral?"

"Verheye, of course."

"Correct. And who takes care of the grave stone?"

"Verheye of course . . . Jesus H. Christ! The idiot used his victim's date of birth!"

"Exactly," she laughed.

"So I was right after all," Van In stammered incredulously.

"Let's hope so," she said softly.

18

Daniel Verhaeghe had been staring spellbound at the ever-expanding crowd on Zand Square for more than an hour and a half.

The turnout had surpassed everyone's expectations. Aerial observers estimated the number of people at fifty thousand. Bruges was indeed a city under siege.

Daniel watched the spectacle with a glass of champagne in his hand, enjoying this ultimate triumph with every fiber of his being.

He turned up the TV with the remote. Almost every European broadcaster would soon be transmitting the bonfire live to the world. Dozens of cameras zoomed in on the paintings, which were displayed on a long, improvised easel. Sotheby's experts discussed the value of the canvases and, as usual, disagreed. Estimates fluctuated between sixty and a hundred million Belgian francs.

Four hundred local and federal police had been deployed to keep order. Their presence seemed unnecessary at first sight as the crowd was exceptionally well-behaved. But the atmosphere on Zand Square was high-spirited. On the road encircling the square, which had been closed to traffic for the occasion, stalls selling hot dogs, French fries, and kebabs had sprung up like dandelions on a freshly watered lawn. Local shop owners were selling beer and sodas on the sidewalk. Greedy curiosity had made the crowd thirsty, and the closer it got to nine o'clock, the rowdier it became. Everyone had his own opinion on what was about to happen.

Patrick Delahaye was waiting in a local police car, a vacant expression on his face. Charlotte had stayed home. She was watching TV and counting the minutes. Her thoughts were reserved for her son alone. She prayed the Lord's Prayer, awkward but sincere, begging God to listen to her plea.

Van In contacted Captain D'Hondt at eight-fifty.

He had received word from Commandant Evrard five minutes earlier. In Schaarbeek police station, officers searched at fever pitch through piles of forms submitted to report the loss or theft of an identity card. They were forced to do it manually because the computer that stored the information was acting up.

They had work on their hands. Everything depended on the date Verheye had reported the ID card loss; then they had to check the addresses of those who would have been eligible for the exchange.

"Hello, Van In here. I have a message for Captain D'Hondt. And it's urgent."

"I'm afraid Captain D'Hondt is unavailable right now," said the duty sergeant on the other end of the line.

His instructions had been crystal-clear. Captain D'Hondt was giving an interview to a BBC reporter. D'Hondt was a huge anglophile, and his heart skipped a beat when he was asked for an interview. Appearing in front of the camera for British television was the greatest honor he could imagine. Some of his colleagues would be green with envy when they saw him, and he would finally be able to demonstrate that he was the only one among them who spoke decent English.

Van In paled around the nostrils when the arrogant subordinate brushed him off. The hand in which he was holding the receiver started to shake. Hannelore could see that he was about to explode.

"Let me repeat my request one more time," he snarled. "I have the minister of the interior here beside me. If D'Hondt doesn't get to the phone in one minute, I'll let you deal with the minister in person."

His words were met with a steely silence, and for a moment Van In thought that the sergeant had hung up on him. Hannelore was in tears and held a handkerchief to her mouth to conceal her laughter.

"Hello, D'Hondt."

The captain's heart was pounding loud enough to hear and he was clearly out of breath from running.

"I need you to delay the spectacle for one more hour," Van In snorted.

D'Hondt registered the words but was unable to grasp their significance.

"What did you say?" he croaked.

"I want you to postpone the bonfire for one more hour. Make up a story for the press, whatever you want . . . but give me one more hour."

"You must be kidding. Make up a story? What story?"

"Put the minister on," Hannelore whispered, still giggling.

"A second, D'Hondt."

Van In racked his brain for a solution. The kidnappers were sure to be watching the whole thing on TV, and Long-legs was almost certainly somewhere on Zand Square. He doubted they would kill the boy for a minor delay, but he wasn't certain by any means.

"Ask Delahaye to pretend to pass out just as he about to put a match to the first painting. Have him carried away on a stretcher and make sure the cameras pick it all up."

"I hope you know what you're doing, Van In," said D'Hondt, who had managed to get his breath back and get ahold of himself.

"Don't worry about me, friend. And one more thing . . . tell Delahaye to make it as realistic as possible."

From nine onwards, the police station in Schaarbeek was in contact with the Federal Records Office, where the computer was working as it should.

Fifteen minutes later, it spewed out a name: Laurent De Bock, Les Heids, Vezin.

As the name was being passed round, Van In was chain-smoking next to a neo-gothic monument in the cemetery of Fleurus. Every thirty seconds he looked at his watch.

Hannelore was close by, chatting with Commandant Evrard. The commandant, a respectable husband and father, found it hard to stay focused on the task at hand. Like so many others, he was convinced that the attractive Deputy didn't belong in their world. He was also taken by her exceptionally melodious French. She could easily make a career for herself in Paris. He was convinced of it.

Bertrand Delahaye was awakened from his feverish anesthesia by the sound of slamming car doors and wheels spinning on gravel.

He had dreamed that he was standing on top of a steep hill. He was on a mountain hike with the scouts and had lost his companions. He had decided to climb higher until he reached the top, but when he didn't find his companions there he figured it best to head back down to the valley on his own. But the hill he had just climbed suddenly appeared incredibly steep. He was standing at the edge of an almost vertical ravine and he was terrified. No one was likely to find him where he was, so he made up his mind not to wait and started his descent step by careful step.

He felt loose stones slip away under his feet and tried to keep his balance. When he started to fall into the empty void below, he suddenly realized that the sound of crunching gravel didn't square with the sensation of free fall.

The sound was coming from outside.

People were surrounding the house.

A force of fifty armed policemen had surrounded the chalet of Aquilin Verheye, alias Laurent De Bock. Van In read the name that had been written on a wooden board and nailed to the chalet wall: *de Molay.*

Every residual doubt evaporated.

Jacques de Molay, he remembered from Billen's lengthy exposé, was the last grand master of the Templars. He had cursed Philip the Fair, Pope Clement V, and Guillaume de Nogaret before being burned at the stake.

Here was the man they were after.

Evrard waited until his men had taken their positions and then winked at Van In and Hannelore. The summer tranquility of the pinewood forest was restored. Everyone held their breath.

"Help, help," they heard someone shout. The voice was weak, but it was clearly coming from inside the chalet.

Van In and Evrard glanced at each other and sprinted toward the front door like a pair of aging joggers. Van In knocked the door from its hinges with a well-aimed kick. Evrard stormed inside, pistol at the ready, somersaulted forward, landed on his belly, and sought cover behind a copper umbrella stand.

It was a comical sight.

The boy continued to shout for help, but the rest of the chalet was quiet and calm.

Van In burst in to the chalet, hot on Evrard's heels, but unlike Evrard he remained standing. He pushed open an interior door and checked out the corridor ahead. Another door leading to the kitchen was half open. Van In went inside and found the old man on the floor. His arm was stretched out in front of him and he had a key clenched in his fist.

Evrard scrambled to his feet when Van In signaled that the coast was clear.

Van In stood over the dead body of Aquilin Verheye. He was forced to break a couple of fingers to free the key.

"You're safe, take it easy," said Van In seconds later as he pacified a sobbing Bertrand and held him to his chest. "The nightmare is over, young friend. I'm taking you home."

Daniel Verhaeghe listened in astonishment to the journalist as he announced with emotion that the kidnapping was over.

The police had freed the boy and one of the kidnappers had been found dead at the scene, of apparently natural causes.

De Kee stood beside him grinning from ear to ear. His hair had been combed back and gelled to perfection.

"Our people have had the case under control for more than twenty-four hours," he declared with pride. "I've been coordinating the entire operation from the outset. We had essential information at our disposal that finally scuppered the kidnappers' plans."

Versavel taped the entire broadcast and handed it over to Van In. D'Hondt searched in vain for the BBC outside broadcast unit, while his men dispersed the crowd with megaphones.

When Patrick Delahaye heard the news, he passed out, this time for real.

Back in Bishop Avenue, a sobbing Charlotte poured herself a triple cognac. The hands that had carried out the most delicate eye operations for years on end trembled like the wings of an emerging butterfly.

The Park Hotel receptionist saw Daniel Verhaeghe storm through the lobby. He had hung around the evening before after his shift to chat with the colleague who was taking over from him and had seen the young man wheel himself to the elevator in a wheelchair. He grabbed the phone and informed the police.

Daniel was just about to start the blue Ford Transit when it was surrounded by twenty police officers.

"Congratulations, Holmes," said Hannelore as an ambulance rushed Bertrand Delahaye to the nearest hospital. "I still don't know how you figured it out, but you've convinced me once and for all that the Bruges police are not only good for writing parking tickets."

Van In crumpled his empty cigarette pack and took her by the arm. He felt lightheaded.

"Can I bum a cigarette?" he asked softly. "My last . . . it's time to stop. Those things are really bad for your health."

She rummaged in her handbag but also appeared to be out.

"I'll buy some for you later. In the meantime, you'll have to make do with the consolation prize."

She threw her arms around him and kissed him on the lips.

Heroes always get the cutest girl, Van In thought to himself. He tried to make the most of the moment.

Commandant Evrard watched from a distance. *Lucky Flemish bastard*, he thought.

On Tuesday morning, the telephone rang uninterrupted until Van In was no longer able to bear the piercing sound.

"It's eleven o'clock," said Hannelore, still half asleep. "We can't lie here forever."

"Go answer it, then," Van In grumbled.

"Next time it rings, Pieter." She turned on her side and dozed off again.

Van In made his way downstairs in his bare feet and answered the phone in a rage.

"The old bastard Degroof shot himself in the head."

It was Versavel, and he was in a bit of a state. At that moment in time, Van In couldn't have cared less.

"Haven't you seen the papers?" Versavel rattled on. "Someone went public with the whole thing."

Van In sat down and looked around for a cigarette. Luckily, he found none. It wasn't going to be easy to stop, he thought. In the meantime he half-listened to Versavel's tale of woe.

Two papers had Daniel Verhaeghe's complete confession; the others were a little more modest, with just the main points of the story. The entire incest affair and the suspect incarceration of Aurelie had been reported down to the last detail.

"Did you know that Aurelie was actually Aquilin Verheye's daughter?" Versavel roared when he sensed that Van In wasn't really paying any attention. "Elisa de Puyenbroucke and Verheye continued to be lovers after the marriage. Degroof found out about it and sexually abused Aurelie for years on end to get his revenge."

"Not incest in the technical sense," Van In dryly observed. "He knew she wasn't his daughter."

"That's one way of looking at it," Versavel whined. "It's easy to relativize. But Degroof senior found the revelation serious enough to put a bullet in his head. Honor and respect meant everything to him," Versavel sighed. "I thought the news would interest you, Commissioner," he added confused.

"But of course it does, my friend. Thanks for taking the trouble. I'll tell Hannelore right away."

"Ah, so," Versavel coughed knowingly.

"Don't be an asshole, Guido. If you're jealous, go look for Captain D'Hondt. Maybe he can console you."

"Bastard."

"Chin up, Guido. See you tomorrow at the office. Ciao!" Van In hung up and walked toward the kitchen counter, deep in thought. He put the kettle on the range and opened a fresh pack of coffee. The smell made him want a cigarette.

You haven't had one since yesterday, he said to himself, *why not today too?*

So it was the baroness who had handed over the alarm code to Verheye and given him the list of paintings. He had originally suspected Anne-Marie, but with Aquilin and the baroness's relationship now confirmed, it was she who had had the ultimate grudge to settle.

As he poured boiling water through the filter, he lined up the events of the preceding eight days.

The motive was now understandable.

Aquilin Verheye, lover of the Baroness Elisa de Puyenbroucke, wanted revenge against Degroof for raping and ruining their love child. Daniel Verhaeghe, the child born of the allegedly incestuous relationship between Degroof and Aurelie, wanted revenge for the injustice Degroof had done to his mother. And while they both wanted to get at Degroof, they used the rest of the family to reach their goal.

Their roundabout modus operandi wasn't the most trans-parent, but it also wasn't so out of the ordinary. The Americans could tell a story or two on that count. But the case was closed, so why was he worrying? He couldn't help himself.

Why had they waited so long, and what inspired Daniel Verhaeghe to . . .

Van In poured too much water onto the coffee. The filter overflowed and the black sludge ran down the sides of the por-celain coffee pot he had dug up for the occasion.

Without bothering about the mess, he headed back to the lounge and punched in Delahaye's number. Fortunately, it was Charlotte herself who picked up the phone.

She was surprised when she heard what he wanted to know, but promised she would call him back as soon as she had the information.

Van In could have asked her anything, given her grateful state.

Hannelore beamed when he appeared in the room with a tray of toast and coffee. He almost tripped on the last stair.

"I'm not used to serving breakfast in bed," he said apologetically.

"I would hope so too, Pieter Van In," she said threateningly.

The telephone rang moments after noon, and Van In rushed downstairs.

"Wouldn't it be easier to have a phone installed up here?" she shouted after him.

The conversation lasted a couple of minutes, and when Van In came back to the bedroom he was shaking his head.

"Problems?"

"No, not really," he sighed.

"Well, say something then and stop being so bloody secretive."

"Finish your coffee first. We need to pay a visit to the baroness. I think it's time she told us the whole story. But promise me one thing: whatever she tells us stays between me and you."

It took a while before anyone answered the door at the house on Spinola Street.

Hannelore whined the entire trip about why he wasn't telling her what his intentions were, but Van In refused to budge and said nothing. She was straining at the leash when he rang the bell for a third time.

Elisa, baroness de Puyenbroucke, had lost her youth, but her beauty and grace were still in ample evidence. She looked just like the photo on the mantel. She was wearing gray slacks and a large-knit woolen sweater, which made her look twenty years younger. There was pain in her eyes, and her slightly stooped shoulders appeared to be carrying a heavy burden. Van In wasn't surprised that there was no wheelchair and that she didn't look sickly and weak as Degroof had implied.

"I've been expecting you, Commissioner. Please come in."

She spoke elegant Dutch with a slight North Holland accent, a remnant from her boarding school days.

"We're not disturbing you?"

She shook her head.

"He didn't have the courage to do it here," she said with a melancholic smile. "He kept his hunting gear at our country house in Vlissegem."

That explained the absence of hustle and bustle around the house. Van In had already asked himself why there were no vehicles from the public prosecutor's office. They were off in the countryside, then, dealing with the proverbial mess.

She led them to the same lounge in which Degroof had earlier received Van In. An enormous vase of white lilies graced the coffee table. The musty smell had more or less disappeared.

"Ms. Martens is Deputy to the public prosecutor. She has been at my side throughout the investigation. But neither of us is here on official business. This is an informal visit."

She nodded and took a seat by the window, far from her husband's chesterfield.

"Did he ever tell you about the circumstances of our marriage?" she asked, unexpectedly to the point.

Van In nodded in the affirmative but let her continue. He and Hannelore sat down uninvited on a couch with flower motif upholstery.

"I was in love with Aquilin and he with me," she said hesitatingly, as if she only now realized that she was talking to complete strangers. "Our love for each other never died, but my family refused to accept him back then. He was poor and so were we. All my father had to sell was his name. He arranged the marriage with Degroof. He was rich, and on top of that I knew him quite well. He was Aquilin's best friend. Now they're both dead: the prince and the beast."

Hannelore was taken aback by the elderly woman's choice of words.

"We planned to elope at first, to go abroad, but I couldn't do that to my family. The only thing I could promise Aquilin was my eternal love. We agreed to see each other on a regular basis, easy enough since my husband was rarely home."

She paused for a moment and Hannelore had the impression that she was reliving those days with Aquilin in her thoughts. She felt sorry for her.

"Aquilin visited once a month, and one day we decided we wanted a child together. He was reluctant at first, but I persuaded him. I wanted his child. It was the only way I could have him with me at all times. We calculated the most suitable date and I resolved to spend the next couple of weeks at my parents' place. I did that all the time, and I knew no one would be suspicious."

The baroness was clearly in difficulty. Her voice faltered, and her eyes were bathed in an ocean of bitter tears.

"We spent a heavenly afternoon together and I was happy."

She pulled out her handkerchief and blew her nose.

"But that evening, minutes after I'd unpacked my bags upon my return, he stormed into the room. I've no idea what overcame him, but I could see in his eyes that he knew. He raped me like an animal for three days in a row."

Van In sensed the beginnings of a lump in his throat.

"But when Aurelie was born, I knew she was our child. She had Aquilin's eyes and that amply made up for the humiliation. Aquilin came to see her every month. To avoid further risks, we arranged to meet at a different place each time. I was so happy with Aurelie that I let the beast sire his own children."

"When did you find out that he was abusing Aurelie?" asked Van In with the utmost caution.

The baroness lost control and burst into tears.

"Her youth was a nightmare," she sobbed. "Aquilin did everything to free her from his claws. He wanted to kill him, but I talked him out of it. If they had locked him up I would have been left with nothing. We were powerless in official terms. I once tried to file charges. When he got home that evening, he beat me black and blue. The public prosecutor had called him and the case, of course, was dismissed. He had them all under his thumb. He would leave her alone from time to time, but he would work out his rage on me instead. He locked me up and told everyone I was sick."

"Did the other children know what was going on?"

She nodded.

"He brainwashed them and kept telling them that Aurelie was making it all up."

"And did he abuse Benedicta?"

"I think so. He was insatiable by this point."

"And Nathalie?"

"Nathalie was our second child," she said with pride.

"What?" Van In exclaimed.

"Before Aurelie fell pregnant to the beast, Aquilin wanted to console me. I was depressed, and if it hadn't been for Aquilin I would have taken my own life years earlier. A child would bring me hope, he figured."

"And did Degroof ever find out?"

She shook her head.

"He was never able to have her. Nathalie had Aquilin's character. She was strong and defiant. She ran away from home, but ended up in the wrong circles. Now she's . . ."

"Now she's heavily addicted to drugs," Van In blurted, but she paid no attention.

"Aquilin didn't want me to give her money."

She looked Van In in the eye.

"Our first daughter is in an institution. Her son is suffering from a deadly condition. Was I wrong not to begrudge Nathalie her drug-induced elation?"

"Daniel suffers from Marfan syndrome, doesn't he?"

She was surprised that Van In knew. "We found out five years ago," she said. "The eye problem was treatable, but then the doctors discovered that Daniel's condition had created a thinning of the aorta wall and that it was inoperable. It is a death sentence."

"And that was the last straw," said Van In. "The plan to give everyone their just rewards was hatched just five years ago."

She nodded.

"Aquilin worked everything out to the tiniest detail. He wanted the beast to know who was punishing him. He wanted to make the beast and his brood pay for what they had done to his daughters and his grandson. The beast had to die, and

Ghislain, Charlotte, and Benedicta had to suffer for their silence."

"You knew that the authorities wouldn't cooperate if Degroof had been faced with a cheap gossip campaign, so Aquilin arranged so much media interest that no one could overlook the facts, at least if they were made known at the appropriate moment."

"Nathalie passed on all the details to the press on Monday evening," she said.

I was right, Hannelore thought. *She was part of the plot after all. That was why she got so angry when I threatened to have her locked up.*

"Aquilin wasn't afraid of the consequences. Even if the plan backfired and the police arrested him, Daniel had nothing to fear. In his condition, there wasn't a jury in the world that would convict him. And my sweet Aquilin: he knew his life was coming to an end. His only ambition was to allow his grandson to witness and enjoy his act of revenge as a privileged observer."

The baroness spoke with vigor and conviction.

"And I regret nothing. The beast's children chose him over their mother and made my life a hell."

Silence filled the room. Time passed. Hannelore fidgeted awkwardly with her rings. Van In stared through the green stained-glass windows.

Sator rotas opera tenet.

But only he and Charlotte knew the truth. When the doctors diagnosed Marfan syndrome, they didn't say that it was a hereditary condition that often was passed on as a result of incest.

There was something Sophoclean about it all.

Elisa and Aquilin had only one child together: Nathalie.

Aurelie was really the daughter of the beast.

Van In looked at Hannelore and at the old baroness. He had no intention of telling them.